WAIT FOR
Me

Cinnamon
Believe
[signature]

USA TODAY BESTSELLING AUTHOR

TIA LOUISE

This book is a work of fiction. Names, characters, places, and incidents are products of the author's imagination or are used fictitiously. Any resemblance to actual events or locales or persons, living or dead, is entirely coincidental.

Wait for Me
Copyright © TLM Productions LLC, 2019
Printed in the United States of America.

Cover design by Lori Jackson Design.
Photography by Wander Aguiar.

For lovers of sad songs and sweet surprises…

To my husband, who wanted a story about the peach orchard where he grew up, and to Ilona, who loved it first.

Prologue

Noel

MY MOMMA WAS TOO BEAUTIFUL TO DIE.

At least, that's what everybody said.

Penelope Jean Harris was the scion of our town's founder and prettiest girl in three parishes. She was head major-ette in high school and homecoming queen and prom queen and every other queen. She was Peach Princess, Teen Dixie Peach, and Miss Dixie Gem. She would've gone on to be Miss Louisiana if my daddy hadn't made her a Mrs.

I was eleven—that strange age between too big to play in the creek in only my panties and too little to sleep without the closet light on. I loved Dolly Parton and butterflies and picking peaches straight off my daddy's trees and eating them, jumping in the lake and running after jackrabbits with my little brother Leon.

In the summer the trees were rich green, and the sweet scent of peach juice filled the air. In the winter they were sparse, bony hands, reaching palms up to heaven. Branches like fingers spread, grasping for hope.

Momma's hazel eyes crinkled at the corners whenever she looked at me or my brothers or my daddy. Her sweet smile was warm sunshine when I got cold.

She would wrap me in her arms and sing an old sad song when I was sleepy or cranky or "out of sorts," which is how she'd put it. I pictured "sorts" as ivory dominoes I could line up and knock down or slap off the table, across the room. I'd pull her silky brown hair around me like a cape and close my eyes and breathe...

Then she was gone.

She went for a walk one crisp winter evening along the narrow, dirt road that runs past our orchard out to the old house on the hill. Frost was in the air; bonfires were burning. The man driving the truck said she came out of nowhere.

He never saw her.

She never saw him.

Six weeks later, in that same orchard with peach blossoms on the trees and dew tipping the grass, on the very spot she died, my daddy took his life with his own gun.

I guess sometimes love makes you forget things can get better.

I guess he didn't see a bend in the road up ahead.

I guess he only saw a straight line leading deeper and deeper into black.

My daddy was the star of his high school football team... but Life threw him a pass he couldn't catch with Momma's death.

Our world changed forever that winter.

Dolly says love is like a butterfly, soft and gentle as a sigh, but from what I've seen of love, I think it's more like a tornado, shocking and violent and so powerful it can rip your soul out of your mouth...

It's faster than you can run, and it blows one house away while leaving the next one peacefully standing.

I didn't know which way love would take me, quietly or with the roar of a freight train. I should've known. I should've realized the moment I saw him.

It was both. It was quiet as the brush of peach fuzz, but it left my insides in splinters. It twisted my lungs and lifted me up so high only to throw me down with a force that rang my ears and flooded my eyes.

It all started the summer before they left, a month before my brother was sent to fight in a war everybody said was over.

It all started in the kitchen of my momma's house…

Seven Years Ago

CHAPTER
One

Taron

"**R**ISE AND SHINE, SLICK." SAWYER SLAPS MY FOOT, KNOCKING MY legs off the couch, and I come up with my fist clenched.

"What the hell..." Defense is an instinct to me, born out of a childhood where I had to fend for myself.

"Be at the truck in seven minutes."

I scrub my eyes with my hand instead of punching. "Seven. It's still dark."

"We're on farm time now." His voice mimics our drill sergeant's and he closes the bathroom door without looking back.

Farm time, military time... no wonder he adapted so easily to basic. Lifting my phone, I see it's only five. *Shit.* Looking around, I try to get my bearings in the large, dark room. The hint of a dream still lingers at the edge of my brain.

Soft skin, soft hair... A scent so familiar, but I can't place it— sweet, but earthy. I want to close my eyes and bury my face in her neck and just breathe...

It was only a dream.

A dream I'd like to finish for once.

With a low growl I stand, pushing down the wood in my

shorts and searching the floor for the jeans and tee I wore on the drive in last night.

We arrived at Sawyer's place after midnight, and I crashed on the couch in the living room, thinking I'd sleep more than five hours. We finished boot camp last week and got our marching orders. We're full-fledged Marines now, with only a few weeks before we head out to South America for an eighteen-month assignment.

Eighteen months if we're lucky.

I find my shirt at the same time something warm and wet smears down my face.

"What tha—!" I shout, falling back on my ass.

My heart is in my throat as the bathroom door opens again, casting a column of light across the floor. A big, black and gray dog with one blue eye and one brown eye stands in front of me. It looks like it's grinning. I'm pretty sure it knows it scared the shit out of me.

"Akela, come." Sawyer's voice is sharp. "Bathroom's yours."

He doesn't stop as he passes, and the fluffy dog follows him to the kitchen. Shaking my head, I stagger toward the light.

Five minutes later, we're in the truck, and I'm no morning person but I have to say, the golden sunrise over the hills covered in short trees heavy with green leaves and ripe peaches is pretty special. A misting of dew makes it shine.

Sawyer has his cap pulled down low as he drives, and he doesn't seem to notice. He's been pretty focused since we left Nashville yesterday evening. I guess coming home can be stressful, even if you own the place and your best friend volunteered to come back and help settle things.

"That's some dog." My elbow is propped on the open window and the warm breeze wraps around us in the cab.

"She's Noel's." He's driving slow down a narrow, dirt road.

He's told me a little about his kid sister, skinned knees and pigtails, chasing jackrabbits.

"Where we headed?"

"Harristown central." He cracks a hint of a smile, and I'm glad to see he's not brooding.

"Where's that?"

"You'll see."

We continue at twenty miles per hour until we reach a paved, two-lane highway. He takes a right, heading into the small town, and I think he'll speed up.

He doesn't.

Looking down at my phone, I see I have zero cell service. "No Verizon out here?"

He casts me a glance. "Who you trying to call?"

"I was gonna let Patton and Marley know we made it."

"I got a landline at the house."

Pressing my lips together, I give him a nod. It's like that. *Great.*

Five more minutes and we're pulling off on a service road, up to a truck stop with a Denny's restaurant attached. Several trucks are parked near the entrance and men in jeans and caps climb out slowly, adjusting the top of their britches and stretching.

"Denny's?" I shoot him a skeptical look.

He just shrugs. "It's how they've always done it."

"Done what?"

"Sorted out the schedule of workers for harvest."

"You don't have your own workers for harvest?"

"I'm about to."

He shifts the truck into park, adjusts his cap, and gets out. I follow him inside at the same slow pace as the rest of the old-timers filtering through the doors. On my mind is our conversation a few weeks back, when we were getting our assignments, talking about leaving the country.

He'd told me all about the hundred-acre farm he inherited from his dad in north Louisiana, and I'd said I'd like to see it sometime.

I don't have much family left in Nashville, besides my buddies Patton Fletcher and Martin "Marley" Randall. We enlisted together hoping to get the same assignment, which luckily, we did.

Sawyer fell right in with Patton, Marley, and me on our first day, and we've been inseparable ever since. When he asked me to come home with him, to help him get everything in order before we ship out, I figured why not? I'd just be wasting time, partying too hard if I spent a month in Nashville waiting.

"Welcome the hometown hero," a voice calls to us from across the room.

"Not yet." Sawyer clasps hands with a man who looks at least twenty years older than us. "How's the team this year?"

"About the same as last year." The man's voice is measured, like my friend's. He nods toward a stout, Mexican man sitting at a booth across the way. "Jay Hidalgo has a good team lined up. We're just discussing price."

Then he looks at me and nods. "How's it going?"

I quickly stretch out my hand. "Taron Rhodes."

He gives it a shake. "Dutch Hayes. I own the cotton fields east of town all the way to Delta."

"Nice." I have no idea how to respond, but Sawyer interjects.

"Taron's a friend of mine from Nashville. We finished basic together."

"Another Marine? With that face?"

My jaw tightens. Being what people consider good-looking has definite plusses and minuses. The plus is easy pussy, although I've never been a man-whore. It's not my style.

The minus, I occasionally bump into dicks who think I can't kick their asses.

Still, I was taught respect for my elders.

"Another Marine," I say through a tight smile.

"Don't let him fool you." Sawyer grips my shoulder. "I'd trust Taron with my life."

Dutch nods. "Brothers in arms."

"Something like that." Sawyer redirects. "Can Digger come by this afternoon? I need to get Noel and Leon squared away before I leave."

A greedy light flashes in the man's eyes when Sawyer's back is turned. He quickly hides it, and I like him even less.

"You get on the schedule, and I'll send him over." They go to where Hidalgo sits waiting with his arms crossed, and I decide to wait this one out.

Sliding into a red vinyl booth, I notice the wireless is working in this place. I quickly tap out a group text to the guys saying we made it. Marley immediately sends back a peace-sign emoji. He's probably already high—Mr. Wake and Bake.

Patton's dad's probably busting his balls. I can imagine him cursing my name for taking off like I did, but he'd be climbing the walls in this place. I'm kind of digging it in a weird, back-to-the-essentials kind of way.

I've just picked up a plastic-covered menu when a woman with strawberry-blonde hair piled high on her head and a brown apron glides up to me. She looks about the same age as my mom.

"Hey there, handsome. Can I get you some coffee?" She gives me a wink, and I see her plastic nametag says *Florence*.

"Hi, Florence." I return her grin. "That'd be great."

She produces a gold-plastic carafe from beside her and fills the small cup on the table in front of me. "You can call me Flo. You're new in town."

"Just visiting the LaGrange Orchard. I'm friends with Sawyer."

"You don't say?" She looks curiously to where he stands with the two men. "Miracles never cease."

I'm not sure what that's supposed to mean, but I'm glad for the coffee. It's been a long morning, and it's not even seven.

"You sticking around or just passing through?"

I sip the weak, brown concoction and nod. "We're here a few weeks then we ship out for South America."

"Ahh…" She slides a receipt out of her book across the table to me. "If you need somebody to show you around, you let me know."

I lift the ticket and see a phone number written on it.

"Hey, Flo." Sawyer is at the end of the table, digging in his front pocket. "You ready?"

I finish my drink with a slug, scooping up the scrap of paper. "How much do I owe you?"

She gives me another wink. "No charge, sugar. You just let me know if you need anything."

"Hang on. If I don't pay, you have to pay it out of your tips, right?"

She wrinkles her nose and shakes her head. "Don't worry about it."

Placing a ten in her hand, I pat her shoulder. "Keep the change."

Her eyes warm. "And I thought southern gentlemen had gone out of style."

"Just paying my bill."

I don't want to get into my family history, but I know how tight a waitress's budget can be.

Sawyer punches my arm. "Come on, Casanova. See you later, Flo."

She nods. "Glad to see you're finally getting around to making friends… And good ones."

We're in the truck heading to the farm, and just like always, he doesn't say much. It's Sawyer's style, though. He's the quiet member of the group. Patton is all ambition, Marley's always after a party, an escape. I'm… still searching for that answer.

The sun is higher in the sky, and the shimmering glow of dawn breaking over the peach orchard is gone. Now it's sticky heat and rising humidity.

He leans forward. "It's going to be a scorcher."

"Did you get your team?"

"I think so. I think Digger will be a good pick to take over while I'm gone. Everything should run smoothly for a while."

"You won't leave your sister in charge?"

"Noel?" His forehead wrinkles. "She's just a kid. Anyway, she'll be starting college. She needs to focus on her studies."

I know leaving the orchard and his siblings is heavy on his mind. I also know he really wants to do something for himself. Now could be his last chance—at least that's what he told me.

He pulls off the narrow dirt road in front of the sprawling farm house. It's the first time I've seen it in the daylight, and I'm impressed by the size. It's a two-story structure with white wooden siding and a large, wraparound porch complete with swing. It's the picture of classic Americana.

We slam our doors shut, and I follow him up the walk, past the small white picket fence and through the front door. My stomach immediately starts growling as the aromas of fresh toast, sizzling bacon, and fried eggs hit my nose.

"Damn, that smells good." I rub my hands over my stomach.

Sawyer's phone starts ringing, and he holds up a hand. "I'll be right there. Head on in and introduce yourself to Noel."

I'm not going to argue. I follow the scent of food, and the closer I get, I hear a high voice, singing an old Dolly Parton song. It's the one that used to be on that TV show. It sounds good.

I push the swinging door open, and I'm almost knocked on my ass for the second time today.

Standing with her back to me, reaching high over her head into an open cabinet is not a kid by any stretch. Noel is petite and slender, with curves in all the right places. She's wearing a fatigue-green tank top and cutoff shorts, and her glossy brown hair is piled on her head with little strands falling down.

I watch as she stretches higher for the plates, and my eyes glide down the smooth skin of her arm to her narrow waist over the curve of her ass and down her silky legs to her bare feet.

Her toenails are painted bright red.

Just as I'm about to offer to help, she hops up with one foot on the edge of the counter and grabs a big, ivory platter and bowl, but they must be too heavy for her. Everything seems to shift into slow motion.

She wobbles, and her song turns into a loud scream as she falls backward. "Oh, no… NO!"

"Noel!" I dive forward, and by some miracle, she lands in my arms, sending me down to my knees.

I'm leaning forward, holding her close. We're both breathing fast, our noses almost touching. Her eyes blink open, and when they meet mine, golden-brown as whiskey, I think I'm falling.

A sharp inhale, and I'm surrounded by fresh spring and flowers. She's soft as silk, her breasts against my chest, and her full, glossy lips part in front of mine.

I could kiss her…

"Sweet Jesus, an angel…" It's a breathy whisper, a little raspy and a lot sexy.

"I'm Taron."

Both plates are still in her hands. She blinks a few times before looking around. "Oh, hell."

She pulls back, and I move to the side, helping her find her feet. When she stands, her legs are right in my face, smooth and muscular, and I resist the urge to reach out and slide my palm against her skin… *Shit, get a grip, Taron.*

"Are you okay?" I stand quickly, lightly touching her arm.

"I think so." She glances up at me and smiles shyly, and I swear the earth moves. "I mean, yes… Thank you. That could've been bad."

Her gaze captures me, and her tanned cheeks flush.

"Noel, Jesus!" We both jump as Sawyer enters the room shouting. "Can you use the damn step ladder!"

I step away from her fast, leaning against the counter, and she goes to where he's standing in the doorway.

"Lord, Sawyer! You almost gave me a heart attack."

"You're going to give me a heart attack if you keep pulling stunts like that. I'm about to be out of the country, and you're climbing around the kitchen like a circus performer with no net."

"Shut up and give me a hug." She reaches up to embrace him.

He glances at me. "Thanks for saving my idiot sister."

"Jerk." She pushes his shoulder. "Thank you, Taron."

She smiles, but her eyes don't quite meet mine. I can't tell if she's embarrassed or shaken up or something else. Either way, she turns and gives me another view of her cute little ass. My hand goes to my stomach, and I rub the sudden ache there.

"I hope you're hungry. I made a half dozen eggs and a pile of biscuits."

"I'm starving." Sawyer goes to the table.

I force myself to stop staring at her like I've never seen a girl before. "How can I help?"

"Just wash up. The table's set." She moves quickly around the small space in her bare feet while I go to the sink and wash my hands.

She skips over to where I'm standing and hands me a towel, and the scent of her wraps around me again, fresh and warm, and my dream flickers through my head.

"Let's eat." Sawyer's voice is sharp, and I join him at the table.

I'm not here for a summer romance. I'm here to help with the harvest. In a few short weeks, I'll be gone, and I can't lose sight of that—no matter how hot Sawyer's "kid" sister is.

"Praise the Lord and pass the biscuits." She sits across from me, and this time when our eyes meet, a hint of a grin curls her lips.

Our gaze tangles like we're sharing a secret, and all my good intentions slip right out the window.

CHAPTER
Two

Noel

HOLY SHIT, TARON RHODES IS THE SEXIEST MAN I'VE EVER SEEN, AND he just saved my life. Or my neck.

Or at the very least, my ass.

Now he's sitting across the table from me, and every time he glances up, it's like going over that hill at the top of the old orchard road at fifty miles per hour. My insides whoosh to my throat, and all my breath disappears.

"I can't leave Caracas to visit you in the hospital…" Sawyer's still going on like some old lady. "I need to know you're making good choices, taking care of Leon."

I take a sip of orange juice, trying to get my stomach to unclench so I can eat. "I won't need a step ladder when you're gone. I'll just be cooking for two."

Taron glances up at me again, and my stomach flips.

So much for breakfast.

He's got the most amazing eyes. I can't tell if they're green or blue. They're this pale blend of both colors, and they stand out under his dark brows and dark hair.

A close beard covers his cheeks. I'm sure he'll have to shave it before he reports for duty—at least that's what I've always heard—still, I'd like to rake my nails through it while I kiss his full lips…

"Pass the eggs," my brother grunts.

Taron and I both reach at the same time, and when our fingers brush, I swear it sparks.

"I've got it." His grin is playful, bad-boyish, and I hold in a sigh at the lines of muscle wrapping his arms as he passes the bowl.

"Jay Hidalgo and his crew will be here bright and early tomorrow morning." Sawyer shovels more eggs onto his plate before dropping the wooden spoon.

That snaps me out of my swoon-fest. "Do I need to feed them?"

Shit, that's a day-long trip to Walmart.

"I told him we don't have time for that. They'll bring their own meals. I need you with the high school kids on the sorter, not spending all day at the store."

That old sadness nudges my chest. Sawyer's been pretty good at keeping me in the loop about his deployment, but I think my brain just doesn't want to hang onto the information. I keep forgetting the details.

"How long before you leave?"

"I'll be here through the harvest, through the peach festival. We report on July fifth."

Right after the holiday. I nod, looking down and pushing my food around my plate. Sawyer's decision to join the military scared me at first. We've already lost so much, and then he went and picked the Marines. That's like the hardest branch of the service. They serve the longest, and they're in the most dangerous places…

"Dang, Noel!" My little brother Leon stomps into the kitchen in his cowboy boots like a one-man gang. "Why didn't you call me for breakfast? You know I'm starving to death."

"Your sister was too busy trying to kill herself." Sawyer reaches out and musses Leon's shaggy dark hair. "Grab a plate, kid."

"I never have to worry about you leaving," I tease as he drops into a chair. "Hoecake'll get you."

"Like you ever make hoecakes." He grabs a cathead biscuit and straddles the chair.

"Shut up and eat," I say gently, motioning to the platter. "Take two."

As much as he eats, he's still skinny as a rail. His jeans fall off his hips without a belt, and his red plaid shirt is loose over a white tank. His hair's too long, and he reminds me of a young horse, messy and wild.

"I know somebody who makes damn good hoecakes." Taron's rich voice joins the conversation.

"You make hoecakes?" Sawyer laughs, and I wonder when my brother got to be such a dad. He's the same age as Taron, but they're worlds apart. "Report for KP at oh-six hundred tomorrow."

A dimple pierces Taron's scruffy cheek and those eyes are back on me. It's like fizzy liquid in my veins. "I don't mind helping you with breakfast."

I look down at my plate, trying to stop all the butterflies. *Seriously, Noel?* You'd think I've never seen a good-looking man before.

"Sure. That'd be great." My voice is quiet.

Leon squints over at him. "You're Sawyer's friend?"

"Taron," he supplies.

I push Leon's foot off the chair. "Sit up at the table like you've got manners."

"Get off me, woman!" Leon shoves another bite of biscuit in his mouth, and I shoot Sawyer a look.

"That's no woman, that's your sister." My oldest brother deadpans.

All three guys laugh, and my eyes narrow.

"Thanks." Sarcasm is thick in my tone, and Leon laughs more, bumping his chest against the table.

Sawyer clears his throat, and I guess because he's a Marine now or maybe because he's leaving, he has the decency to try and salvage the situation.

"Leon." His voice is sharp. "I need you to help Noel while I'm gone. Treat her with respect."

Leon groans like the fifteen-year-old he is. Sawyer must give him a glare I don't see because he changes his tune. "Okay."

"Are your friends coming today?" Sawyer shifts the conversation to business. "We need them ready to sort tomorrow morning. Jay's coming with his crew."

My little brother shrugs. "They said they'd be here."

"Why don't you text them and be sure."

He lets out a groan and pushes out of his seat. "Good breakfast, sis."

"Take another biscuit." I put one in his hand as he scuffs out the door.

Sawyer stands, pulling his phone from his pocket. "I'll check on the crate situation. Thanks, Noel."

He's out the door, leaving me at a table full of dirty dishes.

Taron sits back watching them go before turning to me. He's so damn hot. "Are they always like that?"

My brow furrows as I pretend to think then nod. "Pretty much."

"So you make breakfast, they eat it, give you a hard time, then leave you to clean it all up?"

"Well… I mean, it's what we do. The house is mine." Pushing away from the table, I start collecting the dishes and carrying them to the sink. Behind me, I hear him doing the same, and I turn around. "You don't have to—"

"I came here to help." He gives me another grin, and I chew

my bottom lip, watching him carry dirty plates, his broad shoulders stretching his cotton tee. He's gotta be at least six-two.

"I think Sawyer is expecting you to help with the men's work."

"The men's work?" His voice changes. "Now that is something I would not expect to hear from you."

"How come?" My eyes narrow. "You've never met me."

"True." He nods. "But I know your brother, and he said you graduated with honors and plan to go to business school in the fall."

"I do." Crossing back to the table, I pick up the last of the dirty plates. "And I don't expect to have to lift and carry a bushel of peaches in a board room."

"A bushel." He holds a towel, and I wash the first dish, passing it to him to dry.

"That's fifty pounds." I hand him another clean plate, and he dries it, reaching overhead to return them to their shelf each time.

When he does it, his shirt rises, and I get a glimpse of the lines of muscle in his stomach. *Hot.*

"I see." He looks at me again, and my eyes snap to the soapy water. "On the farm, work is divided by who can carry the most weight?"

"I don't know about farms." I pass him another plate, sliding my eyes to the side for another peek at his abs. "But at LaGrange Orchard, we put everybody where they can be the most useful. Like, you're pretty good at drying dishes, and you claim you can make hoecakes—"

"I make damn good hoecakes. You'll see."

Leaning closer, I catch a whiff of his scent, masculine and clean. "Still, I wouldn't waste your back in the kitchen when you're needed on the loading dock."

I flip the switch for the garbage disposal and help the food scraps down the drain. Akela trots into the room as if on cue, and I toss her the last piece of bacon, then I squat down to rub her fluffy white neck while she chews.

Taron crosses his arms watching us. "She knocked me on my ass this morning."

"Akela!" Laughter tickles in my stomach, and I shake my face at her. She only licks my nose. "Did you knock Taron down?"

He squats beside me to pet her head. "Huskey?"

"Yeah." I give her one more neck scrub and stand. "Somebody dumped her out in the field when she was a puppy. Sawyer said I couldn't keep her, but he's not my dad."

His eyes sober at my words. "Sawyer told me what happened to your parents. That must've been rough."

"It was a long time ago." I don't know why I always say that. No matter how many years pass, losing both our parents the way we did is a pain that never leaves.

Now my brother's leaving home, putting himself in harm's way.

With a sigh, I push those feelings away like I always do. Feeling bad doesn't change a damn thing.

"Sorry all the women around here are throwing themselves at you."

"I'm glad I was here to catch you."

"Me too." I blink up and try to smile.

We share a moment... until the back door opens, and Sawyer sticks his head in. "You planning to stay in the house all day or you coming to help?"

"He helped me with the dishes."

"Hoecake, dishes... Get out here where I need you."

"You'll take that back in the morning." Taron jogs down the steps after my brother.

I walk out to the porch watching his tight end as he walks away. Exhaling a little sigh, I step into my cowboy boots. The teenagers are milling around in the sorting shed, and if Sawyer's prepping for the crew, I need to teach these kids how to sort peaches.

They'll be coming in fast tomorrow, and we won't have time for them to get behind. The next two weeks are going to be insane around here.

CHAPTER
Three

Taron

THE FOREMAN'S COTTAGE IS ABOUT THIRTY YARDS UP THE HILL FROM the house. The door sticks a bit, but Sawyer pushes it open and crosses to switch on a small window unit.

"It's stuffy, but it'll cool off fast." He opens a narrow door at the back corner. "Full bathroom here. Closet there."

I drop my oversized duffel on a chair, looking around the small space. "Not bad."

"You're welcome at the house anytime, and you'll eat with us." He walks to the door, his boots thumping on the pine floors. "But here you'll have some privacy… if you meet somebody or whatever."

My mind tries to drift to Noel, but I catch it. Hooking up, especially with my best friend's little sister, is not why I came to this tiny town.

"Nobody should mess with your stuff, but just in case." His tosses me a set of keys. "Come to the loading dock when you're done, and I'll show you how to use the forklift."

With that, he's gone, and I give the place a quick scan. It's small, but a double bed is in the corner with a nightstand and lamp beside it. A few books are on the shelf—both look like cowboy novels. Across the room, a mini fridge is on a counter with a coffee maker beside it.

Blinds cover the windows, and the chair where I dropped my bag is positioned in front of a small, flat screen television. I look at my phone—still no service.

"Whatever." I've checked in with the only people I care about in Nashville.

It takes me five minutes to unpack, hang my few belongings in the closet and place my toiletries in the bathroom before I head out again, leaving the keys on the small table by the door.

Noel's got a group of teenagers in the enormous peach shed, and I watch as she uses a basket of tennis balls to demonstrate sorting. It's a good mix of boys and girls, and she's encouraging but strict as she guides them through the process of finding the yellow balls with black lines down the sides and sorting them into baskets while stacking the all-yellow ones into crates.

"You need to move fast, but not so fast you miss bad ones." She helps a petite blonde girl turn one of the balls over before sorting it into a waiting crate. "That's a good one."

The next ball bounces off the Lazy Susan and rolls to where I'm standing. The girl beside Noel wails, "I busted that one!"

Noel only laughs. "It's okay! Actual peaches don't get away from you that easy. You're doing good!"

Our eyes catch and she smiles as she walks to where I'm standing holding the escaped fake peach. My stomach tightens, but I push those feelings down, reminding myself why I'm here.

Still, my eyes drink her in as she approaches. The cutoffs she's wearing put her tanned legs on full display, down to the calf-high cowboy boots she's wearing, and her dark hair is still piled in a messy bun on top of her head. She smiles—full, natural lips parting over straight white teeth, and *damn*, she's gorgeous.

"Betsy lost her peach."

I can't resist. "That's the pits."

She blinks at me.

For a moment, she doesn't say a word, and I picture a plane crashing and burning...

Until I see the twinkle in her eye.

Her lips press together, and she holds out her hand. "She's a little fuzzy on the details."

My lips tighten, and I hold out the tennis ball. "She seemed speachless."

"She needs to practice what I peach."

I can't hold back a chuckle, and I shake my head. "You got me."

Her eyebrow arches and she takes the tennis ball, turning on her heel and walking away victorious. "Pitty."

That makes me laugh out loud, and she spins back, laughing. A small dimple is right at the corner of her bottom lip, and I shake my head. *This girl.*

"Hey!" Sawyer's sharp voice snatches my attention. "We need to get these palettes over to the loading dock now."

I follow him out the back entrance, and we spend the rest of the morning lifting and carrying wooden crates across a concrete lot. After a while, they feel like they weigh five hundred pounds each, and I get why Sawyer sailed through basic training.

Sweat rolls down my sides, and my tee is soaking wet and sticking to me when Leon appears with a cooler in his hand.

"Thanks." I reach for a water bottle, and he digs out sandwiches and cokes.

"Noel said there's plenty more if you want it."

I'm unwrapping what looks like chicken salad.

Sawyer has already finished his first sandwich and is tearing the wrapping off a second as he fishes out his truck keys. "I'm heading to town to pick up the last of the crates. I'll back in an hour."

Leon is right on his heels. "I'll ride with you."

His brother puts a hand on his shoulder. "I need you here in case Digger shows up before I get back."

"Digger? Why is that asshole coming here?"

"He knows about running an orchard."

"Into the ground." Leon crosses his arms, and I see a resemblance between the brothers.

"Digger was just a kid when all that happened."

"Still, he inherited the genes. I thought they did cotton now."

"He'll do what I tell him to do." Sawyer turns to the truck. "You'll behave yourself."

Leon walks over and sits on the back of the flatbed, watching his brother get in the Chevy and pull out of the loading area where we've been working.

My hunger is somewhat eased, and I'm on my second bottle of water. "Who's Digger?"

"Some dick who's got his sights set on this place. Sawyer doesn't even see it. Or maybe he does and doesn't care. He is leaving, after all."

He hops off the trailer and starts walking toward the rows of trees stretching over the hill. I glance in the direction my friend just left and decide to take off after his little brother.

We walk up the hill for a bit in silence. I watch as Leon stops occasionally, pushing leaves off the dappled fruit and inspecting each one. He finally picks one that has a split down the side and continues to the next short tree.

"Hey." I stop while he repeats the process, finding another overripe fruit and dropping it into the cooler he brought with him.

He cuts his eyes up at me. "What?"

His curt tone doesn't bug me. "How many do you need?"

"Noel said to bring her ten. She's making ice cream." He finds another split peach and drops it into the cooler.

"Anything in particular you're looking for?"

"Just ones that can't be sold." He picks another one, and I search the limb in front of me.

I'm surprised how long it takes to find a blemished peach. "I guess I thought there'd be more split ones."

"These are Freestone peaches. They'll keep ripening until the end of July." He picks another and hands it to me. "You can eat one."

Turning it over in my hand, I look for signs of insects. "Does it need to be washed?"

"Nah, we use a natural insecticide to control the caterpillars and borers."

"Cool." I take a bite of the split fruit, and the juice is refreshing after the long day hauling palettes in the heat. "It's not as sweet as I thought it would be."

He keeps going, picking several more fruits.

I follow, finishing off the one he gave me. "Should I toss the pit?"

He shrugs. "It won't hurt anything."

I drop the stone and wipe my hands on my jeans. He stops and looks ahead before closing the top of the cooler. It's just after noon and hot as the face of the sun out here. I step on a pit in my chucks and wish I'd packed tougher-soled shoes.

Leon glances down. "We can run by the boot store if you want to get some boots for while you're here."

"Not a bad idea. You can go with me."

"When fucking Digger finally gets here."

My lips tighten, and I have a feeling he's not allowed to drop the F-bomb. Still, I'm not looking to bust his balls. I get he's pissed about Sawyer leaving. "You really hate that guy."

"Hating's a sin." He kicks a fallen peach and a swarm of flies swirls around it then resettles where it lands. I give him a look, and he shrugs. "You'll see when he gets here."

We walk a little farther up the row, and I take a chance. "You're pretty smart. What are you, a junior?"

"I'll be sixteen next week." He looks over at me like it's an accomplishment. "You know I was an accident?"

"Who told you that?"

"It's the family joke." He shrugs. "My name's Noel backward. They said it was because my parents had run out of names. My birthday is exactly six months after hers."

"Wait... but Noel's—"

"She'll be nineteen at Christmas. I just mean her birth *date* is December 25th, so they named her Noel. Mine's June 25th, the exact opposite."

"So they named you Leon." I chuckle, wondering what their folks must've been like. It's hard to square with what I know of them.

He turns and we start down the hill again, toward the house. "I don't really remember them much. I just remember Sawyer working his ass off all the time."

"He said he had to drop out of school for a year."

"He figured it was more important to keep things running here than finish tenth grade. It was right in the middle of planting season. The whole town pretty much pitched in to help us. Church ladies brought us food and clothes."

I think back to my mom, struggling with a waitressing job, doing her best to take care of me alone in Nashville. "Not everybody has that kind of support."

He shrugs. "I guess."

"Your brother really cares about you. He talks about you all the time."

"Then why's he leaving?" He cuts his eyes at me, and I see hurt simmering there.

We're back at the house, and I choose my words carefully. "You said he's been working his ass off since he was your age. Maybe he wants to do something for himself now. While he still can."

"Yeah, well, we need him here. Not in some foreign country where who knows what might happen to him."

"Hey." I catch Leon's arm. "I won't let anything happen to your brother. I promise."

The anger in his brow eases slightly. He shakes his head and starts up the steps, letting the screen door slam behind him. I hear Noel's voice inside and walk toward the shed. I need a shower, but I don't know what else my friend has lined up for us this afternoon. I feel like the walking dead after working all day on five hours of sleep.

A warm breeze blows nonstop through the empty peach shed, and I take a seat on the flatbed, thinking about the promise I just made to Leon. I don't know what's ahead of us when we leave for active duty, but I plan to do whatever it takes to keep that promise. It's what we all agreed when we parted ways. *Family*.

CHAPTER
Four

Noel

HALF THE PEACHES LEON PICKED ARE WASHED, DICED, AND IN THE freezer. The remaining five go in the food processor with honey, lemon zest, and cream for fresh sorbet after dinner.

I pour the mixture into the ice cream maker and gaze up the hill at the large shed where I spent the morning teaching twenty kids the art of sorting peaches. Tomorrow, Mr. Hidalgo's crew will descend on the orchard and clean the trees fast, emptying their haul onto the belts where the teens will sort the bruised or cut ones into baskets for jams, preserves, peach syrup, or peach ice cream.

The unblemished fruits will be stacked into crates, which the bigger boys lift and haul to the waiting flatbed trucks.

Taron will have to eat his words—Brenda Stein, one of the bigger girls, wanted to help the boys haul crates to the trucks, and I said she could. She promised not to overdo it.

My mind filters through the conversations we had today. He's so easy to talk to, so playful and relaxed. I snort remembering our pun war. He should've known I've heard them all.

Wiping my hands on a towel, I walk out the door and up the hill toward the shed. As I approach, I see Taron is lying on his back on one of the flatbed trailers with his ball cap over his face. He's still wearing those converse sneakers, and I just hope he knows they'll be ruined if he wears them to work in the fields.

Without really thinking about it, I go to where he's perched and playfully shove his crossed feet. "Better get some boots, City Slicker—oh! Oh no!"

Taron's feet flop to the side, but they don't stop there. His legs go off the back of the truck, and the rest of him follows, hitting the ground with a thud.

"Fuck!" His low voice is loud.

"Taron!" I run around the end of the trailer to where he's lying on his side, shaking his head.

"What the hell?"

I drop to my knees, putting my hand on his shoulder. "I'm so sorry!"

"Did you just shove me off the flatbed?" Anger flashes in his wolf eyes, and I feel like shit.

"I didn't! I—"

"I think you did." He pushes up to a sitting position, shaking his head.

His face is all covered in dirt, and I want to die. "Here." I hold out the towel still in my hands. "Let me wipe your face. Are you okay?"

He holds my arm and stands slowly, stretching to one side and wincing. "Shit... Feels like I cracked a rib."

I clutch a hand to my mouth. "Taron. I'm so sorry."

He cuts his eyes at me, and I think I might cry. As he studies me, the anger seems to melt. Something different takes its place, something devious.

"Now I owe you one."

My eyebrows shoot up. "You don't..."

"Oh, yes I do." He lifts his shoulder and circles his arm, wincing again as he does it.

My heart beats faster. I'm a little nervous about what payback could be. "It was an accident…"

"You didn't accidentally shove my feet off the flatbed."

Stepping forward, I catch his arms. "I really didn't know you'd fall—"

Our faces are close again, and I feel his breath against my cheek. My eyes drift up and his are cast down, meeting my gaze and sending heat flooding my panties.

It's just like in the kitchen when he caught me. The air around us seems to crackle. His hands span my waist, and his arms are like bands of iron beneath my grip. I feel like peach sorbet melting in the sun under his gaze. My lips grow hot and heavy, and *Oh, lord, I want him to kiss me so bad…*

"Hey, what's happening over here?" I recognize the tenor voice at once and step back, away from the inferno that is Taron Rhodes holding me in his arms.

"Digger?" I shake myself, pushing a stray lock of hair behind my ear. "Are you looking for Sawyer?"

I walk around the flatbed, and I feel Taron watching me as I go. I've felt him watching me all day, and it tingles in my lower belly.

"Hey, Noel." Digger Hayes steps forward to give me a brief hug. He always wants to kiss my cheek, but I dodge just in time.

Taron's deep voice interrupts his greeting. "Sawyer had to drive into town to pick up some crates."

Digger's eyes narrow as he inspects Taron. "I don't think we've met."

"We haven't." Taron steps forward, extending a hand. "Taron Rhodes. I'm here for the harvest."

"Ah." Digger's eyebrows rise, and I see him visibly relax. "You must be Sawyer's military friend."

"Marine. I'm his Marine friend."

"Oh, right." Digger does a little laugh that makes me cringe.

He is such a condescending dick. "And how are you liking our little town so far? I imagine it's a far cry from Nashville."

"I've only been here a day, but I like what I see." His ocean eyes meet mine, and it's like a bolt of lightning straight through my core.

"We're pretty happy with it." Digger puts his arm around my shoulders, and my head snaps around to face him. *Has he lost his mind?*

I step out of his unwelcome embrace. "I'll put on some coffee if y'all want some?"

Taron's eyes narrow. "I'm good. Thanks, Noel."

"Sounds great." Digger smiles, moving to follow me. "I'll walk you to the house."

What is his deal? "No need. I'll bring it out. Sawyer should be back any minute."

"I don't mind." Digger has a pointed look in his eye, and I exhale a sigh.

"Whatever."

Taron crosses his arms, eyes still narrowed as he watches Digger follow me to the back door. I glance back a few times. I want to somehow let him know I have nothing to do with this sudden interest coming from my old friend. My old, annoying friend.

Pushing the door open, I go straight to the coffee pot and pull out the carafe to fill with water. Nothing fancy around here.

"He seems like a nice fellow." Digger looks out the bay window toward the peach shed. "Nice of him to come down to help with the harvest."

"Sawyer's different. I think he's excited." I scoop the coffee grounds into the basket, shove it in place, and hit go. "He's been so focused on this place for so long."

"And what about you?" Digger turns to me, a weird grin on his face. "Are you excited to start business school?"

The way he says it feels like he's patronizing me. "I'm excited to try new things, yes."

"Have you figured out how you're going to pay for it?"

Crossing my arms, I arch an eyebrow. "Is that any of your business?"

"I happen to know the orchard is just barely covering expenses right now."

I won't even ask how he knows that information. Everybody seems to know everybody's' business in a small town.

"I've got plans of my own." Not that I want him knowing them.

"Right. The store." That condescension is in his tone again.

"We get a lot of tourists through here. A lot of people like to eat organics, and clean beauty is a growing industry—"

"I was just thinking…" He places a hand on my upper arm, interrupting. "Maybe you'd like to go out sometime. With me."

Exhaling a laugh, I shake my head. "I'm sorry. Didn't we try that?" Dating Digger Hayes is about the last thing I want to do again.

"Going to the Peach Ball is hardly dating. You're a pretty girl, Noel. I'd love to see you taking your place in society. With me."

"With you." It's not a question.

"Let's have dinner at LaFonda's."

"Only politicians go to LaFonda's."

"You're so cute." He shakes his head, and I swear, I want to knee him in the groin.

"Puppies are cute." My voice is thinly veiled annoyance.

"LaFonda's is the nicest steak restaurant in Harristown. It's a place your momma would've been accustomed to patronizing."

That pulls me up short. "My parents never had any money to go to a place like that."

"I'm talking about your momma's people, about you being Harristown royalty. You're not a shop owner."

"I'm not Harristown royalty. We weren't raised like that."

He leans close enough that his breath skates over my eyebrows. "Maybe it's time for a change. I'd like to bring you back to what you are. I'd like to bring this whole orchard into the Hayes fold, and re-establish what it once was."

I take a step back, my brow furrowed. "Have you been drinking today, Digger?"

"Noel…" He chuckles. "You're so adorable. All I'm saying is think about it. Open your mind and let your imagination roam. We could be the king and queen of this town."

"Oh, look." I point over to the counter. "The coffee's ready. Let me pour you a cup."

He crosses his arms and watches me in a way I don't like. I quickly pour him a cup and grab the cream from the refrigerator. I'm not looking to spend any more time in this kitchen, and where the hell is Sawyer?

"There you go. I made some peach muffins." Reaching into the microwave, I pull out the plate of rose-gold cakes. "Help yourself. I'll just be out at the shed."

I'm about to go when my upper arm is caught in an uncomfortable grip. "Don't forget who you are, Noel. I've known you your whole life. We have history."

Jerking my arm away, I smile, but there's steel behind my eyes. "I might have known you my whole life, Digger Hayes, but that doesn't mean we have history."

"Just keep in mind who'll be here when everyone else is gone."

My insides feel like wooden shutters when a strong wind blows through. I'm rattled and uneasy, and who the hell is Digger Hayes to make me feel this way?

I head down the back steps, but instead of going to the peach shed, I take a turn and head up the hill into the rows. Whenever life gets too much, I've always walked in these trees. They belong to us. They're part of our family, and they keep us alive. A heavy breath and light bark, and Akela's with me.

"Hey, girl." I give her head a scrub. She's five years old, which in dog years is older than me.

Same as these trees, she lifts me up when I'm feeling down. I put my hand on her head and walk until the tension eases in my chest. I've worked hard to avoid complications, to keep my life simple. Maybe Digger is right, and I shouldn't let a guy who's only going to be here a few weeks distract me. But it sure as hell won't be because I'm looking to be the queen of anything.

Turning, I head back toward the house. Whatever happens, it'll be suppertime soon, and I've got hungry men to feed. If I've learned anything about this life, it's that it does what it wants, and the best we can do is buckle up and hold on.

CHAPTER
Five

Taron

"L EGEND IS THEY GOT THEIR NAME BECAUSE FARMERS WOULD FRY THE cakes on the back of their hoes." My hands are wrist-deep in cornmeal, self-rising flour, eggs, sugar, buttermilk, and I'm mixing it all together in a bowl.

"We're not bringing a shovel in the house." Noel is beside me cracking a dozen eggs into a large white bowl. "You're not using a spoon to mix it?"

Today she's wearing another pair of cutoffs and a beige tank top. Her hair is in a high ponytail on her head, and the ends dance in large curls around her shoulders. I want to wrap one around my finger and pull.

"Spoons are for suckers. You're not using a spoon."

She holds up a fork. "I'm making scrambled eggs. I have to scramble the eggs."

"Anyway, as I was saying…" I cut my eyes, she rolls hers, and I want to pull her close. "We'll use a cast iron skillet."

Leaving the mixture in the bowl, I wash my hands and dry them, tossing a drop of water on the black skillet to see if it bounces. When it does, I start opening drawers.

"What do you need?" Noel is holding a large block of cheese and a knife over the bowl of eggs.

"Ladle."

"Top drawer to your left."

"Don't slice toward your hand."

She glances down at her hands then shakes her head. "Mind your business." Still I notice she changes directions with the knife. "How's your rib?"

"Better. I think I just bruised it."

"Oh, thank God! I prayed it would be okay. Sawyer would kill me if you were too hurt to work." She's talking fast, and it makes me grin. Then she squints up at me. "So there's no reason to get even now."

"Think again. You shoved me off a flatbed."

"It was an accident!"

"Yeah, right."

"I see you got some better shoes."

"Not because you tried to break my neck."

When Sawyer came back and took Digger the Dick into his office to talk, Leon and I drove to Boot City where I got a pair of pretty basic work boots. Leon reminds me of how I felt so many times at his age, after my mom left Nashville, and I felt like I was a wart on my uncle's butt that he wished would go away.

Before I met Patton and Marley.

Before we joined the military.

Now I feel like I have a family. I feel like I can make a difference and count for something... If only I didn't have this itchy feeling I might have found something just as fulfilling right here in this tiny kitchen.

Holding the bowl over the skillet, I carefully ladle batter in four little cakes.

"You *do* use a spoon." The smug look on her face makes me tug her ponytail.

"Strictly for measuring purposes."

"Ow!" She bats at my hand.

"That didn't hurt."

With an exaggerated sigh, she dumps the egg mixture into an adjacent skillet on the stove and watches it bubble, spreading it around with the fork.

"Who taught you to make hoecakes?" Her head tilts to the side, and for a minute, I'm caught by her bright eyes, curious and sweet.

"Paula Deen," I blurt, and she laughs. "It's the truth. Unlike you, they're the only thing I know how to make."

Last night she prepared a dinner of fried pork chops, green beans, and mashed potatoes with peach muffins and peach sorbet for dessert. It was the best food I'd tasted in my life—or maybe I was starving from how hard we worked all day. I wanted to be better company, but after one beer, I was doing my best to keep my eyes open.

The only thing that stopped me at the front door of the foreman's cottage was looking back toward the house and seeing the light in Noel's window, watching her moving around. I couldn't help thinking she might be the perfect woman. Last night I chalked the idea up to utter exhaustion.

The tightness in my stomach standing beside her now, teasing, making breakfast, fully rested, makes me wonder if I might be right.

"You're burning that one." She points with the fork, and I jump, snatching up a spatula and flipping the hoecakes fast before they all burn.

"Thanks."

Sawyer and Leon banging into the kitchen puts an end to our joking. They start grabbing plates, and I look out the window to see a truck full of men pulling into the lot. A few teenagers have started to arrive, parking their pickups and hatchbacks in the lot behind the shed.

"Time to get busy." Sawyer's voice is all business, and I know he won't let me hang around to help with dishes.

It doesn't seem to matter as the entire place shifts into work mode. Sawyer takes one team of men, Digger takes another, and I take a third. We're either in the fields helping pick fruit or on the dock helping load crates onto the backs of the trailers.

We lift the heavy crates, one by one, onto the backs of the trucks that will take them to the distribution center. My shirt's off, but unlike yesterday, I don't feel like the walking dead.

When we hit eight hours, Sawyer calls it a day for the teams. Noel's still with the teens on the sorters, finishing up what we've just harvested. I've been watching her all day, unable to keep my eyes from her smooth body, her cute little ass as she bends and lifts crates and carries baskets of damaged fruit.

Her cheeks are pink, and the strands of hair falling from her high ponytail stick to her neck. It gives me an idea.

Taking a cup of ice water, I walk over behind her at one of the large lazy Susan's, and quicker than she can move, I drop a large chunk of ice down the back of her shirt.

"Taron!" She screams louder than the heavy machinery and poor Betsy drops a peach.

I take off running, but she's right behind me, snatching a solo cup of ice water off the ledge. Akela starts to bark and chase us, and we don't stop until we're down the hill, breathing hard and laughing. She tosses the water at me, but I don't even care it's so damn hot. The dog just stands at attention, waiting excitedly for what the hell we're about to do next.

"What do you guys do to cool off around here?"

"Well…" Her eyes trickle down my bare chest in a way that kicks the temperature up another thirty degrees, then she glances back toward the shed. "They're just wrapping up. Come on."

I follow her around the shed to where a three-wheeler's parked, watching as she throws a bare leg over the seat and pushes down on the starter. It roars to life, and she gives me a grin.

"You getting on?"

I guess I am.

I climb on behind her, bracing my feet on the pegs and holding her waist as she zips over the hills as fast as this thing can go. Akela keeps pace with us the whole way, barking excitedly.

Noel's body weight compared to mine is not enough to keep me on this seat, and with every bump, I feel like I might fly off the back.

Still, her hair whips around us, and she's calling to her dog. She rises off the seat with every bounce, and I do my best to keep my thoughts focused on old lady underwear, scowling politicians—every boner-killer I can imagine.

Finally, we're there. My hands slide from her waist to her hips, and she quickly steps off to the side. Akela stands waiting.

"Fun, huh?" Her eyes sparkle, and her ponytail is wild.

"I'm surprised you didn't leave me on the road a ways back," I tease her. "Where are we?"

"Come on!"

She takes off running up a small rise, Akela right with her, and I hop off the three-wheeler to follow them. When I reach the top of the small hill, we're looking down over a pond shaded by tall pine trees. At one end is a swirl of small currents, and farther below us, deeper in the dark shadows, I see another swirl.

"What is this?"

"It's the Bates reservoir." I watch as she toes off her boots, my stomach tight and my insides humming. "It could be a million degrees out here, and the water's always like ice."

She jogs down into the shade of the trees and dips her feet in the shallows, letting out a squeal. "Freezing!"

"How deep is it?" I follow her lead, toeing off my boots and grinning like an idiot watching her.

"About five feet, I think."

She's still dancing around the edge with her dog, barely getting her feet wet, when without thinking, I race down to where she's standing and sweep her over my shoulder.

"Taron!" She screams at the top of her lungs. "Don't you dare!"

"Payback time!"

"Nooo!" She beats on my lower back as I charge into the water, Akela right with us barking, and *holy shit*! It *is* like ice.

I don't let it stop me. I keep going until it's mid-thigh, when I circle her around.

"Don't you dare!" Her eyes throw daggers, but she can't get a grip on my arms.

I toss her forward like a sack of potatoes into the water. A short shriek breaks the quiet before she crashes through the surface, going all the way under.

She's up just as fast, gasping and screaming. "Are you trying to give me a heart attack?"

"Now we're even." Turning my back, I walk out of the frigid water to where the sun beats down with a vengeance.

It actually feels pretty good standing in the scorching heat after that ice bath. My limbs are loose from the running and the laughing and the adrenaline, but as I watch her wading toward me, water running down her beautiful body, hair clinging to her cheeks and neck, I start to feel a different kind of adrenaline.

The beige tank she's wearing is transparent, and I can see her thin lace bra under it and the dark circles of her areolas crowned by her hardened nipples.

Heat races below my belt, and I have to turn toward the pine trees while I push down the sudden wood in my pants.

"Oh, what? Now you're going to act like nothing happened?" Noel's voice is mad, but playful.

She jogs up behind me and wraps both her arms tightly around mine, soaking my backside with her frigid, wet body.

"How does that feel, Mr. Bruised Rib? Huh? How does it?" Her voice is so adorably taunting, like she's going to fight me or something.

I kind of can't take it anymore. Turning around, I swoop her up by the waist, putting her face directly level with mine. She gasps as our eyes meet. Her hands are on my shoulders, and all the pent-up heat, the nagging chemistry, her hard nipples pressing against my chest, all of it swirls into a fusion of lust and need.

"I want to kiss you." My voice cracks roughly. I barely recognize it.

She nods, and I stretch up as she meets me halfway. Our lips brush, and it's like two flints striking. Sparks swirl between us as I push her mouth open with mine.

I lower her to her feet so I can cup her face in my hands, and our tongues slide and curl together. She tastes like cold, fresh water, and she feels like diving off the top of a cliff into a bottomless ocean.

Her small body fits perfectly in my arms, and I pull her closer to me, wrapping my arms around her. She exhales a high noise, and my lips move to the top of her cheek, to her temple, to her brow. I don't want to stop kissing her, holding her. I've never felt this way—desperate and hungry and so satisfied.

She slides her hands up to my neck, and she drops her forehead to my bare chest. I lower my nose to the top of her head and breathe.

"Taron." Her soft voice sounds as bewildered as I feel.

How is this happening to us? Has this ever happened to anyone before? Is it possible? It feels so specific.

Her head lifts, and her golden-brown eyes are warm. "What are you doing?"

The question makes me grin. "Something I've wanted to do for two days."

She blinks down as her cheeks flush. "I wondered why I didn't do it when you caught me in the kitchen." Her nose wrinkles, and she squints up at me. "Isn't that what ladies do when they're saved by handsome princes?"

"I'm not a prince."

"But you are handsome." A tease is in her eye.

Sliding my thumb along the top of her cheek, I lean down to kiss her lips once more. "If you ever need saving, I want to save you."

Somehow I'm certain Noel LaGrange can take care of herself no matter what. Still, everybody slips off a kitchen counter sometimes.

"And I'll save you back."

I pull her to my chest, wanting to kiss her again. "It's a deal."

CHAPTER
Six

Noel

ARON'S FULL LIPS COVER MINE, AND MY INSIDES TURN MOLTEN AND slippery. He tastes like salty sweat and fresh water, and he feels like a wall of granite. His hot skin is beneath my hands, and I want to wrap myself around him, feel every ridge and line of muscle. I want to trace my tongue over his collarbone and nip his broad shoulder.

All day today I've stolen glances at him working with the other men. He stomped around the shed in those boots with his faded jeans hugging his ass like a dare, making me sigh and shift in my seat.

Occasionally, his blue-green eyes would catch mine from under the brim of his ball cap, and it was like brushing against a live wire. I'd look away to keep from blushing, but I could feel the electricity simmering in my skin.

Digger also stalked in and out of the shed, his eyes on me like some kind of vulture. Every time I saw him, I'd immediately become engrossed in working with Betsy or Leon or Brenda or one of the other teens. When Taron pulled his shirt off in the midday heat, I'm pretty sure every female in the shed took a moment to appreciate the beauty of God's creation.

Digger's oversized frown almost made me snort. *Jealous much?*

I had to fight a swoon, watching the muscles in Taron's arms flex and bulge, the sweat tracing lines down his neck every time he'd lift a crate of peaches. Muscles rippled across his sides and down his back, and I wondered how it was possible to be so fine.

Now I'm holding him, and everything is hot, including my panties.

Our gaze meets and tangles. His eyes seem darker, and he slides a large hand over my cheek, pushing a lock of wet hair behind my ear. I think he's going to say something, want something, and I know I'll say yes. I'm playing a dangerous game.

Clearing my throat, I force myself to step out of his arms. "We should get back. I kind of ditched out on the teenagers. Sawyer's probably wondering where we are…"

He grins as if he understands what I'm thinking, and butterflies flood my stomach. I'm not sure my older brother would like me making out with his new best friend—or all the X-rated thoughts I'm having.

"This time I'm driving." He takes my hand, pulling me close to his side as we walk.

It's so possessive and unexpected, I forget to care what Sawyer thinks. I just want to stay here with him. I pull on my boots and climb onto the back of the three-wheeler.

My arms wrap around his waist, and I rest my cheek against his warm skin, closing my eyes and imagining this gorgeous man as my boyfriend… or something.

Akela is in dog heaven, barking and running the whole way with us. She probably thinks we've lost our minds charging into that icy pond… or she might think we've lost our minds not staying there. She is a cold-weather breed, after all.

Taron pulls up fast behind the small house, and we hop off, jogging around and up to the peach shed where only a few people still mill around.

"Where have you been?" Sawyer's voice is sharp, and I look down at my drenched clothes, realizing my shirt has gone transparent.

My face flames hot as a firecracker. Gripping the fabric in both hands, I pull it away from my body, going to where he's standing, Taron right behind me.

"It was so hot, and Taron asked me if there was a place to cool off. I thought we could go to Bates—"

"You're supposed to be supervising the teenagers, not running off with Taron."

"It was my fault," Taron starts, but I interrupt him.

"You said we were done. We were off the clock—"

"Noel." My brother's hazel eyes flash.

I don't even know why I'm arguing with him. This isn't my first harvest. "Sorry. I'll check on the kids and tell them when to be back tomorrow."

"I've already done that. Go inside and make us something to eat. Mindy's waiting for you."

I take one last look to where Taron is pulling his tee over his head. He catches me and gives me a fast wink, which sends a grin splitting my cheeks.

I snap my head away so my brother doesn't see us flirting and jog up to the house. Halfway through the door, Mindy's on my case.

"Who is THAT?" Her voice is too loud, and she stands in the window staring outside at Taron. "Holy shit! Is there a missing Hemsworth brother I didn't know about?"

Standing beside her, I watch as he walks toward the shed with Sawyer. His damp hair is messy around his face, and I think about how the muscle in his square jaw moves when he's thinking. I shiver remembering his kiss…

"I don't think so." Heading to the fridge, I pull out the dinner prep.

This morning I'd put four New York strips in a gallon-sized Ziploc with Worcestershire sauce and garlic to marinate all day. I put the plastic baggie in the sink and take the cast-iron skillet out from under the cabinet and put it on the stove.

"Did I see you riding up behind him on the three-wheeler just now?" Mindy's green eyes sparkle even more with the deep tan in her olive skin, and I know she knows.

"It was so dang hot today. I just showed him the Bates reservoir."

"I see… Is that why your clothes are all damp?"

"Sort of. How's things at the nursing home?" I take out a bunch of asparagus and give them a quick rinse, changing the subject.

I have no idea what's going on between Taron and me, so I can't be expected to explain it to my best friend.

Mindy pushes a lock of spiral-curly brown hair behind her ear and saunters to where I'm quickly cutting the hard ends off the stalks. She really is stunning. "Your aunt's doing good, considering."

I pause mid-slice, my eyes flying to hers and fear trickling into my chest. "Considering what? Did something happen? I was planning to come see her—"

"She's fine!" Mindy puts her hand on my arm. "She's fine… I just meant considering, you know… she's in her own world."

"Oh." I spin around and grab a small package of mushrooms, quickly wiping them with a damp paper towel before dicing them. "I'm glad you're there with her."

I've known Mindy all my life. Her family and mine have always been close, and her mom was one of the main people to step up and make sure we made it through the worst winter of our lives— along with my dad's older sister Doris, who's now in the Pine Hills nursing home, where Mindy works as an administrative assistant.

"Not that she knows it." Mindy slides the woody ends of the asparagus into her palm and tosses them in the trash. "Did you get your class list for fall yet?"

"Not yet. Did you?" I quickly remove the steaks one by one, giving them a light coat of salt and pepper before putting them in the hot skillet.

After a quick sear on both sides, I remove them and add the asparagus and mushrooms to the pan, sautéing them quickly. Once they're ready, I return everything to the pan and put the whole thing into the preheated oven.

"Girl, I swear, you need one of those TV shows. You must be the fastest good cook I know."

I wave her away as I take a paper package of dinner rolls from the refrigerator. They have three little lines in the tops, and I put a quarter-pat of butter on each one before popping them into the oven as well.

"It helps Sawyer and Leon are pretty clear about what they like and what they don't like."

Her eyebrows rise. "Rachel Ray has nothing on you."

The rich aroma of cooking steak fills the air, and I switch on the vent. "They'll be in here soon. Did you get your schedule?"

"No. Bea Johnson said she and Mavis got theirs today. I just wanted to be sure I didn't do something wrong."

"Well, if you did, I did too!"

We're starting at the small college in town this fall, along with several of our friends, and I'm thinking it'll be a good distraction with Sawyer away and Leon in school… and my brain still trying to figure out what to do with the Taron situation.

The back door opens, and three men charge in like a herd of buffalo. The kitchen is suddenly very crowded with all three of them crowding for plates and asking what's for dinner.

Mindy waves from the back of the room. "I'm taking off. I expect the full story on this later." She points over Taron's head behind his back, and I narrow my eyes.

If she gets me in trouble with Sawyer… but my brother's way more focused on steak than what my best friend is doing. Taron's right behind him, and I think men forget about romance when they're hungry.

After dinner, Taron recruits Leon to help him clean up the kitchen while I "take it easy." Sawyer acts like this is a ground-breaking idea, and I internally shake my head. I know Sawyer feels bad Leon has no clear memories of our parents. I feel bad about that too, but not so bad I'd let my youngest brother grow up to be a spoiled brat.

With a sigh, I head to the shower. We're all beat after this day, and the next two weeks will be no different. Still, I've got work to do before I can sleep.

A few hours later, I'm sitting on the floor in my bedroom watching a YouTube video about how to make peach body lotion when a soft tapping on the window almost jumps me out of my skin.

Akela's head pops up, but her ears soften just as fast.

Taron is outside my window grinning in his naughty-boy way, and my insides clench. Holding up a hand, I wait to see if anybody's coming before going and slowly raising the glass.

"What are you doing?" I ask, stepping back as he sits on the sill and swings his feet into the room.

I moved my bedroom downstairs to the master suite last year—primarily so I could have my own bathroom and some privacy from the boys, but also for the Internet cable. Sawyer refuses to set up the wireless because he "doesn't want us on our phones all the time," but I've got a surprise for him once he leaves.

"I wanted to see you again." Taron catches me by the waist, pulling me between his legs. "You took off after dinner."

"I was just getting ready for bed." I put my hands on his shoulders, and the way he's holding me, I'm very aware I'm only wearing a thin tee and boxer shorts. "I can't believe you got Leon to help with the dishes."

"It wasn't so hard. I think he really wants to help more."

"I think he likes you—which is saying a lot." Tracing my fingers along the ends of his hair, I think about who else likes him… "You're trying to spoil me."

"I want to spoil you."

I study his blue-green eyes studying mine. He's so pretty, it hurts.

"Well, I'm not getting used to it." It's a light tease, but secretly I want to cry thinking he'll be gone soon. It seems so unfair.

My laptop is still playing on the bed, and he lifts his chin. "How are you getting such good service?"

I step out of his hands and walk over to hit the pause button. Then I lift the cord running out of the wall. "Cable."

"Ahh." He nods. "What's that you're watching?"

"How to make peach body lotion," I read the title proudly.

"For your store?"

"Yeah, check it out." I go to the bathroom and grab two small jars off my vanity. When I return to the room, he's still sitting on the ledge, smiling at me. "I made this sugar scrub."

Opening the jar, I hold it out to him. "Smell." He takes it while I screw the top off the smallest one and slide my finger across the face.

"You made this?"

"Yep." Reaching out, I slide my finger across his full lips, thinking how good they felt on mine.

His eyes narrow, and he pulls back. "Did you just put makeup on me?"

"It's a hydrating lip masque. How does it feel?"

"Hmm…" He presses his lips together. "Moist."

"Gross!" I give his arm a push, and he laughs, pulling me to him again.

"I've never seen your hair down. It's pretty."

Feeling self-conscious, I push it behind my shoulder. "I should cut it, but I can't find a style I like."

"Don't." His brow furrows. "I like your hair long."

Another gentle tug, and I'm closer to him, our faces a breath apart again. The heat between us sparkles in the air. My eyes go from his chin to his lips... to his eyes, which are hungry and tempting.

"Can I kiss you again?" He speaks, and heat floods my lower body.

Closing my eyes, I lift my chin and kiss him first, lightly, carefully. He takes control at once, parting my lips and sliding his tongue along mine.

I never knew a kiss could feel this way, like I'm on fire from the inside out, like I want to rip my clothes off and rip his clothes off and do all sorts of dirty things with him.

I've kissed guys before, of course. I've even dated a few guys more than once—Digger Hayes being one of them, total mistake.

I've just never been touched or kissed this way. Kissing Taron makes me understand what the songs and books and movies are about. Now I know why people lose their minds and do crazy things for other people.

His soft lips are on my cheek, and his warm breath is in my hair. "You smell good."

"You taste like peaches." I touch my lips with my tongue.

He presses his together a few times. "I like it. You'll have to make some for me."

Stepping away, I go to my laptop.

"Sawyer thinks a store is a waste of time. He says we have enough to do around here without having a bunch of tourists poking around in everything."

Taron sits beside me on the floor so our legs are touching. "What do you think?"

"I think it's a potential goldmine. Everybody wants organic products, visitors want souvenirs... I think they'll pay top dollar for this stuff."

With a few clicks, I show him the research I've done on cosmetics and all-natural products and the growth in the market.

He studies it all with an interest that makes me fall for him a little more. "Is this what you want to do?"

"Dolly Parton says you'll never do a whole lot unless you're brave enough to try…" I feel self-conscious quoting my icon. "Anyway… I like a challenge."

"I bet you do." He smiles at me with something like pride in his eyes, and I feel so excited and optimistic that he believes in me.

"Is that why you joined the military? For the challenge?"

"I don't know." He slides a piece of hair off my cheek. "I didn't have anything else in mind. All my friends were signing up. I figured I'd go and keep my eye on them."

"Who are your friends? Besides Sawyer, I mean?" I want to know everything about him, how he can come into my life so quickly and feel so seamless, so irreplaceable.

"Patton, Martin… We call him Marley."

My nose wrinkles. "Why?"

"He loves Bob Marley, and I guess…" Taron blinks down, seeming embarrassed. "He smokes a lot of pot."

A laugh bubbles in my chest at his protectiveness. Or maybe it's just the fact of him here, sitting in my room, talking to me this way.

"I love Bob Marley, too."

He reaches for my computer and types something quickly. A few clicks, and the song "Is This Love" starts playing. Just as fast, he's on his feet, pulling me up with him. I'm wrapped in his arms, and we sway to the beat of the reggae tune.

It's like the lyrics are revealing my thoughts. *Is this love that I'm feeling?* Taron's hand slides along the hem of my shirt, finding the skin of my lower back. When he touches me, my eyes close. I dissolve into the words. *I want to know now…*

Lifting my chin, I search for his mouth, and he kisses me

again. Our lips seal together, and his palms flatten against my back, holding me securely against his hard body. I feel the hardness below his waist, and my head gets light.

My hands rise to his cheeks, and I drag my nails through the sides of his beard. He lets out a low groan. A soft moan rises in my throat as a response.

We're moving faster. I'm off my feet. His hands are under my butt, and I wrap my legs around his waist. My nipples harden against his chest. I want to pull off my shirt and feel his skin against mine. I want him inside me.

My head is a fog of want and need and primal instincts when a loud banging on my door makes me yip.

"Noel!" Sawyer's voice is loud outside. "It's late. Turn the music down."

My feet hit the floor, and I drag Taron to the window by his wrist. I've never needed my brother to tell me to go to bed, but I think it's a good thing he did tonight.

"You'd better go. Tomorrow comes early, and it'll be just as hard as today."

We're standing at the window, and Taron slides his thumb along the line of my jaw. We're both breathing fast, and I'm trembling all over—only, it's not from fear.

"Okay." He smiles like he knows something I don't. Leaning down, he kisses me once more, tugging my lips with his, before stepping through my open window and hopping down to the ground.

I watch him dash across the lawn, wishing I could call him back.

He pauses and looks over his shoulder once more, giving me a wave. I wave back before resting my cheek on my hand, feeling the glow radiating through my skin.

CHAPTER
Seven

Taron

LYING IN MY BED, I CAN STILL FEEL HER IN MY ARMS, STILL SMELL HER hair, still feel her soft lips against mine. *Noel LaGrange…* I don't know her middle name. It should be something beautiful like her.

Something with long, silky brown hair and golden-brown eyes. Her skin is so soft under my touch, her nipples hard against my chest.

I think about other girls I've been with. Some were interesting, some were funny, some were smart… None of them were her.

She looks at me like she feels the same way I do… like we've found something special. Like I'm the best thing she's ever seen. Like the world has shifted and everything's different.

I want her dreams to be my dreams. I want to hold her in my arms all night. I want to explore her, taste her, be inside her. I want her on top of me, under me…

I wonder how she'll sound when I make her come. I picture my lips against her shoulder, my face in her soft hair, inhaling the scent of peaches and coconut on her skin…

I've found her.

She's with me, drifting into my room on the soft night air. I cover her small breasts with my hands, pulling a nipple into my mouth. With my knee, I slide her thighs apart, and as I plunge deep into heaven, she exhales a moan, soft and low.

Our bodies move together in a rhythmic wave, I thrust deep, and she rises to meet me. We move faster, grasping and pulling, straining to place our mouths on shoulders, collarbones, necks...

I'm so close, I want to hear her come...

One more thrust...

The obnoxious buzz of my phone alarm shatters my dream.

Sunlight breaks through the window, and I only hesitate a moment before getting out of bed, shoving down my morning wood and staggering to the bathroom. I jerk my jeans over my hips and pull on a tee, quickly brushing my teeth and step into my boots before heading out the door to the house.

Akela meets me, and I give her head a rub, jogging with her the rest of the way to the back door, where Noel is already at work in the kitchen. Hesitating on the back step, I watch her moving around making us breakfast in those cutoffs. She's wearing a dark purple tank this time, and her hair is piled on top of her head again. I can't think of a better way to start the day...

Our eyes meet, and I'm through the door, ready to pull her to me for a kiss when Leon and Sawyer burst into the room, breaking the moment. We only get to touch hands, steal longing glances when their backs are turned.

Jay's crew arrives before we finish, and while I want to hang back and help her clean up, Sawyer hustles us out the door before I can start. I'm in the field with the men before she leaves the house.

The rest of the day is the same as the one before—hell, the whole week is the same, except the sun beats down hotter. We're exhausted by mid-afternoon, but at night, I slip across the yard to her bedroom window. She shows me what she's working on, and

I hold her in my arms. Akela lies on the floor watching us happily while Noel mixes the raw ingredients—things I've never even heard of, shea butter and jojoba—and makes me pick my favorite scents.

She lets me kiss her, hold her, but she always sends me out the window before we can do more.

At night I dream about her. I bury my face in her hair, inhaling her soft scent, until I wake up in the morning hot and bothered and pulling on my clothes so I can get to the kitchen before her brothers, Akela running and jumping beside me all the way. Even if the guys beat me, I get to be near her, touch her, before we start another long, hot day.

"There's got to be a place to swim around here that isn't cold as the devil's backside." I'm sitting on the flatbed on Friday afternoon, Noel's standing between my knees looking up at me.

Today she's in a thin flowery dress that ends at the top of her thighs. Her long, dark hair is up in a ponytail, and I run my finger along the thin strap going over her shoulder, catching the ends of her hair in my fingers.

Leon led the high school crew today, and I barely saw her as she dashed around, gathering the baskets of discarded peaches and taking them to the house.

Her head tilts to the side. "My aunt used to go fishing at Hayes Lake."

"Hayes… as in Digger's family?" I don't like that guy.

He always acts polite and respectful to Sawyer, but I catch him watching Noel as she works. Lechery is all over his face, and I want to punch him in the nuts. Leon doesn't like him either. Hell, even Akela shows her teeth whenever he's around.

"I don't think anybody fishes there anymore…" Noel seems oblivious. "It's right out in the sun."

"Will anybody care if we swim in it?"

A mischievous light hits her eye. "One way to find out."

"Meet you at the truck."

An old red Chevy is parked behind the shed for anyone to use. We take it, and Noel scoots to the center of the bench seat beside me. Her head is on my shoulder and my hand is between her knees as we drive the back roads connecting the properties.

Akela runs with us the whole way, bouncing in the black-eyed Susans growing in clumps beside the road. We leave the truck in the center of the field, and I help Noel down then strip off my shirt.

We jog to the pier extending out to the center of the lake, Akela right at our heels. Our feet make thumping noises on the wooden planks as we run, and our hands are clasped as we take a flying leap into the placid, brown water.

It's as warm as a bath under the burning-hot sun. A large pipe rises from the center, spraying water in the air like a geyser, keeping it oxygenated, and I reach out, pulling Noel to me, our skin sliding together, slippery as a bar of soap.

She feels so good in my arms. I claim her mouth, pushing her lips apart and finding her tongue. She melts like peach ice cream, and I kiss her deeper before moving my lips to her ear. Her nipples are taut against my chest, and I know she feels my hardness on her stomach. I'm sure she's felt it before.

When I find her eyes, I look deeply into them. "What are you thinking about?"

She blinks down and hesitates. "I never asked if you had a girlfriend or anything back home."

This makes me smile. "Not much point having a girlfriend when I'm about to leave." Her face falls, and I wish I could take back the words. "I just mean… No, I don't. It wouldn't be fair to ask somebody to wait for me."

She traces a finger along the line of my jaw not meeting my eyes. "What if somebody wanted to wait for you?"

My insides churn. I don't know if she means her—as in,

she'd wait for me. I don't know if I want to hope she would. "Nobody has yet."

Moments pass. She doesn't say anything, so I give her a little squeeze. "What about you? You're not dating one of these country boys?"

A little shrug. "Digger's the most persistent."

"That guy." My voice is more of a growl than I intend.

Her eyes meet mine sparkling. "What's wrong with Digger?"

"He's the worst."

"He's not so bad."

"He is *so* bad." Leaning forward, I catch her eye. "You wouldn't date that guy, would you?"

Her lips twist, and she gives me a sheepish grin. "I kind of already did."

I loosen my hold, and she lunges forward, squeezing me around the shoulders. "It was a long time ago! One summer after harvest... I think the sun had melted my brain cells."

She laughs, and I pull her tighter to me. "Do you guys always work this hard in the summer?"

"Just since we lost Daddy. Up to then, we always had hired help."

"You didn't have any uncles or anything to take over for him, run things?"

"My momma was an only child." She props her elbows on my shoulders. "Her family pretty much disowned her when she married my daddy. My grandfather acted like we didn't exist most of my life."

Anger tightens my throat. *How could anybody not want to know this beautiful girl?* "His loss."

She nods absently. "My grandma died years ago, and he was alone afterwards, always. All because my momma didn't marry a doctor or a lawyer..."

"Your daddy owned this huge orchard! What's wrong with that?"

"He didn't always own it. His people were sharecroppers. My

daddy was a poor kid from the wrong side of town. His daddy died of a heart attack when he was only fifty-five."

"Shit." I pull her into another hug.

She manages a smile. "But look what he did. He married the woman of his dreams, he built this huge orchard, he got everything he wanted…"

Her voice trails off, and we don't continue down that road. I don't want to think about how he had it all and ultimately lost everything.

I want to think about right here, right now.

I want to think about having her with me and life and love. "Tell me about this peach festival coming up."

She blinks up at me, her smile returning. "It's sort of the annual town gathering. We do it every year at the end of the harvest."

"Are you saying I'll get to meet the whole town?"

She laughs. "I don't know if the whole town will be there, but a lot of people go. They have pie-eating contests and car shows and pageants and crafts. Mrs. Jenny Ray, Mindy's mom, is going to put some of my beauty products at her table for me to sell."

"Hey! That's a big deal."

"Why do you think I've been working so hard every night?"

"Hell, I don't know." I was too focused on her to wonder about what she was doing or why. "I thought you did that every night."

"No." She shakes her head, laughing.

"Well, I'll be there with my money in hand."

"You don't need beauty products." Her arms are around my neck again, and she kisses my nose. "You're pretty enough without them."

"I have to get more of that lip stuff."

"What's wrong with your lips?" Heavy-lidded eyes slide to my mouth, and it's enough of an invitation for me.

I pull her to me, parting her lips, nibbling and kissing them, loving the rise of heat between us as our chests move together, only separated by thin cotton. Her skirt floats around us, and I put my hands on her thighs, sliding them higher, wanting to explore her secret places.

She inhales sharply as I find the line of her panties. She trembles in my arms, and I kiss her deeper now, moving my tongue to hers as I slide my finger back and forth across her clit.

"Taron…" Her thighs tighten around my hand.

I'm rock-hard and desperate to be inside her… Still. "It's okay." My breath is hot at her ear, and I start to take my hand away.

"No…" It's a soft plea, and I grin, finding her eyes. Our gazes lock, and her cheeks flush.

I back us to the pier post, bracing her as I move my hand again to her warm pussy, massaging and fingering the sweet heat between her legs. Her eyes squeeze shut, and her grip tightens on my shoulders. I keep going, watching as her breath grows faster, shallower.

"Right there… right there…" It's a soft hiss, and her hips rock.

She rides my hand, biting her lip and bucking her pelvis. I circle faster, and she holds my arm, focused on what I'm doing to her. I lean forward to kiss her ear, lightly touching it with my tongue, and she breaks with a loud moan.

"Oh, yes!" She's crying out, thrusting, fucking my hand like a goddess, and with every stroke, she moans and shudders. "Taron…" She exhales sharply. "It feels so good…"

My arm is around her shoulders, and I cradle her against my chest. "I want to make you feel good."

She holds me a bit longer, riding out the afterglow. Then she stretches up and kisses the side of my jaw, biting it lightly. It's fucking hot. My hand is out of her panties and on her cute little round ass, cupping it to me. I want her to feel my cock. I want to sink into her so bad right now.

She hugs me tighter. "I've never done this before with a guy."

I'm not sure I understand what she means. Still, I don't want to break this moment. She's here, just like my dreams. She's in my arms, and her hair is against my cheek.

Kissing the side of her face, I whisper in her ear. "I love holding you this way."

Her body moves, and she pulls back slightly. "I need to tell you something…"

I smile, pushing a damp lock of hair behind her ear. "This sounds serious."

"Just so you don't think I know how… I mean, we don't have much time, so I'm trying—"

"Hey." I put my fingers over her lips gently. "You don't have to feel pressured because of time. I don't want that."

"But I do." Her eyes are wide, pleading. "I do want it. I just need you to show me how… I'm not sure exactly what to do."

My brow furrows. "What do you mean?"

"Ah, this is so embarrassing… Don't make me say it."

"Say what?" I'm horny as hell, and still she's able to make me laugh.

Her chin drops and she says it fast. "I… I'm a virgin."

CHAPTER
Eight

Noel

EVERYTHING GOES QUIET LIKE I SHOUTED A SWEAR WORD IN CHURCH. Even Akela doesn't make a noise—not that she ever does. The only sound is the constant churning of the aerator in the middle of the pond, and I feel Taron's eyes on me even if I don't look up to meet them.

My cheeks are hot, and I want to die of embarrassment. Naturally, I assumed he wanted to have sex with me. Is it possible I was wrong?

We have been kissing pretty hot and heavy every night this week before I send him out the window, which by the way, takes the strength of Hercules. He did just make me come right out here in the middle of the lake—and oh, God, did he ever make me come…

I shiver. I might be a virgin, but my body is ready.

"Say something." My voice is quietly cringey.

He only shakes his head. "Okay."

"That's it?" My eyes flash to his.

"You're only eighteen, Noel. You live in this tiny town. I'd be surprised if you weren't a virgin."

Pulling away, he takes my hand and guides me to the shallow

waters then leads me out to the truck. My stomach sinks to my feet.

"Does that mean you don't want me?"

"No." His voice is low and strained, and it's a thrill in my stomach.

Still, I'm confused. "Where are we going?"

"We need to head back." He still holds my hand warm and strong in his, and when we stop at the truck, he looks down at my wet dress. "I don't guess you have a towel or anything."

"There might be one in the glove box." I wait, watching him dig around then come back empty-handed.

"Here." He pulls his tee over my head, covering my transparent dress.

His jeans are soaked, but he helps me in the truck and jogs around to the other side. We drive back the way we came—me sitting in the middle with my head on his shoulder. Him looking ahead, his hand between my knees.

How I wish his hand would move higher, stroke me, and make me come like he did a few minutes ago. Instead, as I feared it would, my confession threw cold water on everything. I expect he won't touch me again the rest of the week…

Then he'll be gone.

We get back to the house, and he walks me to the back door. "See you in a little while." With that he kisses my cheek before jogging down to the cottage where he stays.

I mix up the ingredients I'd set out for dinner, boiled corn on the cob, shake and bake chicken, and fresh tomatoes. The men wolf it down, while I watch them not really hungry. As usual, Taron shoos me out while he and Leon do the dishes. He's friendly and gives me sweet smiles, but he seems to have completely withdrawn.

My chest is heavy, and as much as I hate to admit it, I cry in the shower. I hate being a baby. I'm too old to cry over a boy, but it still hurts.

Lying on my bed, I'm not in the mood to work on my cosmetics stock tonight. I've almost met my quota for Mindy's mom, anyway.

Snatching up my phone, I send a text to my friend. **You around?**

Staring at the face, I wait for her to reply. I *need* her to reply.

A few seconds pass then I see the gray dots bouncing.

What's up?

Nothing. Everything's down. I find the perfect guy, and he's too nice to punch my V-card.

More gray dots as I wait.

I KNEW IT!!!

"Jeez, Min!" I crossing my arms, staring at the phone a second, then I pick it up again. **No shouty caps. I'm in pain.**

Mr. Hemsworth won't give you his gift? (crying-laugh emoji)

No, Digger. Who else? (gag emoji)

She replies with a string of emojis—the gag one, the green-faced vomit one, the one with Xs for eyes.

I shake my head and tap back. **What do I do? I told him the truth, and he shut down on me.**

GOOD. You're not ready. Are you even on the pill?

Chewing my lip, I think about this... I hadn't really considered birth control. *Way to use your brain, Noel.* Where would I even get birth control? Everybody in town will talk if I go to Dr. Fieldstone...

My friend doesn't miss a beat. **I'll take you to the clinic in Shreveport tomorrow. Meet you at eight.**

I'm starting my reply when a tapping on my window makes me throw the phone on my bed. Akela doesn't even flinch. My eyes fly to the glass, and Taron is outside, smiling like always.

I go to him and slide it open. "Hey."

Everything feels quieter tonight.

"Hey..." He swings his legs into the room and pulls me

between them like always. "You're not making any lotions or lip balms?"

My hands are on his shoulders, and I study my fingernails. "I don't feel like it."

He doesn't say anything, and I steal a glance at his face. He's looking away, and he seems to be struggling with something.

My sadness melts into anger. Was he hoping I'd be an easy lay before he left for South America? Is he trying to figure out how to let me down now? I don't let anyone make me feel inferior. Ever. Dolly Parton says a strong woman looks a challenge in the eye and winks.

"You'd better head on back to the cottage now. Morning comes early." Mentally, I pull up my big-girl panties and prepare to push him out the window, out of my heart, when he catches my arms.

"I've been thinking all evening about what you said." His blue-green eyes are so earnest, I almost feel ashamed for thinking bad thoughts about him. "I can't take that from you and leave, Noel. It's the same as asking you to wait for me. It's not fair…"

"You didn't ask me to wait for you." My voice is quiet, and our gazes mingle in a swirl of longing and sadness and reality hitting us in the face.

"It doesn't mean I don't want to." His voice drops lower. His hands grasp mine, and I lower my eyes to them—long fingers, neatly trimmed nails. He's gorgeous, top to bottom.

Lifting my chin, my voice is sassy, defiant. "Whatever happens between us is as much my decision as it is yours."

"Yes, but I have more experience with this than you do."

"You've slept with a lot of women?"

"No," he answers fast. "When it happens, it matters. Especially the first time."

"Well, thank you for being so considerate." I start to move away. The last thing I need is another know-it-all guy telling me how I feel.

"Stop." Taron pulls me firmly against his chest. "Be mad at me if you want—I'm telling you the truth. I won't hurt you."

I see the break in his eyes, and it breaks something in me. I understand deeply he's not rejecting me. After all we've shared, I don't know how I could ever believe he was.

Reaching out, I thread my fingers in his hair, looking deeply into his blue-green eyes. "I've waited so long for you to appear. You can't hurt me."

Strong hands cup my cheeks, and he pulls my mouth to his. Our lips part, and our tongues entwine. Tears heat my closed eyes, but I won't allow them to escape. I won't give him any reason to think I'm not strong enough for this, even if the idea of saying goodbye leaves my insides in shreds.

He pulls back, looking deep in my eyes. "I'll see you tomorrow."

With that, he's out the window, heading back across the yard. As I watch him go, I can't help thinking, *Yes, you will. You'll see me every day as long as you're here.*

The teams don't come on the weekends, but that doesn't mean the work stops. I run down before anyone is up and whip up a batch of pancakes. I cut up fresh peaches and put them in the refrigerator and stick a note on the microwave saying I'll be back after lunch.

Sawyer will be bitching, but this appointment is too important to skip. I've never visited a Planned Parenthood. Everybody around here thinks they're evil, but I know a lot of the workers' wives go to them for free birth control. An hour later, I'm driving home with Mindy and a round, plastic pack of pills in my bag.

We pull up to a quiet house, and Mindy lets me out at the back door. "Doesn't look like they're home."

"Probably off picking up more crates." It's just as well. I don't need a bunch of questions about where I've been. "I'll see you tomorrow. Tell your mom I'll have everything ready for her Wednesday."

"She's real excited to see how your line sells."

"Me too." I give her a hug and dash up the back steps, going straight to my room and hiding the pills in my nightstand.

From there, I head to the kitchen, bringing in baskets of bruised peaches and putting them beside the sink. I spend all day cooking them down for preserves and jelly or cutting them up and throwing bags in the freezer for ice cream and sorbet.

The festival opens Wednesday night, and it'll take me all week to make enough for selling at Miss Jenny's table. It's my last chance to prove to Sawyer a store is a good idea before he leaves, and I'm hoping to make a killing.

That night, after stir-fry beef and peach salad, Taron recruits my brother to help clean up and appears as always at my window, affectionate as ever and ready to say goodnight before things get too hot between us.

It's the worst.

The next morning, I dutifully take my pill before heading to church. I'm not even discussing this with Jesus. He put this gorgeous man in my life, and I'm not wasting the opportunity.

Another night of chaste kisses and Taron's early departure from my bedroom has me almost ready to climb the walls. I'm not worried, though. I have a plan, and the next morning, I get up and take my pill.

Leon takes over supervising the high school team while I prepare for the festival. In the afternoon, when the men are tired, I carry a silver metal pail out to the shed with peach ice cream in it.

Digger is standing at the back, looking over a ledger with Jay, and Taron is sitting on the flatbed watching me like he wants to have me for dessert. I'm convinced this distance between us is killing him as much as it is me. *Soon...*

I walk right up to him, confident after all we've said and done. "See what you think."

Holding out the spoon, I watch as he slips the bite of peach ice cream between his full lips.

They curl into a smile that reaches all the way to his pretty eyes. "Delicious. Did you dip your little finger in it?"

That makes me laugh, and he catches me around my waist. For the first time in days, I feel light.

"Taron, put me down!"

Digger watches us with a scowl. "What's that, Noel? Peach ice cream?"

"Yeah." I give Taron a nudge with my hip and walk to where Digger is standing.

He takes the spoon, dipping it in the pail I'm carrying. "Not bad. You used your momma's old recipe." The way he says it, using that know-it-all tone, makes my skin crawl.

I look over my shoulder, and Taron's frowning as well. "How could you remember that? We were just kids when Momma passed."

"I remember when you were Princess Peach." Digger taps me on the nose. "I remember when I took you to your first Peach Festival Ball."

"You got that wrong. I was never Princess Peach. It was the one time I let my momma down... that I know about."

"You never let your momma down." He gives my cheek a little pinch, which irritates me more. I see a light flash in Taron's eyes, and I know it irritates him. "It's nice to be with people who know your history and share your values."

I don't like his implication. I don't like his ideas about my place in society. "Just because somebody is from your hometown doesn't mean that person shares your values."

"Nonsense. Besides your brothers, nobody knows your history better than I do, Noel."

"I doubt it." Does he sit at home at night studying my past?

"You're so adorably stubborn. Go with me to the peach ball again this year. It'll be just like old times."

I'm caught off guard by his invitation, but that doesn't mean I'm not prepared. "I'm not going to the ball. We've got too much to do with Sawyer leaving and needing to prepare and all."

"Nonsense. You have to go to the ball. It's tradition. You're the co-owner of one of the largest peach orchards in town."

"If it's a tradition, it's one I don't know about."

"I told you." He takes my arm in his. "It's time we re-establish your family's place in society. This is one of the ways to do it, by going to the ball and showing your interest."

Reaching back, I pull my arm out of his. "Everybody knows us. I appreciate your invitation, but I'm not in the mood for a ball this year."

Taron stands up, and Digger releases me.

Digger crosses his arms over his chest, stretching that seersucker blazer. Who wears seersucker to a peach shed? "I'll talk to Sawyer about it."

His tone implies my older brother tells me what to do, but instead of letting him get under my skin, I turn on my heel toward the house. I'm not wasting time on Digger Hayes.

"My ice cream is melting." I trot down the steps and jog up the hill toward the house.

I've never been more annoyed in my life. Digger Hayes thinks he's going to tell me what to do? He's got another thing coming.

I'm at the door when I realize a tall figure is right behind me. Taron's large hand covers mine, and I turn as I step into the kitchen. "You startled me."

"Sorry. I figured I'd better follow you before I did something I'd regret."

"Regret?" I take down a freezer-safe container and spoon the rest of the ice cream into it.

"Something Sawyer wouldn't like is more what I meant." He catches the back of my ponytail, twirling it around his hand. "You really dated that guy?"

"People thought we were a good match." Shoving the ice cream in the freezer, I'm still pissed at the implications of Digger's words.

"You didn't win Princess Peach?" I look up and Taron's smiling down at me. It melts the anger I'm feeling just a little.

"I never liked pageants. Momma won every pageant she ever thought about entering, but it just wasn't my thing."

He leans against the bar with a chuckle. "No wonder you're so pretty."

His compliment is like tingling electricity in my veins, and I admire how the sun has put gold highlights in his dark hair. His skin is tanned, and if it's possible, he's even more handsome. It's time, and I'm more than ready.

"I'd better get started on dinner." Rising on my toes, I kiss his soft lips.

My insides are humming just thinking about the special dessert I have planned. It won't be long now…

CHAPTER
Nine

Taron

DON'T KNOW HOW SHE DOES IT. FOR SUNDAY DINNER, NOEL SERVED US braised brisket with bourbon peach glaze. Tonight, she gave us pork chops with grilled peaches, and when I stop by her bedroom before saying goodnight, she's back to mixing up her homemade organic beauty products.

She's amazing, and she dismisses it all out of hand.

"Cooking is just practice. I've been whipping up those same meals a couple times a month for as long as I can remember."

It's after ten and we're in the kitchen whispering. I stand behind her watching as she carefully pours candle wax into small, labeled jars.

"You should write them down and sell a cookbook along with all this other stuff." I kiss the side of her jaw, and she lets out a little noise that registers straight to my cock.

"You're going to make me spill wax everywhere."

"Am I distracting you?"

"You know you are." She lifts the pan and turns her face to kiss me gently on the lips.

I swear, leaving her alone in her bedroom these past few nights has been about the hardest thing I've ever had to do. It's taken many cold showers and much jerking off to relieve the pressure.

"So I was thinking about what you told Digger in the shed—about how you don't want to go to the ball with Sawyer leaving and everything happening…"

Her lips tighten, but she doesn't respond. Her eyes are focused on filling the small jars.

"Did you just say that to put him off or did you mean it?"

She finishes the last pour then her whiskey eyes meet mine. "What's it to you?"

Clearing my throat, I look down at my shoes, remembering all the reasons I've been doing my best to keep my distance. In a few days I'll be gone… Is it fair to keep pursuing her?

"I was wondering how you felt about all that stuff he said."

"He knows a lot about the business. I guess that's why my brother hired him. Is that what you meant?"

"Are you interested in him?"

"I never have been." She carries her candle supplies to a large pail in the sink and carefully places each item inside. "Still… He's not a bad-looking guy. I guess if I were on the market—"

"You're not on the market," I snap.

Fuck fair. Hearing her say those words stirs something deep inside me.

Something primitive.

"I'm not?" Curiosity is in her eyes now, and I'm pretty sure a little mischief. "How come?"

"You're going to the festival with me—and to that ball. If you want to go."

"I usually go to the festival with Leon. It's his birthday."

"I'll talk to him about it tomorrow. He can ride with us if he wants."

"Okay." Her voice is soft and a hint playful.

I'm still riled up and angry, but I don't know why. We've

settled it. She's going with me to the festival and not that asshole Hayes.

Reaching out, I catch her by the waist and pull her to me roughly. Her body is pliant under my grip. She lifts her chin and threads her fingers into my hair when I find her mouth, pushing it open and tasting the sweet mint on her tongue. Desire is in her kiss, and it makes me feel even more frustrated.

Pulling back with a growl, I turn for the back door. "I'd better head on." Tonight, I don't know why, but I don't feel like I'll leave as easily if I don't do it now.

"Sleep well," she calls after me, a lilt in her tone.

The way she's being tonight, playful and teasing, has me wound up tight, and even though we worked harder today than we did any day last week, I'm not sure I'll fall asleep.

Frustration courses through my limbs as I lie on the bed on my back staring at the ceiling in the darkness. I have the window-unit on, but this fire is in my veins, it's in my blood. It's like a force driving me.

Glancing at the clock, I see it's almost midnight. I've got to sleep.

Pressing my bent arm over my eyes, I try to think of soothing things... Noel's silky hair, her gentle smile, the way she concentrates when she's reading a recipe for peach lotion or peach ice cream or... peaches.

Her soft, round ass floats through my mind, and my dick hardens... Soft as a peach. A peach I want to taste, lick, suck, eat... I want her crying out my name like she did in that pond.

The small hairs prickle on my skin when I realize I'm not alone.

Dropping my arm on the bed, I squint into the darkness. The door is open, and in the glow of the moonlight, I see the one thing that can give me relief.

"Noel?" I sit up, letting the sheet fall to my waist where I'm sporting some serious wood. "What are you doing here?"

She doesn't speak. She closes the space between us, reaching up to push the robe she's wearing off her shoulders. My forehead collapses, and I let out a low groan. She's standing in front of me completely nude, and the light from the telephone pole across the yard casts a soft glow around her curves.

"I'm ready now."

"Close the door."

All my thoughts of waiting, my concern about leaving her disappear in the face of Noel straddling my lap, cupping my cheeks in her hands, saying how much she wants me.

"Kiss me, Taron." Her voice is a rasp, demanding, and my hands clutch her soft ass that I've dreamed of every night.

I'm hard as a rock as she drags her nails through my beard, as our lips seal together.

She pulls my lips with hers. She bites and exhales a soft purr. "Don't you want this?"

Her lips move to my cheek and up to my eyebrow before she pulls back to meet my eyes. Her beautiful, whiskey eyes... intoxicating.

"I don't want to hurt you." It's a strained whisper, the last of my resistance.

"Then don't."

She moves on my lap and the moonlight glows on her skin. I whip the sheet away and catch her around the waist, turning her so she's beneath me. She exhales something between a laugh and a sigh, and I cover her mouth again with mine.

Our kisses are hungry, demanding—fueled by every touch denied, every tease wasted, every time we've come so close only to push apart.

My mouth moves from her lips to her chin, to her neck, down to the soft curve of her breast. Rising up on my heels, I look down at her small breasts rising and falling rapidly. Her gorgeous body is spread out before me on the bed like an uncharted land I want to claim. Her hair ripples around her shoulders in dark, silky waves. My mouth waters. My dick aches. I'll never forget this night.

"You're so beautiful." My voice is quiet awe.

Her knee bends, and she rubs her thighs together. "Do something." Her whisper is laced with nervous laughter.

It makes me smile.

Leaning down, I touch my lips to her flat belly, and her fingers thread in my hair. I follow a line to her hip, grazing my teeth over the soft skin there. I'm rewarded with a whimper.

She's a virgin. I've never been with a virgin, but I've been thinking about it ever since she told me. I don't want to hurt her. I want it to be as pleasurable for her as possible.

My lips move lower, to the top of her pubic bone, and she trembles.

"Will you... Ahh..."

Her question disappears as I cover her with my mouth, sweeping my tongue inside to taste her innocence. She's sweet, delicate, ocean water and soft musk. I'm ravenous, tracing my tongue around her clit, pulling and sucking the tiny bud hidden there.

"Oh, God... oh, it's so... Oh..." She jerks, twisting and pulling in the sheets.

Lifting my chin I look up and see her back arched and her skin flushed. Her hand goes to my face, and I'm back on her, hungry for her orgasm. I want her drenched in desire when I take her for the first time.

Another pass of my tongue, and I slide my finger inside to test her. She bucks and whimpers, and she's so wet. I slide another finger inside her...

"Taron... Oh my God." Her knees rise, and I feel the small shudders rippling in her legs.

I lean down to kiss her again, deeper, tonguing her again and again, and on the final pass, she breaks. Her body rises, and her legs clench. She moans my name, writhing in the sheets as I grab a condom and quickly roll it on.

Kneeling above her, I move her thighs apart. "Open for me, baby."

She tries to do what I say, but I know she doesn't understand how far… "Do you trust me?" It's a gentle, loving question.

Round eyes are on mine, and she nods. Her soft neck is at my lips, and I kiss it, pulling the skin between my teeth gently, making her shiver. I hold her thighs, parting them more and lining my cock up with her dripping core.

"Hold onto me." My lips graze her ear and my voice breaks.

Her hands grip my shoulders and I thrust completely, all the way inside her and hold. Fuck me, she's so fucking tight.

"Ahh…" She cries out, and I wait, feeling her body moving slightly, dying inside as I hold back my instinct to take her.

She feels so fucking good.

It's been so long.

I'm overwhelmed by the intensity of my feelings for her.

Through the fog of it all, my brain manages to form a coherent sentence. "Are you okay?" It's a strained whisper at her ear.

Her hands move to the tops of my shoulders, and she nods. "Yes… yes, it's so… Big."

My hips move, slowly at first. The first thrust makes her cry out, a shaky whimper, and I hold still again, fighting every natural urge in my body.

"Still okay?" Lifting my head, I see her eyes are closed.

She nods. "I'm good… It's good. Keep going." Her golden-brown eyes open, and they're heavy with lust, with longing.

"You sure?" I lean down to kiss those rosebud lips, her bottom lip bigger than the top.

"I'm sure. I want this… I want you."

It's all I need to hear. My arms go around her, gathering her to me as my hips rock harder, thrusting in and out, sating my consuming desire for her.

My eyes squeeze shut, but I feel it when she joins me. I feel her hips beginning to move, rocking in time, taking me in, meeting my thrusts with her own.

Releasing her from my embrace, I rise up to kiss her, to claim her mouth and stroke her tongue with mine.

She grasps my cheeks, kissing me back with equal fervor, and I'm lost to my orgasm. Thrusting again and again, I'm driven by how good she feels, so tight, so wet. My ass clenches, pleasure snakes up my thighs. It all centers where our bodies are joined. Sweat drips down my cheek, and I come with a loud groan, hard and long.

Holding deep inside her, I groan again as my dick pulses, as I fill the condom. I hold onto her as my anchor to this world. My mind is blank, and all I know is her and me sharing this experience. It's incredible.

Gradually, the world starts to come back in focus. I'm breathing hard, and I blink my eyes open to see her smiling up at me. She rises up to kiss my neck, and I cup the back of her head, holding her to me. I wrap my other arm around her upper body, flattening her soft breasts against my chest.

I understand the concept of two becoming one in this moment. I feel like she's become a part of me. I'm her first, but she's my first virgin. I feel protective of her, like she belongs to me now, as fucked up as that might sound.

Something inside me clicks, and I'll never let anything bad happen to her. I never want to let her go.

She starts to wiggle, and I loosen my grip. "I'd better get cleaned up. I might bleed all over your sheets."

I want to say I don't care. Then I realize these sheets actually belong to her—as does the bed. "Sorry." I stand and help her to the bathroom. "Can I get you anything?"

"Make sure the bed's not ruined. I didn't even think to get a towel."

She dashes to the bathroom, and I check the sheets—all clean. The frustration and anger in my chest have dissolved into contentment and calm. "Get out here so I can cuddle you and shower you with affection."

The door opens, and she's holding a towel, smiling up at me. "Are you making fun of me?"

Leaning my arm on the doorjamb above her head, I lean into a kiss, pulling her lips with mine. "Never. I want to hold you… and maybe do it again."

"Ah…" She grins, stretching up to kiss me again. "That sounds more like it. You're going to have to hold that thought. We've got to sleep tonight."

She starts for the door, but I catch her waist. "Wait."

A big smile is on her lips as she turns around to meet me. It fades into warmth, and she puts her palm against my cheek. "What is it?"

"I want you to stay with me. I'll set the alarm early. I want to hold you tonight."

Blinking several times, she nods, following me to the bed again. I crawl in first, lying on my back, and she climbs in, resting her cheek on my chest. I thread my fingers in her long hair, sliding my thumb along her soft shoulder. This is what heaven must be like.

Heaven is finding the thing you can't live without and being able to hold it.

Hell is knowing you'll have to let it go.

CHAPTER
Ten

Noel

TARON IS WAITING IN THE KITCHEN WHILE I FINISH PUTTING ON MY makeup. I've chosen a peach eyelet sundress with an empire waist that stops mid-thigh to wear to the festival. This dress doesn't allow for a bra, so I opted for no underwear as well. I get turned on every time my thighs swish together. I can't wait for him to find out…

Leon informed us he's taking Betsy to the festival, and he doesn't need us to chaperone him. He has no idea he'd be the real chaperone going with Taron and me.

I've heard that old expression about taking the lid off the jar… or maybe it's taking the genie out of the bottle? Either way, it applies a hundredfold to having sex with Taron.

We've spent the entire week barely able to keep our hands off each other. We only did it once Monday night, but by Wednesday, we'd done it a million more times.

I told him I'd started the pill, and he ditched the condoms. He said they all got tested at the start of basic, and he's clean, which meant we've been sneaking around, doing it anywhere and everywhere.

We've had sex in his bed every night, in my bed twice, in the old red Chevy once, in the lake every day… The hottest time was when we were in the kitchen together, and I was cutting up peaches to make preserves.

I'd held up one of the blush-pink fruits and asked him what it reminded him of… Yes, I was being naughty, and when I saw the fire in his eyes, I dragged him into the pantry. He spun me to face the window, and I gripped the ledge while he flipped my skirt over my peachy ass.

Feeling him behind me, working to get his pants down made me hotter than asphalt in July, and my pussy was so wet, by the time he thrust into me, I was coming on his dick.

One hand slipped under my shirt, cupping and squeezing my breast, rolling my nipple between his fingers. The other went between my legs, circling and massaging my clit, turning my knees to liquid.

I dropped my head back against his shoulder, losing myself in the sensations buzzing from the arches of my feet to the place where we came together.

He groaned and thrust so hard, I went up on my toes, at times leaving the ground, and the noise he made when he came vibrated in my bones. He pulsed deep within me, and his come mixed with my wetness was slippery on the back of my thighs.

From there, we took the three-wheeler down to the lake to clean up. Holding hands in the water, he told me he wasn't sure what the future will look like now that we've found each other. I couldn't tell him the feelings swirling in my chest and in my heart toward him. I was still afraid to even think them.

He's my first love. He's my first real kiss. He's my first everything…

I don't know how I'll let him go in two days. I only know I'll have to, and I don't know what will happen after that.

When I walk into the kitchen tonight, I stop to take in his handsome form, standing in front of me in dark jeans and a short-sleeved polo.

He lets out a low whistle, and I pause in the doorway feeling self-conscious.

"You're so beautiful." His voice is hushed, and he walks slowly to where I stand.

My hair is styled in large curls cascading down my shoulder, and he leans down to kiss my cheek, taking a deep breath of my hair.

"You smell good... Is that one of yours?"

"It's the lotion you helped me mix, remember? You picked the scent."

It's light coconut, peach, and rose, and it almost smells like a day at the beach—with fresh peaches on the side.

He cups my cheek and kisses me slowly, possessively. Our lips pull, and that familiar, delicious heat ignites beneath my skin.

We're the only ones in the house, and I want to take his hand and slide it under my skirt... Only, I know if I do that, we'll never make it to the festival, and I have to check in with Mindy's mom.

"You kiss me, and I forget everything." My hand is on his cheek and when our eyes meet, we smile.

"I'm just the opposite. I start getting ideas." He gives me that bad-boy wink, and I start to laugh.

"Come on." Tugging his hand under my arm, I lead us out the back. "I can't wait to see if people buy my stuff. I can't wait to show Sawyer my untapped market."

His hand is around my waist, and he walks me to the old red Chevy. "I fully intend to tap your market."

"Is that so?

"You know it." The low rumble of his voice does crazy things to my insides.

"Let's check on the actual market then I'll let you in the secret market a little later."

"Secret market." He grins and kisses me again. "I'm intrigued."

Shaking my head, I climb into the truck and scoot all the way across so I'm right beside him. I realize just how serious I am about this store when his hand rests between my knees and I don't even slide it higher.

The Bible says there's a time and a place for everything, and it's time to see if I'm going to make a success of this organic products business.

The peach-eating contest is well underway when we pull up in front of the town civic center and city hall. Tents line the perimeter, and a big funnel cake booth greets us at the entrance.

Taron pays the ten dollars to grant us entrance, and we head straight for Mrs. Jenny's booth. Mindy's mom is shorter than me, and about forty pounds heavier. Her dark hair is cut close to her ears and hangs in sausage curls around her cheeks. Tonight, she's wearing a purple dress with little flowers all over it.

"We're almost sold out of those peach-scented candles." Mrs. Jenny's clear voice rises above the noise of people talking and the live band playing zydeco music at the end of the row.

"Sold out!" My voice goes loud, and my heart jumps to my throat. "It's only the first night! I don't think I have enough left over to go through Saturday."

"That lotion you made is a big hit, too." She hands me a green vinyl bank bag containing checks and cash. "People are saying they love the scent."

Looking up at Taron, I press my elbow into his side. "That's the one you did. The one I'm wearing tonight."

But instead of being excited for me, his brow furrows. "You're selling that one? That one's just for you. It's your signature scent."

"Taron!" My voice goes louder. "I'm trying to launch a business here."

"Yeah, but I only want that smell on you."

"There's more than three hundred million people in this

country. I don't think the few who buy my lotion are going to take away from you smelling me."

"I'll smell you." He leans down and gives my neck a sharp inhale then a little bite, and I squeal a laugh. Happiness bubbles in my stomach. I've never felt so optimistic.

Mrs. Jenny's left eyebrow rises, and she looks from me to Taron and back to me. "Noel Aveline, you haven't introduced me to your beau."

"Aveline." Taron's voice is low at my ear, sending goose bumps skating down my arms.

"Oh, Mrs. Jenny Ray, this is Taron Rhodes." I hold out my hand from him to her. "He's Sawyer's friend… from the Marines."

"Is that so?" She smiles and nods, and I feel embarrassed all of a sudden, like she knows what we did in the pantry.

"Nice to meet you Mrs. Ray." Taron shakes her hand so politely.

"You're in the Marines with Sawyer?" Her voice has that edge like it did when she caught Mindy and me sneaking out of Mindy's bedroom window.

"Yes, ma'am."

"So you're being deployed with him at the end of the week?"

"Yes, ma'am."

Her dark eyes move to mine, and I feel that painful knot in my throat. A soft voice is in my head, *We weren't going to talk about this, remember…* Only that was just something Taron and I unofficially decided between the two of us.

As if that would stop it from coming.

"It's too bad we won't get to know you better."

Heat rises in my eyes, but I blink it away fast. Tonight is for holding hands and being in love and celebrating the fact I have a market for my store, not crying.

Taron doesn't miss a beat. "Autumn's bounty? How did you come up with the name?"

I focus on the white label with a peach outline of the sun over a tree. "I like the name Autumn. Mindy helped me with the design."

"I love it." He gives me a wink then turns to Mrs. Jenny. "I need a couple of those lip balms there."

Mrs. Jenny picks up two tiny jars and holds them out. "These are selling like hotcakes, too. You'd better be careful, because they'll walk away."

My eyes widen. "People are stealing them?"

"Not on my watch. I'm just saying." She waits as Taron passes her a twenty, and I try to decide if I'm pissed or flattered. "It's also higher than people are used to spending on lip balm."

"It's priced for the market—" I'm about to defend myself when Taron catches my arm.

"I want to see the pie eating contest if we haven't missed it." His expression tells me not to argue.

"You okay, Mrs. Jenny? Do you need me to stay?"

Her eyes glide from me to Taron, and she softens. "No, honey. You go on and enjoy the festival. I'll let you know if I need anything."

Stepping around the table, I give her a tight hug. "Thank you."

My hand is back in Taron's as we walk across the rows of tents, past the zydeco band at the end playing "Jolie Blonde." I hesitate a moment. It's my favorite zydeco song... But Taron gives me a tug, and we continue toward the pavilion, where picnic tables are arranged in a line and a group of ten kids to grownups sit in front of peach pies with bright red and white checked bibs tied around their necks.

We watch the first round, with me gagging and laughing. Then Taron spots the antique car show. He pulls me to a row of cars from old beaters to slick race cars. He's especially interested in the glossy Model T. The owner, a man from Ferriday, is glad to tell him all about it. Watching them talk, I'm surprised to learn my man is a car geek.

My man... the words sprang into my mind unbidden.

Can I call him that? My heart says an emphatic yes, but we've never had the conversation... Am I his?

While they talk shop, I survey the fair grounds. Banners are all around celebrating the 70th anniversary of the festival. I catch sight of my brother standing with his arms crossed beside another, older man inside the Official Peach Grower's tent. The way he talks, considering, thoughtful makes me miss my daddy.

Daddy always loved the Peach Festival. It was his favorite time of the year—and not just because it signaled the end of our hardest-working days. It was symbolic of what he'd accomplished. He'd gone from nobody to being a leader in our small community.

An old, familiar ache is in my bones, and my brother's eyes catch mine. He smiles, and I do a little wave. Taron walks up behind me, putting his hand on my waist, and I see the change in Sawyer's expression, like he's just seeing for the first time what's been under his nose for two weeks. I'm not sure if I should be worried or glad.

"What else do you want to do?" I blink away from whatever my brother is thinking and smile up at his friend.

"Oh, I've done this a hundred times. What would you like to see?"

He narrows his eyes as if he's thinking. "Princess Peach. I want to see what kind of supermodels they have competing this year."

"It's a pageant for six year-olds."

"Which you didn't win. Those kids have to be on beauty-pageant steroids to beat you."

"That's not a thing."

"I still want to see what kind of rigged system they're running here. You could win a pageant soaking wet in a burlap sack."

I shake my head, laughing. "I didn't want to be in it."

"Stop making excuses and lead the way."

We're intercepted by a hawker guiding us to the Ferris wheel—something I'd so much rather do than revisit my childhood failure.

One look at my face, and Taron buys two tickets for us to go all the way to the top and come back down again. We're in our car, and I scoot in close to his side, wrapping his arm over my shoulder and thinking about all the good things... my product line being a success, having this wonderful man on my arm... I overheard Sawyer saying we'd had our best harvest in years, thanks to the extra hands. So many good things. My heart is so full of gratitude.

The wind blows in short gusts laced with the metallic scent of rain the higher we rise. A storm is moving in, and I think about what's building between Taron and me. Our love is wild like a tornado, consuming and fierce... yet at the same time, it can be soft and gentle like a butterfly, like the way he's touching my cheek right now.

My eyes flicker up to his, and he smiles. "Noel Aveline LaGrange." So much love is in his eyes, it takes my breath away. "You're the prettiest girl I've ever seen."

Dark lashes frame his pale eyes, and I slide my thumb over his full bottom lip. "You're the prettiest boy I've ever seen."

That gets me a sexy smile. "Can boys be pretty?"

"You can." Scooting closer, I put my chin on his shoulder. "I've never been so happy in my life."

"I'm pretty happy, too." His arm tightens around me. "I wish..."

His voice trails off, and my chest aches. I know what he wishes. It's what I wish for every night he holds me as we sleep. I wish he weren't leaving. I wish we could be together always. I wish the best things in my life didn't always seem to end.

I wish our love would last.

Lifting my chin, I meet his earnest gaze. The lights flicker in his eyes like a million promises we have yet to make.

He catches my cheek and pulls my mouth to his, pushing my lips apart and tracing his tongue along mine. My insides catch flame, and I feel my stomach rise as the wheel moves, taking us back down to the ground.

Lightning illuminates the clouds, and I guide his wrist to my knees, under my skirt, tracing his fingers higher to the apex of my thighs. His gaze darkens when he discovers my secret, and my stomach tightens. I love the hungry look in his eyes.

"Come with me." His voice is rough as sandpaper, and he pulls me quickly from the car, down the steps, and across the short distance to the civic center.

The pageant is in the final rounds, and music blasts, accompanied by the voice of Mr. Newman the MC announcing the names of the five finalists.

Roaring is in my ears, and my focus is on one thing as he leads me quickly into a small room, an empty office with only the exit sign providing pale green light. We spin inside, and he backs me against the door, dropping to his knees and lifting my skirt.

My hand flies out to brace the wall, and I wouldn't stop him if I could.

His nose nudges at my bare pussy, and my knees go liquid. "Taron…" It's a strained whisper as his warm tongue makes its first pass over my slippery clit. "Oh, God… Yes…"

Strong hands grasp my thighs, lifting me higher. He spreads me wider as his mouth goes deep, covering me, then sliding his tongue up again, focusing on my clit.

His beard scratches my inner thighs, and my hips buck involuntarily. My head drops back against the door, and a blast of music covers my moans.

He makes me come so hard, my thighs shudder in his grip. Wild moans ripple from my belly. A million fireworks shoot off through my veins to a variation of the Miss America theme, and what he's doing to me is better than any pretend crown.

With a final kiss to the seam of my leg, he rises, covering my mouth with his and muffling my moans. My hands struggle with his to unbuckle his pants, to shove them down, and free his massive cock.

I ache for him.

My need for him is deep in my bones.

He doesn't make me wait.

With one strong thrust, he's inside, letting out a low groan. My arm is around his shoulders, holding his neck as he pushes me higher, thrusting deeper as I'm pinned against the door, and it's so good. I want to hold him forever, hold him so tight, and never let him go.

The friction between us drives me up and over the cliff with him again. Our bodies grasp and pull, we groan in unison as we ride out the sensation. It's incredible… our breath labored, holding each other so close. I can feel his heart beat against my chest. The music outside dies down, and it's only us in this space.

These last few days, what's happening between us is about lust and need and obsession with each other's bodies, but it's also about young love, fierce love, a love so strong it might be able to survive…

And having that looming shadow right alongside it. The clock running out, like Cinderella at the ball. The pain of knowing in only a few short hours, everything will change, will go back to the way it was before, and we won't be able to hold each other this way for a long, long time.

CHAPTER
Eleven

Taron

'M STANDING IN THE BACK OF THE ROOM WATCHING THE MAN CROWN A little girl with orange-red hair Princess Peach, and I have to confess…

She looks like a peach.

The child prances down the stage in a leaf-green ruffled dress, and the music rises. Everyone claps. After all the days I've spent with her, flying on the three-wheeler, jumping in the pond, running through the groves with Akela, working quietly behind the scenes in the kitchen, on her product line, on the store… I realize this is something Noel would never be happy doing. Not that there's anything wrong with it.

It's absolutely not her personality.

Light streams across the dark corridor, and she emerges from the bathroom. Her hair is over one shoulder, and a smile curls her lips… She's so beautiful. She's the best thing I've ever seen, and the truth hits me like a freight train.

I'm in love with this girl.

She pauses to chat with a lady holding a sleeping toddler. The woman nods and smiles, and Noel pushes a strand of dark hair behind her ear with long, elegant fingers.

She only makes it a few more steps in my direction when an older lady stops her. The woman shows her a bottle of Autumn's Bounty body lotion, and I can tell by the animated way she's speaking it's a rave review.

As much as I hate that asshat Digger, he's right. Noel is royalty in this place. The way she carries herself, the grace she shows everyone who approaches her. She's not just beautiful and smart and damn sexy, she's special.

I'm standing beside a line of men along the back wall with their arms crossed, watching the pageant and the spectacle surrounding it. I recognize some of them from that first meeting at Denny's. A few I've seen talking to Sawyer in the fields, and I realize they're part of the community of growers.

What would it mean to build a life here with them? It's miles away from Nashville, but it feels more like home than anything I've ever experienced. Warmth is at my side, and I look down at my girl smiling up at me.

"Seen enough?" She's happy, and I love seeing the glow in her eyes when she looks at me.

"I get it now. That little girl actually looks like a peach."

Her chin rises, and she nods as if I've cracked the code. "Next year you can be a judge." The words catch her short, and a splinter of pain cuts my chest.

I don't want to think about next year and where I'll be or how far away. I put my arm around her waist and turn her to the door. "Let's get out of here."

I want to spend the night holding this beautiful creature in my arms.

The yellow cake turns golden brown, and I look over her shoulder. "Just a few more seconds."

Noel is in front of me, holding a spatula as she watches her first batch of hoecakes frying in the pan.

"It's just like making pancakes." She reaches out and quickly flips all four of them, perfectly browned.

I kiss the side of her neck, holding her waist, loving the feel of her back against my chest. The weekend is here, and Sawyer told everybody to sleep in—which naturally means we've been up since dawn stealing every moment we can find together.

Last night I held her so close to me as she slept. My face was in her hair, and I did my best to memorize her scent, feel her body against mine, doing everything in my power to imprint her on my mind. I never want to forget how she feels in my arms.

The Peach Ball is tonight, and she said she'd go with me. We've done our best to stay in the moment, but we can't avoid the truth any longer. It's my last night in town. Tomorrow, I leave before dawn, and it feels like a lead weight pressing on my chest.

My face is at her shoulder, and I take another deep inhale as she plates the small corn cakes. Then she turns in my arms and puts her hands on my chest.

"I decided to change the scent on the one I sell." Her head tilts to the side and she smiles up at me. "I'll still make this scent, but it'll just be for me."

I don't know why this makes me so happy, but it does. "Will you send me a bottle?"

"I'll give you the one I have. I'll put it in your bag."

Raking my fingers along the side of her hair, I lean down and kiss her cheek, just as the door swings open and Leon storms into the room. We step apart, but I'm sure he saw me holding her, kissing her.

Either way, he doesn't say anything about it. "Breakfast ready?" He pulls down a plate without making eye contact.

Noel is back at the stove, spooning four more cakes onto the hot griddle. "Almost. Unless you want eggs."

"Nah, this is good."

I put a few strips of bacon on to fry and walk over to restart the coffee pot. My eyes are on Noel moving around in those cut-offs I love. I'm making a mental picture when Sawyer joins us, growling about too much noise in the house to sleep.

Noel cuts up the last peaches in the refrigerator, and we have a quiet breakfast. I think it's about more than simply the end of harvest and exhaustion. I think it's because the fact of what's coming is settling in. I'm leaving in the morning, then a few days later Sawyer will leave. Neither of us will be back for a long time.

Breakfast is over, and we all carry our dishes to the sink. Leon immediately starts to load the dishwasher, but Noel stops him, pulling him into a brief hug.

"It's your birthday weekend. Go pick me some peaches, and I'll make ice cream." He starts for the door, and when our eyes meet, she nods. "Go with him."

A sweet smile is on her lips, and I head out the door, following Leon up the hill. It takes longer today, searching the near-bare trees. Primarily under-ripe fruit is left, but we're able to find a few new ones that have turned since the pickers left.

We celebrated Leon's actual birthday a few days ago, but the festival seemed to take over everyone's attention. He's been un-usually quiet the last few days, and I wonder if it's because of a certain teenage girl.

"So..." We're walking side by side past the short trees. "You and Betsy?"

He doesn't answer right away. His brow is still lowered, and he searches a branch, finding two more peaches.

After putting them in the bucket I'm holding, he cuts those hazel eyes up at me.

"So, you and Noel?" His sharp tone catches me off guard.

I'm not sure how to answer him or why exactly he seems so angry. I take a few steps to another tree and search the branches, coming back empty-handed.

Clearing my throat, I look over at him. "Something like that."

Crossing his arms, he glares at me. "How long?"

Rubbing my hand across my chin, I start slowly up the hill. "Almost since the first day." I grin, remembering her falling off the counter right into my arms.

She was like a gift from heaven.

"You love her?"

Love. It's a word I've thought more than once, but I've never said it out loud. Here, in this fragrant grove with this kid who reminds me so much of myself, I decide it's time to be honest.

"I do."

"Have you told her?"

My lips press together, and I shake my head. "No."

"Why not?"

"Ah… I don't know." Exhaling a deep breath, I level with him. "It's not fair to tell her I love her and leave. It's not fair to ask her to wait. I don't know what might happen in the next eighteen months."

"You were pretty sure of yourself when you got here."

"Was I?" I think back fourteen days… it feels like a lifetime ago. I feel like a completely different person from the guy who rode in here in the middle of the night, fresh out of basic with Sawyer.

"You said you'd take care of my brother. You said you wouldn't let anything happen to him."

I hadn't thought he was listening to me.

Lifting my chin, I meet his eyes. "I meant it."

"You'll have to take care of yourself if you plan to keep that promise."

The side of my mouth lifts with a grin. "I guess I will."

He turns and starts down the hill toward the house. "Noel's a serious person. She's got plans, and she doesn't fall in love with just anybody. In fact, I don't think she's ever had a serious boyfriend."

"Okay." I won't say I'm sorry to hear it.

"Whether you ask her or not, she's going to wait for you." He reaches over and takes the bucket of peaches. "I'll kick your ass if you hurt my sister."

Emotion hits me hard in the chest. Slowing my stride, I watch him stalk away from me, jogging up the back steps and into the house.

Noel is there, but I don't go to her. I need to think. I need to decide my next moves and what I'm going to say. Either way, I've got to tell her the truth before I go.

CHAPTER
Twelve

Noel

THE PEACH BALL SOUNDS LIKE A BIG EVENT, BUT IT'S REALLY MORE A reception with live music and dancing. It's the final event of the festival, and the organizers go all out with a cash bar and heavy hors d'oeuvres… Still, it's not an evening-gown and tuxedo type of thing.

Either way, I got a new little black dress to wear, and I'm hoping to make it a special night… A memory I hope will last us a while.

Taron is down at the cottage, and I've done my best to hold it together all day. Last night he slept in my bed, which is a first. Usually, I slip down to his place late in the evenings then back to my room before the sun comes up. It's safer that way.

Sawyer knows something's going on between us. He knows we slip off to the pond and the reservoir, and we make breakfast together every morning and sit up talking at night. He knows Taron's taking me to the ball tonight, but I don't know what he'd say if he knew we were sleeping together. I don't want to fight with my brother before he leaves the country.

So I've been being careful, secretive, but I couldn't stop Taron last night. He got in my small bed and curled around me like a koala. This morning, he taught me his signature hoecake recipe, which he says he got off the Food channel on TV. We had ice cream, and we rode the three-wheeler down to the pond once more. Now I'm waiting for him to come to the house to "pick me up."

Leon is taking Betsy, and he left about thirty minutes ago. As part of the growers association, Sawyer took off after lunch to help set up or tear down or basically just be a presence. Mindy Facetimed me wanting to see my dress, which she helped me pick out the day I told her I was going with Taron.

"Oh my gosh, it's gorgeous!"

"You think?" Turning side to side, I look at the short black dress only held up by thin straps crossing my back.

I want tonight to be perfect. I want everything to go just right.

I need everything to go just right. It's a memory I'll hold for a long time…

My dark hair is styled over one shoulder, and I put on water-proof mascara. God, I don't want to cry, but I'm afraid I might.

"Now I'm wishing I was going." My friend is in her bed in bright red pajamas eating popcorn from a big green bowl.

Her curly dark hair is in a bun right on top of her head, and any other day, I'd be right there with her.

"What are you doing tonight?"

"Binging *Pretty Little Liars* for the third time."

"Is it bad that I think Alexander Skarsgård is so hot in that?"

"Alexander Skarsgård is an actor." Mindy adopts a clinical tone. "You can appreciate his hotness even when he plays a horri-ble character."

"Noel?" Taron's voice in the kitchen makes my stomach jump.

"Gotta run!"

"Have fun tonight! I want to hear all about it!" She blows me a kiss, and I hit the end button.

Giving myself one last look in the mirror, I grab my special lotion and rub a quick pump on my hands and shoulders before opening the door.

Taron takes my breath away. He's standing in the hall in his boots, dark jeans, and a navy button-down shirt with a tan blazer on top.

"Damn." He exhales the word on a hot breath.

His blue-green eyes glow with desire. They travel like a caress from my hair to my shoulders and down my legs.

"You like it?" My voice is small, quiet, and he closes the space between us, pulling me into his arms.

For a moment, we hold each other. My arms are around his waist, and his are around my shoulders. I'm completely engulfed in his rich scent of clean soap and cedar. Our breath rises and falls together. *Don't let go…*

I think of the words we've never said. The words our bodies have spoken so many times—every time we've touched each other, teased each other, kissed each other or made love… The words echo in my head and in my aching heart.

Akela's nails click on the wood floors as she trots into the room and sits beside us, waiting, as if she knows this is our last night as well.

Taron's arms relax, and he clears his throat. "We'd better take off if we're going."

His chin drops and he wipes a hand across his mouth. He almost seems like he wants to say more. I want to say more… So much hangs in the air between us.

"Wait a minute!" I dig in my purse and pull out my phone. "My arms aren't long enough."

He takes it from me and holds it up. I do my best to help him get us head to toe beside each other. It's a crooked shot, but we're smiling, our cheeks are together, and all those feelings glow in our eyes. He gives it back to me, and I take one more selfie of just our faces before slipping it back in my tiny handbag.

"Now?" Lacing our fingers, Taron guides me through the kitchen and out the back door to the old Chevy truck.

Inside, I scoot all the way across like always, so I can rest my head is on his shoulder. The lap belt is across my waist, and I hold his hand with our fingers still threaded.

We don't speak. On the radio is an old country song about a man who loved a woman until he died, and I close my eyes, wondering if such a thing is possible. If Taron might love me until he dies. I know I'll love him…

It hurts so much, but I'm determined not to waste these precious moments borrowing heartache from the future. He's still here with me. I can still touch him, smell him. He's still mine right now. I'll have plenty of time to miss him when he's gone.

The civic center is transformed for the party. White twinkle lights are wrapped around potted trees lining the room. Tables are arranged on one half of the hall with white tablecloths and small candles in the centers. A band is playing a mix of country, rock, and standards at the other end, and people are dancing.

I catch sight of my brother talking to Dutch Hayes, and I can guess what's going on there. Sawyer's been worrying himself sick over what's going to happen with the orchard while he's gone. I wish he'd talk to me about it. I'm perfectly capable of keeping things up and running, but he likes to follow the old ways.

He gets up every morning at the ass-crack of dawn, gets in his truck, and drives twenty miles per hour to meet with the old timers at the Denny's in town and talk about the almanac predictions and whether or not the migrant workers will be back next spring.

Spoiler alert: They always are.

"Want some punch?" Taron's smiling down at me, and I let my annoyance with my brother go.

"I'd rather have a Coke, if they've got it."

He lifts my hand and kisses my fingers before leaving me standing beside a tall table at the perimeter of the dance floor.

I look around for anybody I know while I wait, and I see Leon hugged up with Betsy on the dance floor. My brow furrows, and I wonder if I should have The Talk with him. I wonder if Sawyer's already done it... He's just so distracted these days, and he still thinks of Leon as a little kid. I'm sure my youngest brother already knows how sex works, but I hope he's being smarter than I was about birth control. *Jeez... What would I do without Mindy?*

Digger's smooth, unwelcome voice breaks my reverie. "You look as beautiful as I imagined you would."

"Digger." I hold out my hand, hoping to block his usual hug and kiss on the cheek.

I fail.

He pulls me into a stiff embrace and kisses my cheek, leaving behind the heavy scent of his lemony cologne.

Looking past him, I see Rachel Bishop with her arms crossed, standing at his left flank and glaring at me. I really want to tell her she has absolutely nothing to worry about. *At all.*

"Hi, Rachel." I reach out to wave her in closer, but she turns to chat with Andie Stevens at the next table.

Rude. But I guess I don't blame her. Just because I can't imagine ever dating Digger doesn't mean nobody else might. Some girls actually find him attractive, and I guess his dad does have a lot of money.

"You're here with Taron." It's not a question. Digger's nose curls. "At least he'll be gone in twenty-four hours."

"Gone isn't forgotten."

"You think he's something, but he's not. I checked. Taron Rhodes is nothing in Nashville. No people, no family." He looks over my shoulder to where I assume Taron is getting me a drink. "Don't set your heart on a guy like that, Noel. He *will* let you down. Believe me."

My voice is practiced calm. "I couldn't be less interested in what you think."

He's about to say more when a warm hand catches my arm, and I relax at the familiar touch. "Is this guy bothering you?"

His voice is a tease, and I look up into Taron's handsome face. "He talks too much. I'd really like to dance."

"Done." He puts our drinks on the table and lifts his chin at Digger. "Sup, Hayes. Bothering my girl again?"

That makes me laugh, and I slide my hand into the crook of his arm. Digger's dumb expression is enough for me. I put my face against Taron's chest, and we sway into the middle of the couples dancing to an old Patsy Cline song. It's the one about having a picture of the one you love... only he's with another girl.

We sway side to side several bars, and I can't resist. "Your girl?"

"Yeah." His voice lowers, and the air around us seems to change. "That's right."

He leans forward, pressing his lips to my brow, and I close my eyes, feeling all the emotions vibrating in my chest. He lifts his head and looks down at my face.

"I was talking to Leon today, and he said something. It kind of stuck with me."

Not what I was expecting. "Leon?"

He exhales a chuckle at the surprise in my tone. The song ends, and he takes my hand again, threading my fingers and leading me toward the door.

Outside, the air is warm and humid, and a group of smokers is congregated a few feet away. He changes directions, walking us toward the Chevy.

When we get there, he rotates me so my back is against the door, his arms caging me. "I couldn't say this before... I didn't think it was fair to say it and leave, not knowing how long I'll be gone, what might happen—"

"Stop." I reach up, putting my fingers lightly against his lips, my thumb touching his cheek.

He catches my wrist, kissing my hand briefly. "It's so beautiful here, so much more than I expected." Exhaling, he looks down. "I fell in love with this place, the work, the good times, even the heat. It's a simple life, but it's rich."

Listening to him, I can't hold back anymore. I blink, and a tear falls. He scoops it away with his thumb. "I fell in love with you. I love you, Noel Aveline LaGrange."

My throat hurts, and I'm ready to say the words that have been burning in my chest. "I love you."

It seems to settle him, like he decides in that moment. "I have to leave you tomorrow, but I'm coming back... for you—if that's something you want."

I turn his hand in mine, lifting it to my lips this time, kissing each knuckle.

Promises. If we're making promises, I'll start with the one I made our first night together.

"I'll wait for you." My voice is soft, but determined just like his. I've decided, too. "I've waited for you my whole life. I'll wait for you as long as it takes."

Cupping my face, he covers my mouth with his. We seal our words with a kiss. Our lips part, and his arms move to circle me, drawing my body close against his. Our warmth flows together. Our hearts beat together. Our words are real and true.

"You look so beautiful... your hair, this dress." He looks down, our love glowing in his pretty eyes. "Do you mind if we call it a night?"

Smiling, I shake my head no. "I only want to be with you."

We drive home, my head on his shoulder the whole way, and he takes me to my bed. We make love in a way that's different from the other times. It's deliberate and slow, worshipful, underscoring the words we've spoken with a union so elemental, so human.

He holds me all night, and when I wake the next morning, he's gone.

Sawyer's presence keeps me from falling apart the next few days—as do Taron's constant texts and calls. We Facetime every night at the same time as when we used to sit in my room and talk, his knee against mine, watching me work on my dream.

He looks so good, but I just want to touch his face once more. I just want to feel the warmth of his skin. It gives me strength, but even still, I'm so lonely for him it aches deep in my bones.

The day Sawyer has to leave is almost more than I can bear.

After losing our parents, the three of us formed a bond so tight, I thought we'd never be apart. Of course, we'd get married and have our families, but I always believed we'd be in the same place, nearby each other. We'd bonded through a trauma so intense, how could we be apart?

He tosses his pack in the back of his Silverado and gives Leon a hug. My little brother doesn't want to cry in front of us. He wants to be a strong man. He tells Sawyer goodbye and takes off, jogging up the hill into the grove.

My brother understands.

"I'll take care of him." I blink away the tears, giving him a brave smile.

Sawyer looks really good going off to serve and protect our country. He's a handsome man. He has our daddy's dark hair, square jaw, and strong build, and our mother's full lips and hazel eyes.

Girls in town swoon over him, but he only ever dated Tatum Ray, Mindy's older sister. When she left to follow her dream of becoming an actress, he put his head down and focused on the orchard.

Now he's leaving.

He clears his throat and looks over his shoulder toward the groves. "I told Dutch I was leaving the place in your hands."

His tone is even, decided, but you could knock me over with a feather.

"You did?" My eyes are wide.

"I asked him to look out for you like he did for me when I first took over, but it's your place. You're the boss while I'm gone." Hazel eyes meet mine, and I'm sure he sees the shock there. His brow furrows. "If that's okay?"

It only takes a second for me to snatch my jaw off the ground. "Yes! That's great!"

He nods in that quiet way of his. "I watched you this summer. You've got what it takes to be in charge. Leon can take over with the high school kids… You'll have to hire somebody to work as a foreman, Digger or someone else."

"Sawyer!" I step forward, hugging him hard, feeling the tears leaking from the corners of my eyes. "Thank you."

Strong hands go from my sides to around my back, and he hugs me firmly. "I believe in you, sis. Make me proud."

My nose is hot, and it takes every bit of will-power I possess, but I suck it up. "I will. I promise." I wipe my face with my hand. "Come back safe to us, okay?"

His lips curl into a smile, and he does a short nod before climbing into his truck and driving away.

CHAPTER
Fourteen

Noel

September

"**S**O I SHOULD FORM AN LLC AS SOON AS POSSIBLE?" I'M LYING ON my bedroom floor, leaning on my elbows over an accounting textbook, and Mindy's beside me eating popcorn.

"Why is this so hard for you?" She crunches loudly. "I think you have a mental block."

Before Sawyer left, I got him to agree my idea for a store had merit, primarily because everything sold out at the festival, and I made almost four thousand dollars—enough to cover half my first semester's tuition.

I officially launched Autumn's Bounty as an online store, and I've already been inundated with orders. I sold out of the candles and lip balm in the first twenty-four hours, and I only have a few bottles of the lotion and sugar scrub left—not to mention the fragrance melts and taffy.

It was good in two ways, actually. I didn't even get out of bed after Sawyer left. I started sleeping in the foreman's cottage, wrapped up in Taron's sheets and crying myself to sleep... Akela stayed at my feet with her head on her paws as if she knew I was grieving.

Leon finally brought me around—mostly because he ran out of leftovers and said he was going to starve to death if I didn't get out of bed and start taking care of us.

Slowly, I came back around. I stripped the sheets off the bed in the cottage and washed them... except for the pillow case, which I still keep under my pillow every night. My class schedule arrived in the mail, and I called Mindy, who came over at once to compare and rearrange.

Then she helped me get the online store up and running.

Now she's making straight *A*s in all our business classes, whereas I'm studying my ass off and still feel lost.

"I guess I thought it would be easier."

My best friend sighs loudly, shoving her hair behind her shoulders. "With a single-employee S-Corp, you are responsible for everything, but the limited liability protects you from being sued if anyone's hurt by your business."

"Sued." The word makes the blood drain from my face. "Like if I make somebody sick?"

"Or if somebody claims you made them sick. Bitches be crazy!" She cocks her head, sitting straighter in her *Floss like a Boss* PJ pants and navy tee. "Your store is a great idea. Your cosmetics are a hit. The bigger it gets, the more vulnerable you become. How is the orchard set up? I'm sure it's an LLC."

"Hell, I don't know!" I fall onto my back, throwing up my hands. I'm in a pink flannel button-up and leggings, and I feel very ignorant. "Sawyer never told me anything about that stuff. He just let Johnny take care of it all."

"Well, Johnny can keep taking care of it, but you have to pass this accounting course."

"Why did I want to be a business major again?"

"Because you're a smart, independent woman, and you're running a business now."

The Facetime app on my laptop starts to ring, and my whole body perks up. "Taron!"

My bestie levels her green eyes on me. "We have to study."

"Whatever." I hop up and give myself a quick look in the mirror, flicking my fingers through my hair.

She stands, giving me an exaggerated sigh and tapping on her phone as she leaves the room.

"You're going to be stalking the new guy anyway." Satisfied with my appearance, I hit the green button on my computer.

"It's called moving on with my life," she yells back.

"Moving on?" Taron's magnetic gaze hits me, and my stomach tightens. *Never…*

"Mindy's checking out the new guy in our finance class. He's from Dallas." His brow furrows, and I shake my head. "Don't worry—he's not my type."

"What's your type?" His voice drops to sexy, and my insides sizzle.

"Hmm…" I grin, leaning my head on my hand, wishing I could snuggle my nose against his neck. "Tall… dark hair, magnetic eyes…" I run my eyes around the screen as if I really have to think about it. "Playful, but strong… Catches me if I fall…"

"Good luck finding that guy." That makes me laugh, and Akela trots in the room. "Hey, Akela! There's my girl."

Her ears quirk back, and she sits, making a soft noise almost like a whine, like she's still confused why he's in that small rectangle and not here with us. I pet her head before turning back to the screen.

"You're early tonight! You interrupted my accounting torture session."

"Sorry. We finished up early, and I guess I was missing you. Check this out." He holds the phone up, and I see a vast canopy of green trees and mountains. "Isn't that something?"

The guys were diverted to Mexico to assist with peacekeeping along the border. Taron says it's pretty boring, mostly walking around and being visible. I worry someone might try to take a shot at them. The situation is so tense—at least it feels tense from where I'm sitting.

"They keep saying we're headed to Caracas soon, but it feels like we might be stuck here a while." As he talks, he walks into a beige building.

"I'm stuck in accounting. Mindy's pretty good at explaining it to me, but there's so many tax laws!"

He goes into a small room and lies back on a bed, putting his arm behind his head. His bicep flexes, and I want to put my head on his chest. "Doesn't your brother have an accountant?"

"Yeah, but to be a proper business major, apparently I need to know all this stuff, too."

"How's your business going?'

"Good! I'm running out of everything, though. I have no idea how people are finding out about me. I haven't had time to do much marketing at all."

"You said it yourself, people are looking for clean, organic products." He holds up the small, round jar of hydrating lip masque. "I'm almost out of this."

"I'll make a little care package for you."

I immediately start a mental list of all the things I'll add to it. Prints of those pictures we took before the Peach Ball—I have both of them framed on my dresser. A little book of peach puns I found in a gift shop. A tennis ball with a line on it...

"I talked to Sawyer last night." His voice is quiet, and he immediately has my attention.

"What do you mean?"

He shifts position, sitting up. "We had night watch, and we were pretty much trying not to fall asleep... He asked me if we were serious."

"What did you say?" I don't know why my chest feels tight.

"What do you think I said?" Taron's pretty eyes crinkle with his grin. "I said yes."

"How did he take it?"

"Just like Sawyer. He nodded and didn't say much. I think he's okay with it, but I'm watching my back."

He's joking, but I'm chewing my bottom lip. "I wonder why he didn't ask me?"

"Probably because Leon already threatened to kick my ass."

My jaw drops at that. "Leon? He… did what?"

"I told you he cared about you."

That makes me sit back on my butt. I look to the side, thinking about my two brothers and how unexpected they are. Leon stomps around complaining about how he's starving to death and is a general pest, but he hasn't stopped helping me clean up after meals. He's actually started pitching in even more since the guys left, running errands and keeping track of his schedule better.

Sawyer left the whole orchard in my hands, and now this.

"Well, I'll be."

"Don't say anything to him. That was between us."

"I won't."

Loud voices fill the background, and Taron looks over his shoulder. "The guys are coming. I guess it's too late for you to show me your tits."

"Taron!" My voice goes loud, but a tingle is between my thighs. "I'm sure Sawyer would not appreciate that."

"He doesn't have to know everything we do."

"And Mindy's here."

His full lips press into a line. "Sounds like a no."

"I miss you."

"I miss you, too, princess."

"I was never a princess."

"I'm still not a prince."

Leaning forward, I kiss the air in front of the camera. "You're still handsome."

We say goodnight and sign off, and I sit for half a second

before hopping up and running to the bathroom. With my back to the door, I unbutton my shirt and take a quick picture of my bare breasts and text it to him.

My stomach is tight, and I feel like I'm being insanely bad. I get an immediate text reply. *Gorgeous. Just what I needed.*

I type a quick reply. *They miss your kisses.*

Now you're just being cruel.

"Where the heck did you go?" Mindy's voice outside the door makes me jump. "Are you in there crying?"

"No…" I finish with a heart emoji and a kiss.

He replies with an eggplant, and I laugh, sending him a peach, to which he replies *Dat ass*.

I love you.

Love you back.

I quickly delete the selfie from our text string and turn off my phone. I've got to get back to work, but I have an idea for bringing him a little closer.

CHAPTER
Fourteen

Taron

December

A MATCHBOX-SIZED RED CHEVY TRUCK IS IN THIS MONTH'S CARE package, along with a photo of Akela looking down at a burned hoecake. Another picture of Noel holding the sides of her hair out over an accounting textbook makes me laugh, and a newspaper clipping of that little red-haired girl holding an Autumn's Bounty candle.

A two-page, handwritten letter explains everything, how Noel hasn't been able to make a decent hoecake since I left, which I don't believe. How accounting finals are this week, and how the local paper did a feature on her product line—endorsed by the new Princess Peach.

The red Chevy needs no explanation...

I trace my finger along the swirls of her handwriting, thinking how valuable such a thing feels to me now. We text little notes to each other every day, all day, and we Facetime every night. Still, this is special. Things she forgets to tell me or saves for these monthly missives. Holding it to my nose, I take a long inhale of her signature scent, and my longing for her is soul-deep.

"Dad wants to know how much longer we'll be in Mexico."

Patton Fletcher is in his bunk across from mine scoffing at his most recent letter. "He's not impressed by the lack of danger in our mission, says we should inquire about getting out early, since we're clearly being used for National Guard duty."

"He's busting your balls."

"Maybe… but not entirely."

"He's worried the Nashville business community won't find decent real estate without you."

Patton's dad owns Fletcher Properties, and for years, he's been claiming he'll retire and give the company to his son. I'll believe it when I see it. George S. Fletcher, Sr., is the Queen of England when it comes to his fledgling enterprise turned multi-million-dollar corporation. They'll pry those reins out of his cold dead hands.

"He still doesn't understand why we're here." Swinging his legs off the side of the bunk, Patton walks over to the desk and wakes his laptop. "He thinks I enlisted so I could run for senate."

My brow quirks. I never thought of that. "Did you?"

Black eyes cut to mine. "I have no interest in politics… other than how it affects my business." He shifts that laser focus to the computer screen. "We came here to make a difference."

His words became a sort of mantra between us. I remember us sitting around at the Y after a day of shooting hoops. Patton always wanted to do more. We'd see military observances, and he was always interested. As the world became more chaotic, more obsessed with appearances and possessions, he'd talk about how the military kept it simple, grounded—serve and protect.

It was unexpected coming from him, the kid who grew up with the silver spoon in his mouth, but I agreed with him. My home life hadn't give me much to be proud of, and I didn't have many prospects. Hard work and discipline didn't scare me, and the idea of the three of us doing it together seemed like a good plan. We spent most of our time together anyway. Then we met Sawyer.

Then I met Noel.

She's so beautiful. She has dreams and so much ahead of her. I want to bring something to the table as well. Sure, I can never be a prince, but I could be a hero. I've trained for it. If I could do something, come back with a medal, a badge of honor, no one could say we don't belong together. I want to give her that. I want to deserve her...

And I really want to be with her on her birthday.

Nights of talking through the computer screen or seeing her beautiful body on my phone are wearing on me. She's going to be nineteen in a few days, and I'd give anything to be there with her.

"Wish we could get a few days leave."

Patton looks at me like I've lost it. I'm frustrated we're still on the border. We go where we're told, but this mission feels more politically motivated than strategic. Primarily because we're not seeing much action.

"What the hell are you interested in doing? Visiting your mom? Jerome?"

He knows after my mom moved back to the mountains, I pretty much lost contact with her. My uncle is someone I have no intention of visiting ever.

"Just feeling cooped up. Antsy." Deployment in my mind was going to be more active and farther away—Afghanistan or Venezuela like we'd been told, not right here at the edge of our own country.

"You know what would be great right now?" Marley comes in, dropping on the foot of my bunk. "Edibles."

Pulling my leg up, I give him a shove. "I told you not to spend your leave partying. Now you're withdrawing."

"Cannabis is not addictive."

"Maybe not, but I imagine you get used to being high all the time."

"Not all the time."

"You're a Marine." Patton cuts his eyes at our friend. "You don't wake and bake."

"Marines smoke. They drink. Pot's legal now."

"I have a better idea." Patton leans back, rubbing his fingers over his mouth. "Something for after this. Something that will use all our skills."

"Go." Marley sits up. "Anything's better than staring at the jungle all day and night."

"Fletcher International."

Marley groans and Sawyer enters the room. "What'd I miss?"

"Patton still believes his dad's going to retire and give him the business."

"He will, and when he does, I'm making us all filthy rich."

Marley snatches a golf ball off Patton's desk and tosses it in the air. "I thought we came here to get away from all that."

"We came here to serve and protect," Patton agrees. "And when we leave, I've got us covered."

"I'm covered." Sawyer's voice is quiet.

"Yeah, Sawyer's got a hundred acres back home." Marley gives me a shove back. "You were there."

"Sawyer enlisted so he could have a break." I'm teasing along, but he cuts a glance at me. I told him I was serious about his sister, and I meant it.

"That's a long way off." Marley tosses me the golf ball. "I didn't come here to sit around dreaming. I'm going to find something to do."

CHAPTER
Fifteen

Noel

April

DOLLY PARTON SAYS WHEN YOU'RE FEELING LOW, PUT ON YOUR FAVORITE high heels and stand a little taller. I've spent nine months getting up every morning and slipping into a different pair of heels.

I went through the motions of cooking, cleaning, making sure Leon had what he needed and got to school on time. Mindy kept up with me, invited me to college functions, but it was hard to be interested in extracurricular activities.

Students would get so excited about football games and homecoming and beating our big rivals, but I couldn't seem to muster the energy to care. I did manage to pull off almost all *A*s in my business classes, with my only *B* in accounting.

My birthday was a day-long, off and on, Facetime call with Taron. He sent me a birthday care package, which we opened together—a big box of Mayan chocolate, a sterling silver and turquoise ring he said is from Taxco, a blown-glass ombre heart, and a small wooden skull decorated in flowers and brilliant designs for Día de los Muertos. I held up each one and raved over how beautiful and thoughtful his gifts were. I promised I'd never take the ring off my finger.

Sawyer called me, one of the two times we've talked since he left. As usual, he was direct, to the point. *How's the orchard, how's Leon, how am I...* My answer was good to all. He said it was pretty quiet where they were, and he said he and Taron were looking out for each other. He didn't say anything about their conversation concerning me.

I wished I could give him a hug. After nineteen years, I've learned while my big brother doesn't say much, his feelings run deep. Sometimes the only way he can express himself is through a hug or a pat on the back or a smile. I miss him more than I thought I would.

Leon's present to me was a "Get out of Work Free" card... which meant he did all the cooking and cleaning on my special day. He made our breakfast—or McDonald's did. He cleaned up and said he'd be back with dinner, after he took off to spend the day with Betsy. Betsy's mother sent dinner.

I didn't really mind.

In the afternoon, I drove up to the Pine Hills nursing home and dropped off a basket of peach muffins, fudge, and surplus items from my online store. Aunt Doris passed a few weeks back, and while it was sad, I was glad she was at peace. It was difficult seeing her drift further and further away from us in her mind.

Mindy wasn't there when I arrived, but I sat and chatted with Miss Jessica Priddy, the old spinster who used to live in the house next door to us. She doesn't have dementia, but she says her health is too poor for her to live alone. She's small and birdlike, and she wears her hair in a little bun at the nape of her neck. She's usually wearing lip gloss and a fancy smock over her clothes, and I wonder what it would be like to have only friends to take care of you.

After a lonely dinner in front of the fire, I ended the day in my bed, talking to Taron until we fell asleep. The next morning, I woke to a dark screen and cold sheets, and I stayed under the blankets with tears in my eyes until well after noon.

Months passed, and it started to feel like the heaviness would never leave, but as always, time turned out to be the healer.

The peach blossoms opened their petals along the branches of the trees all across the rolling hills of our orchard, and a light seemed to appear at the end of my long tunnel.

This morning, I'm not wearing heels.

I'm in my boots and a sweater, and I stand at the top of the hill, watching as the sun touches the pink blossoms with golden light.

"Good to see you're not crying anymore." Leon's voice appears at my side, and I put an arm around his shoulders.

"I'm not crying." I exhale slowly. "It's time to get busy. What needs to happen here?"

He shrugs out of my embrace, stepping over to break off a small twig sticking out of the trunk of a tree. "Sawyer handled the pruning in July, so we should be good. Maybe head into town and see what the old timers are saying about frost?"

"Yes." I nod, the knowledge seeping into my memory. "Late frost is bad."

We have special windmills throughout the orchard to pull warm air from the ground to protect the young crop.

"I'll drive to town and see what they're saying."

"Good luck." Leon laughs, shaking his head. "I've got to get to school."

"You need anything?"

"Nah, I've got it covered."

Holding a skinny branch, I make a decision. This is my land, and I won't let my brothers down.

I'm at the Denny's next to the truck stop in under an hour, but it's deserted except for a few weary travelers. Glancing at my phone, I've only got twenty minutes before I have to be across the highway in class.

"Morning, Sugar. Coffee?" Flo walks up to where I stand beside a vinyl covered booth.

"I was just looking for Mr. Hayes and the rest of the men."

She gives me a short laugh. "You have to get here earlier than this to see those guys."

Shit. Chewing my lip, I nod and hurry to the door. "Thanks, Flo."

My best friend has a pencil stuck in the bun on her head, and we're whispering in management class. "Frost?"

"Yeah, what have you heard about a late frost this year?" I'm thinking about my lack of management skills the first half of the year and feeling guilty.

Mindy looks at me like I just sprouted an additional head. "Are you serious right now?"

"I'm trying to do a better job keeping track of things while Sawyer's away."

Our professor gives us the homework assignment, dismisses us, and our voices grow louder over the roar of departing students.

"I'm glad." She stands, and we make our way to the end of the row, where I see Deacon waiting at the door.

He's hard to miss, tall with dark brown hair and brooding eyes. As usual, he's dressed in jeans and a blazer. I don't think he means to exude wealth. I think it's just his normal state of affairs.

"I thought he went back to Dallas?"

"He did." She glances over and gives him a little wave. "His family pissed him off again, so he came back."

"So are you dating now?" I squint at her. She has never made anything official between them.

"I don't know." She does a little shrug. "I'm not sure he's my type."

Shaking my head, I give her a squeeze. "He's somebody's type."

"Are you coming by to see Miss Jessica today?"

"Right after classes."

"See you then."

"Oh, I love the smell of this foot cream." Miss Jessica sits on a vinyl couch in the recreation hall rubbing my lotion on her feet. "I can't believe this didn't sell." She slips a fluffy sock on and leans back studying the bottle.

She's become one of my best customers, and I bring her favorites from my discontinued line along with new things I'm trying. Of course, I never make her pay for anything.

"Maybe I didn't name it right." I reach into the small bag I have today. "Like I didn't think this sugar scrub was going to do well, but I named it Peach Passion, and it flies off the shelves."

"I guess it's hard to be passionate about feet."

"I think having *foot* in the name is a problem."

She takes the jar of caramel-colored scrub from me and opens it, giving it a sniff. "I'm glad you brought me more of this. It works great on my elbows."

I take out another small jar. "This is some eye cream I'm trying. See what you think."

"Oh, I love eye cream." She takes the tiny pot and unscrews the lid, applying a smear as we sit side by side. "Feels good… I wish I knew how to use that Internet so I could tell everybody how great your products are."

I laugh, and she reaches out to hold my hand. "You seem happy today. Is it because of Taron?"

"I don't know." My brow furrows as I think about what changed in me. "I think maybe it's spring."

Her spotty old hand pats mine roughly, and she nods. "When my brother Bill was in the service, the first months were always the hardest. We only had letters in those days, and it felt like a little eternity passed between each one."

"I can't imagine." Taron and I don't Facetime every single

day anymore, but our texts are pretty nonstop. "Maybe the peach blossoms did it. I saw them popping out on the trees, and I decided it was time to get back in the game."

She nods. "The game being your business?"

"And running the orchard. And focusing on my classes." I think about all the orders coming in every day for my products. "But mostly my business. I have to stay on top of it if I'm going to keep making a profit, which is the only time Sawyer seems interested."

"You will." She smiles, giving my hand a squeeze. "When your brother gets back, and Taron gets back, you'll have your store."

She makes it sound like they've just gone away for a few days. *I wish.* "Maybe. Sawyer won't let me build anything in the orchard. He doesn't want tourists all in the way. I have to show him they're valuable customers."

Her brow furrows as if she's thinking about this, and I collect the items I made for her into the bag again. My movements draw her attention. "How much do I owe you for these?"

"Oh," I smile and exhale a laugh. "Don't worry about that."

"I do worry about that, Noel Aveline." Her craggly voice goes high. "You're never going to grow your business giving stuff away, and I always pay my bills."

"Tell you what." I pat her hand. "I'll ask Mindy to deduct it from your account." *Her imaginary account.*

The old woman nods. "Okay. Get Mindy to do that."

"I'll take care of it now. Then I have to get back to make dinner for Leon."

"You'll be back next week?"

"If not sooner." I give her a squeeze. "Let Mindy know if you need anything."

That night, lying in my bed, I think about our conversation as I tap out a text to Taron. **Miss Jessica asked about you today.**

I introduced her to Taron using my Facetime app a while back, and you'd have thought I'd shown her the moon landing. Gray dots bounce as he replies. **Tell her when you're sick of me, I'll start dating her.**

His teasing makes me smile. **I'll never be sick of you.** It's hard to even imagine such a thing in our current situation. **She said when Sawyer gets back, I can open my storefront.**

You don't have to wait for that do you?

Chewing my lip, I study my phone. I don't want to bug him about his plans, but I hadn't considered we might be separated like this over and over for years and years. Can I say goodbye to him indefinitely? The alternative makes it easy to say yes but so hard to imagine. Is it possible to get used to this life?

I'd need help with an orchard, a store, and school.

I watch the gray dots as he taps out a reply. **Are you unhappy with being online?**

"Taron…" I sigh his name out loud. Tapping the camera icon, I wait as it rings. I need to see him for this.

A moment later his gorgeous face appears, and I want to cry. "Hey, princess. You okay?"

My eyes scan his surroundings. "Are you in a closet?"

"Half bath. I thought we might need privacy." His eyes crinkle with a grin.

I didn't call for the reason he's thinking, and now that I see his face, I'm having second thoughts about my own. Maybe we should wait to discuss the future. I'm acting like he asked me to marry him or something, which he didn't. "I needed to hear your voice."

He leans to the side, and his face gets a little closer. "It's not getting easier."

Heat filters into my eyes. "No."

The smile melts from his cheeks, and his expression turns serious. "Are you having second thoughts?"

"No!" Akela jumps on the bed at the sudden rise in my voice. I put my hand on her head and she licks my nose. "I'm still waiting. I only thought... I was wondering... how many times you might do this."

He exhales a laugh. "Patton's already making plans for when we get out."

I'm not sure what that means, but I know Patton lives in Nashville. "Are you having second thoughts?" My chest is so tight, I can hardly breathe.

"No." The warmth in his voice puts more tears in my eyes. "I'm still glad I did this, but maybe I'd have made a different choice if I'd met you first."

"You wouldn't have met me if you hadn't done this."

His head tilts side to side. "Catch-22." Blinking down, I quickly swipe the tear off my cheek. I don't want to cry every time we talk. "We're almost there, princess. Can you stay with me a little longer?"

"Yes." My voice breaks on a whisper, but I mean it with all my heart.

"I love you, Noel."

Nodding, I close my eyes. "I love you."

Digger meets me at the door of the Denny's when I get out of the truck the next morning. "Noel? What are you doing here?"

It's still dark outside, and I'm wearing faded jeans and a long-sleeved gray tee with a blue baseball cap pulled over my head. My boots and a barn coat complete the look. "It's time I showed up at these meetings."

"But it's so early."

My brow furrows, as I study him. "You're here."

"Yeah, but you don't need to be. You should get your beauty rest."

"I've rested enough." Once upon a time, Digger didn't bother me so much. Now every word out of his mouth sets my teeth on edge. "Sawyer's going to be gone a while—if he doesn't re-enlist."

"He won't do that." Digger chuckles as if I'm a child. "He told my dad he'd be back by the time you finished college."

Again, I want to growl at my older brother. *Why didn't he tell me that?*

"Either way, the place won't run itself for four years."

Reaching for the door, I'm ready to push past Digger and go inside the restaurant. He stops me, putting his arm around my shoulders.

"You need to hire a foreman and let him handle everything. I'm right here, ready to do it for you."

"You are not my foreman." I wriggle out of his grip. "Sawyer left me in charge. I'll decide what needs to happen on my place."

He exhales an amused noise, and I continue to where Ed Daniels stands beside a booth where a few of the older guys are sitting, sharing coffee. When I walk up, they all stop talking and look at me.

"Noel?" Mr. Daniels straightens, adjusting his cap. "How are you this morning?"

"Fine, thanks." My voice sounds too small, too inexperienced to me. "I was wondering if you know if there'll be a late frost?"

The man chuckles. "I'd be a rich man if I could predict a late frost."

Digger joins us. "Noel wants to have coffee this morning."

The way he says it makes me wonder if he's already told these men he's my foreman. "Sawyer left me in charge. I thought I best know what's coming."

"I thought you were making beauty products." Ed's smile doesn't reach his eyes, and I wonder if he agrees with my brother about bringing tourists onto the farms.

"I've started my own business, if that's what you mean."

Jeff Priddy pipes up. "That's right. My aunt Jessica called last night. Said she wants to give Noel the old feed shed to turn into a store."

"She did?" A blend of surprise and confidence fills my chest at this announcement.

"It's probably full of rats, but she said you can have it if you want it."

"I do want it. Thank you." As disgusting as the prospect of rats might be, I've got a dog, and the old feed shed is only a quarter-mile from the orchard. I'll be making an extra special care package for my number one customer tonight.

"As for frost, it's best to watch the news… and the sky." He continues, and I wonder if he might be on my side after all. "Moisture keeps the chance of frost forming low, so more rain means less frost. Clear skies are a warning sign."

"Thank you again." I nod, and when Flo appears, I hold up a finger.

She brings me a cup of weak coffee, and I take a seat at one of the tables across from the booth where the men sit. I listen as they discuss the latest news. I never cared about politics or what happened at the border before, and I do my best to absorb all they say.

Sawyer said Digger's dad would watch out for me, but I don't want Digger being too close to my business. As they continue, I think about what Miss Jessica has done, giving me her old shed. I wonder how much work it will take to turn it into a real store. I'll have to wait until summer to work on it, until after harvest, but at least I can check it out.

The men start to break up, and I make my way over to Jeff, hoping to get a handle on what needs to be done to transfer ownership. I might have to hold it for a few months, but I don't want to let it go. One thing I know for sure is you never know what might happen.

I'm still holding those words in my mind when my whole world tilts.

CHAPTER
Sixteen

Taron

July

"**D**AMN, YOU LOOK AMAZING." I'M LYING ON MY BUNK LOOKING AT Noel wearing nothing but a beauty pageant sash.

Her small breasts hang in luscious handfuls, rosy nipples hard and pointing upward with a thick white sash draped across the center.

"You're the first person I thought of when I saw it at the party store."

"I wish I was there." She slides her palms up her ribcage, cupping her breasts. "I want to see you touch yourself."

She gives me a naughty wink. "It's part of my evil plan to make you beg for leave."

"Actually," I sit forward, adjusting the boner in my pants. "That's why I called. They're finally moving us to Caracas, and we have the option to take a short one."

The phone drops, and for a minute, the screen goes crazy giving me views of her bedroom before it's back on her again. She's pulled the thin white shirt over her beautiful body.

"You're coming home?" Her pretty amber eyes are watery and an ache hits my throat.

"I'm coming to you."

"Taron..." She blinks down, and two crystal drops hit her cheeks.

I want more than anything to gather her in my arms and hold her tight. "I'm going to love you so hard, we'll never leave the bedroom."

"Is Sawyer coming with you?"

"Yeah, we all get four days."

"That's all?"

"Hey," I force a grin. "Let's focus on the good part."

Her dark head nods, long waves bouncing around her shoulders. "I'm sorry. I just... I miss you so much."

"Don't say you're sorry. I miss you." My voice is warm. My arms long for her. "I've got so much to tell you. So many things I want to say."

"I can't wait to hear them all." Her eyes look tired, and I want to slide my thumbs under them, dry her tears. "You made it through harvest."

"We did." A big smile takes over her face. "I was so scared we couldn't do it without Sawyer. I ended up hiring Digger to be our foreman." Her cute nose wrinkles. "But Leon and I both made a vow it was the last time. Next year, it's just me and him... and maybe one other person, but no more Digger."

That makes me laugh. "That bad?"

"He's just so freakin annoying. You can't imagine."

"I can imagine. But hang on..."

Her brow furrows. "How did I lose my sexy pageant show?"

"Oh." Her chin drops, and she looks up at me through heavy lashes. My dick immediately springs to life at the sight of her. "Were you talking about the grown-up Princess Peach."

She traces a finger down the front of her shirt, sliding the sides apart and letting her beautiful breasts peep out.

"Shit, yeah..." My voice is rough, hungry, and we spend the

next several minutes on a Facetime call so dirty, I'm covered in sweat and weak in the knees when it's over. "I'll never use this sock again."

Noel's lying on her back, her dark hair sticking to her naked, sweaty body. "You make me come so hard."

"I didn't even touch you. Just wait until I'm there."

She rolls over to face me, her pretty breasts hanging down on her bed. "How long before you're here?"

"If everything goes through, we should be able to leave by the weekend. Of course, travel days count against our leave, so I'll only have a few days."

"I'll be so glad to see you." Her voice is soft, sleepy.

"I love you, princess. Get some rest."

"I love you."

We disconnect, and I unlock the door before staggering to the shower. A few minutes later, I'm lying on my bunk, scrolling through the gallery of nude Noels on my phone. She is so damn fine. I can't wait to have my mouth all over her body and my dick deep inside her.

The door flies open, and I quickly shut off my phone. "Taron!" Patton's eyes are wide, his expression panicked. "Have you seen Marley this evening?"

My brow furrows, and I sit up. "No... he went on a fuel run after lunch, and—"

"He didn't come back. Connor says he was at a fuel station that came under fire at sixteen hundred. It's possible he was taken hostage."

"What the fuck?" I'm on my feet, pulling a thick brown Cammie over my white tee. "Why would they take him hostage?"

"Guns, money, both." Patton's voice is fierce, and I know he's worried. We're out the door, heading down the hall toward the communications station.

Kidnapping a Marine is pretty serious shit. "How's it being classified?"

"Don't know yet." He leads me into a large tent where Sawyer is already talking to the major.

He pulls back, coming to us. "His phone was recovered in a ditch halfway to Victoria. They're waiting for contact."

"So they're expecting some kind of ransom?" I rub the back of my neck thinking of what this could mean.

"If they were going to kill him, they'd have found his body in the ditch. They think it's some local thugs."

Patton leaves us and goes to our field commander. I watch as they speak in animated tones. He's asking for us to be assigned the rescue and recovery mission. Tugging at the back of my hair, I hate to think it, but the words come unbidden—*so much for going home.*

I want to hit somebody. I want to roar and throw things, flip tables and break something. More than anything, I want to find these thugs and beat the shit out of them. Sliding my hands over my face, I try to get calm, but all I can think about is Noel.

CHAPTER
Seventeen

Noel

August

A YEAR.

One year I was able to speak to him whenever I wanted. I could see his face, hear his voice. Now it's gone completely dark.

My insides tremble, and instead of crying, all I do is shake.

Marley was kidnapped. That's as much as I know.

Taron called me, and his voice was strained. He told me what they knew and how it changed his ability to take leave.

Having the promise of seeing him, touching him, holding him, even for one day taken away was like having my bones crushed.

He told me Patton insisted they be assigned the rescue mission. He said no one would be more dedicated to Marley's rescue than them. I told him I love him. He told me he wasn't sure when he'd be able to contact me again.

We ended that call, and the clock started.

Two weeks pass in silence until my brother breaks it.

I'm sent a special number and a special code. It's all very top secret and high security. My eyes flood with tears the moment I see his face, covered in a scruffy beard. He speaks, and his voice is a balm to my trembling insides.

"They let me call you since I'm considered the head of the house." Sawyer's voice is apologetic, as if he knows I want to hear from someone else, which I do, but give me a break.

"I'm so glad you called me." I can't help the fear in my tone.

"I don't have much to say other than we're okay."

"That's enough." My throat aches, and tears blur my eyes. "Thank God you're okay."

"Taron's fine, but Marley's..." He turns his face to the side, and I can tell by the flex in his jaw it's bad. "We're going deep to get him back. I might not be able to contact you for a while."

"Please be safe." Desperation is in my voice. "Take care of... all of you."

"I will." He nods. "You and Leon okay? You need anything?"

We need you. "We're good. Don't worry about us. Nothing ever changes around here. You know that."

"I love you, sis." His hazel eyes meet mine, and my heart beats faster. Anxiety twists my chest.

"I love you, Sawyer." I don't want to hang up. "Please call soon... or anything, send me a letter... And please just... Tell Taron—"

"I'll tell him."

The line goes silent, and I drop my face in my hands.

It's the last I hear for another month. Leon starts his senior year of high school. Classes begin at the college, and I do my best to show up mentally and physically. Miss Jessica comforts me with stories of when her brother was in Vietnam. Stories along the lines of "the darkest hour is always before dawn." I love her so much, I don't want to tell her they don't help at all.

I should start cleaning out her old feed shed. I should introduce more products to my line. I should talk to Digger about having the peach trees pruned... So many things I should do. All I do is wait.

The sun comes up every morning, breaking golden over the rows of green-leaved trees. The sun goes down every evening, casting long shadows with no answers or relief.

I go to church every time the doors are open. I go to bed and pray God will please not take another person I love from me. My prayers are always the same. *Please, God. Please let me have lost enough.*

Every day is one long line leading into the next, until the day comes.

I'm standing on the hill, looking out toward the horizon. My eyes follow the narrow dirt road that runs past that old house on the hill, and right where the blue meets the beige I see a faint cloud of dust rising.

My heart leaps to my throat, and I'm running down the hill. Leon's in the yard, and he calls to me, but I don't stop. I don't feel the ground beneath my feet. I don't notice the scenery as I pass. It's all a tunnel of blur centering on the Chevy Silverado growing closer at a rate of twenty miles per hour.

Tears coat my cheeks, and I see the vehicle stop. The door opens, and a dark figure steps out. His hair is messy, long, and a beard covers his cheeks. I don't stop running until we're in each other's arms, hugging each other long and hard.

"Sawyer…" I can only say his name. "You're alive."

His large hand grips the back of my head, and I listen to his heart beating. "I'm home. I'm home for good."

CHAPTER
Eighteen

Taron

SWEAT COATS MY BODY. WE'RE IN A PLACE SO HOT, IT'S HOTTER THAN the summer days in the peach shed.

A shed. I'm in the canopy of darkness. Slick leaves surround us, and the cinder block hut hides in the banana trees and vines. It's my job to test the door. My rifle is in my hand, and Patton is directly across from me in the undergrowth. Sawyer is covering the back of the house, and I'm making my way across the face, ducking under empty black windows devoid of glass.

The cell phone signals, the satellite imagery, the IP addresses, all of it led us to this place. Weeks of torture videos, of watching Marley being beaten, strapped to a chair… We're here to set him free.

My heart beats in my ears. Anyone could be on the other side of that door, and it's my job to open it. Reaching out, I see Noel in my mind's eye one last time.

I rap hard on the wood and pull back, allowing the cement blocks to shield my body.

Silence.

The noise of cicadas rises around us. The scream of a bird somewhere in the distance. I wait, looking deep into the forest until I find a pair of black eyes. Patton has my back like always.

He gives the signal, and I step back, lifting my leg and kicking the door open before dropping to a knee, my gun at the ready.

Again, silence is the only greeting.

Then I see him.

My stomach plunges. Our friend, a guy I've known as long as I can remember, who I grew up sharing my dreams and fears with when nobody else cared, is tied to a chair with ropes cutting through his skin.

Throwing the rifle on my back, I lunge forward, whipping out my knife and cutting him free. I rip the heavy bag off his head just as Sawyer enters the small space.

"We've got him." His familiar accent sounds over the receivers in each of our ears.

Patton joins us, and he catches Marley as his knees hit the floor. "We've got you. You're safe now."

Blood drips from his mouth, and he's incoherent. He's been beaten unconscious, and I pray we get him to help in time to prevent lasting damage. I'm lifting him to his feet, ready to haul him over my shoulder when the air changes.

A woman screams at my left shoulder. Her eyes are blazing green like a cat, her dark hair fanning around her as she races toward us, machete raised.

"Jesus!" I don't have time to think. Reaching for my left ankle, I jerk out the pistol hidden in my boot and fire.

She drops with a dull thud, a spray of blood fanning behind her, the large knife still gripped in her hand. She's slim and young, full lips and long, wavy hair, green eyes staring vacant at the ceiling.

I killed her.

"God, no..." My breath freezes in my chest. *What have I done?* I can't stop staring at her lifeless body.

"GO!" Patton's order snaps me out of my shock.

Throwing Marley's arm over my shoulder, I help Sawyer

walk him out of the shack, but my chest is tight. My heart beats too hard, and I think I'm going to be sick.

I killed that girl.

Two steps outside, and I go down hard.

"Fuck!" I scream as the stabbing of a knife hits me right in the lower back.

My eyes close, and I can't breathe while I feel warm wetness covering my skin. I'm bleeding. Patton is in front of me, and I hear Sawyer yell for him to stop. It's a trip wire he somehow missed on the way inside.

I found it and fell with Marley on top of me on the broken trunk of a sapling. Sawyer throws Marley over his back. Patton jerks me over his shoulder, and we race down the hill. Mission accomplished.

I'm bleeding all over myself and all over my friend. We reach the trucks as the blackness sets in. The pain in my back is so intense, I lose consciousness. I hear Patton telling me to stay with him, but I'm not with him. I'm back in that hut looking at her dead body.

CHAPTER
Nineteen

Noel

I DON'T CARE IF YOU'RE HURT. I JUST WANT TO SEE YOU. IT'S THE SAME TEXT I've sent every day since my brother returned.

Still, no reply.

My brother came back, and after holding us all close for several minutes, during which all three of us broke down and cried, he went to his room and stayed there for several days.

They were all given medals and sent home, and even though my brother doesn't have any visible injuries, he won't tell me what happened on their rescue mission. He handed me a letter from Taron and said no more about it, which I've come to expect from Sawyer.

Can't see you anymore…

Everything has changed…

Can't ask you to wait…

Don't deserve you…

I don't deserve you? These are words I cannot accept.

Taron should know I won't accept them.

If he wants to break up with me, he can do it to my face. Another week passes, and the anger in my chest has effectively burned away the grief I feel.

Sawyer joins us for lunch, and I have a bag packed. "I'm going to Nashville."

His dark brow furrows, and his eyes cut up to me. "Why?"

"To see Taron."

"He's not coming back, Noel." My brother's voice is quiet, definite, and my heart rips in two.

I want to scream. I want to throw things.

My hand shakes so hard, I can't drink my coffee. I set the cup down with a bang. "Then he can tell me to my face."

"It's not like that." Sawyer's eyes change. They become pleading, holding mine as if he's begging me to understand. "He's not the same. He's changed. We all are."

His voice trails off on the last part, but I won't be denied. "If he's hurt, I'll help him heal."

"You don't understand—"

"*You* don't understand!" Standing, I take my dishes to the sink. *We made promises. I made promises...* "I know Taron better than anyone. Maybe even him."

"I'm not trying to hurt you." His words are the same ones Taron said to me so long ago, right before I gave him everything. "This is something you can't fix, sis."

"Maybe not, but he belongs to me. I'm going to get him."

It's dark when I arrive at the address Sawyer texted me. I spent the three-hour flight wringing my hands, wondering if my brother was going to give me what I asked of him.

He said I should wait, but it's the last thing I intend to do. I'm pissed at him for letting Taron shut me out. He's supposed to be on my side, the protective older brother. Instead, he won't tell me anything other than giving me Taron's letter.

I'm furious with both of them for acting like I'm not strong enough to handle whatever might happen. Like I didn't sacrifice these last almost two years.

Now, standing in the lobby of the high-rise apartment, I wait for the silver doors to open. My brother said Taron lives with Marley. Patton arranged for them to take jobs at his dad's commercial real estate firm, and set them up in a penthouse apartment.

None of it makes sense. Taron said he grew up with nothing, the only child of a single mom who moved back to the mountains when he was in high school, yet here he is living like a king. At least, that's how it looks from the outside.

The elevator door opens to a beige lobby with deep brown, mahogany accents. I step across the small foyer and wait, trying to calm my breathing before I knock.

My hand shakes as I lift it, but my eye catches the turquoise ring on my finger.

I promised.

Squeezing my eyes shut, I knock hard and firm.

No response.

My breath is so loud in the small space. I take a trembling *inhale, exhale* then do it again—this time with my eyes open. I knock louder, longer, then I wait.

Even my heartbeat aches. I haven't seen Taron in person in so long. My brother said he's hurt; he sent me a letter telling me not to come. I'm so impulsive.

A trickle of fear, cold as ice filters through my chest. What if I find something I don't want to see? What if his face is mangled or he's in a wheelchair? What if his brain is damaged? What if he lost a limb?

I never actually considered the possibility. I assumed he'd be like my brother—physically whole, internally suffering.

These thoughts bombard my mind, but a calm reassurance fills my chest. It doesn't matter—we can face any of these challenges together.

I love this man.

"Who is it?" His voice is stern through the door.

"Taron?" Mine is clear, cutting the fear.

It's quiet on the other side.

My eyes go to the peep-hole in the middle of the door, and my breath stills. *Is he looking at me right now? Will he open the door?*

The seconds tick past on heartbeats... *one... two... three...*

Anxiety builds, tightening my chest until I hear the bolt turn. The door slides open quietly, and my eyes fill with tears when I see his beautiful face, his hypnotic eyes.

"Taron." Rushing forward, I'm in his arms.

His scent surrounds me, and it all comes flooding back. All the nights we spent hanging on each other's voices, living for just the sight and sound of each other like oxygen. All the times I lay in my bed, memorizing his face through the flickering screen. All the teasing and flirting, all the wishes and promises.

"You're here." His voice vibrates my very core.

His strong arms are around me, and my head is sheltered against his chest. I hear his heart beat, his breath swirl in and out.

"You're real." Tears stream down my cheeks.

I hug him with all my strength, wishing I could bleed my soul into his, give him whatever he needs, heal whatever's hurting him, whatever's making him say words he doesn't mean.

He steps back, guiding me into his apartment and closing the door, turning the lock. His eyes are so weary. Small lines mark the corners, and his beard is thicker. He's lost weight. He's still tall, towering over me, but my brother's right. He's changed.

"Noel..." He slides his fingers along the line of my hair, and more tears flood my eyes.

His touch is the same.

I hold his cheeks, guiding his face to mine and kissing him. He leans into me, pressing his hand against the door behind me. His mouth opens, his tongue slides along mine, but his muscles are stiff, like he's holding back, fighting against something.

Wrapping my arms around his neck, I lift my lips to his ear. "I've waited so long to feel you in my arms again."

His shoulders collapse, his resistance crumbles, and his arms go around my waist, gathering me to him. So much time has passed. I know he aches for me as much as I do for him. I remember the night we thought he'd come home, the twisting of my heart in my chest at the thought I might see him again.

It's all here right now.

We don't speak. He kisses me again, and the heat we've always shared flares to life. His hands move down my back, sliding under my shirt, finding my skin. A noise seeps from my throat, and I pull my shirt over my head.

With every kiss, every touch, we've been moving, stumbling backwards, until now we're in his bedroom. He winces as he removes his shirt, almost like he's been in a fight. I scan his chest for scars but see none. The lines in his torso are deeper. Yes, he's lost weight, but he's still so ripped.

My face is in the middle of his torso, and I rise to press my mouth to his broad shoulder, planting a kiss against his hot skin. Salt is on my tongue, and I feel his palm against my back, his other hand fumbling with my bra. Reaching around, I quickly remove it, and our bare bodies press together.

"I've dreamed of this so many times," he groans.

His hand is on my face, and I feel his hardness pressing against my stomach.

"I couldn't live without you one more day." My voice is a gasp, and my hands are at his waist, unbuckling his belt so fast.

The space between my thighs is hot and pulsing. I'm electric all over, every touch stoking my need hotter.

"Noel..." He groans a weak protest I cover with my mouth as he sits on the side of the bed.

Shoving my pants off, I climb onto his lap in a straddle, feeling his thick cock against my thighs. I'm throbbing and hot. I've touched myself so many times, given myself so many long-distance orgasms to his face on a screen, his voice on my laptop.

His fingers glide lightly over the skin of my ass, and I rise up on my knees, dropping firmly, seating him fully inside me.

His groan is pure desire that curls my toes. I rise onto my knees again and drop, feeling him deep inside me, savoring the sounds of his hunger, his hands gripping my ass. He's moving me now, pulling me up and down his dick, groaning as I ride him, chasing the orgasm rising in my stomach. With every noise he makes, my body flames hotter.

Our chests slide together, sweat and heat and hundreds of nights of need. My breasts bounce, and he catches one, guiding it to his mouth and kissing my hard nipple.

My head drops back, and I moan loudly. "Taron... yes..." My hips buck forward as my orgasm breaks, thundering through my insides.

I shudder and rise, wrapping my arms around him, kissing my way up his neck to his cheek and into his hair. He continues rocking me a bit longer, pulling me closer, burying himself to the hilt as he holds, groaning and pulsing, filling me deep.

We're gasping, wrapped in each other's arms, slick with sweat, and shimmering in afterglow. Scooting higher into the bed, he holds me against him, curling me in his arms as we slip between the sheets.

I realize his bed was unmade. "Did I wake you?" My voice is quiet, higher than his.

He lets out a short breath and shakes his head. "I wasn't sleeping."

Our bodies are flush, my breasts flat against his hard chest, and we breathe together. I slide my fingers along his hairline and he does the same, looking down at me in wonder. I'm sure my eyes are filled with the same emotion.

"What are you doing here?" His voice is tender, sincerely asking.

"Did you think I wouldn't come?"

"I told you not to." His eyes shimmer, and the thought of his tears squeezes my chest. "My beautiful princess. You're so good."

"My handsome prince." I smile, but his eyes flinch.

"So far from a prince." His chin drops as he lifts my hand, kissing the ring on my finger. "Your ring."

"It fit perfectly. I never take it off."

A sad smile curls his lips, and he kisses me again along the jaw, up to my ear. Desire hums through my skin. I could make love to him all night and still not be satisfied, but this heaviness hangs in the air around us.

"Are you okay?" My palm is flat against his cheek.

"I am for now."

It's not enough, but I wrap my arms around him, pulling him against me. I want to feel the weight of his body pressing me down. It's so good. His large hands slide along my sides, and it isn't long before he slips inside me again. Our mouths unite, and we rock together, slowly at first before picking up speed.

He rises over me, thrusting faster. A drop of sweat trickles down his brow, and my hands slide up his strong arms. My fingers follow the lines of his muscles, and I lift my hips to meet him, riding out the orgasm, feeling it in the tips of my toes when he comes with a loud shout. Hard thrusts, deep thrusts.

Our breathing is heavy as we come down once more. I'm sure we're just beginning our reunion. He turns me, strong arms secure around my waist, and I smile as my back presses against his chest. I'm lulled into a false sense of security in his arms as I drift to sleep.

I have no idea it won't last.

I awake before dawn alone. At first, I'm disoriented, then I remember I'm in Taron's room. Climbing out of bed, I make my way to the small carry-on suitcase I brought with me. I wheeled it inside the door, but that's where it stayed. Now I'm feeling around for clothes to cover my naked body.

Wrapping myself in his shirt, I inhale deeply of his scent, clean and masculine. I stagger into the living room, expecting to find him in the kitchen.

It's empty.

"Taron?" My voice echoes in the empty space.

No reply. Nothing. He's just gone. Picking up my phone, I quickly send a text. **Midnight pizza run?**

No gray dots, no missed call, no note. Fear prickles through my veins, and I grab a throw off the back of the couch, wrapping it around me. I sit for a long time, staring out the glass doors of the balcony overlooking the Nashville skyline. The interstate wraps through the tall buildings, and cars like fireflies stream past them.

My eyes grow heavy as the horizon begins to pale, and I doze.

I'm still alone when I open my eyes again, and I grab my phone, dialing Taron's number. It goes to voicemail, and I leave a message. I'm worried and anxious, and *where the hell is he?*

Another hour passes. I walk around his apartment, looking through drawers, searching for any clues. I find a lighter and rolling papers. I'm concerned, but I remember what he said about Marley and pot. Would that have changed after the military? I don't know. I find a business card for Fletcher Properties. Could he have gone to work?

I don't know what he does in real estate, but maybe he's on a deadline? He was asleep when I arrived... Maybe he'd planned to pull an all-nighter?

My fingers hover over the keypad on my phone, ready to dial when I hear a noise at the door. With a sharp inhale, I turn to see him walking into the apartment. He's still wearing the clothes he had on last night—faded jeans and a long-sleeved tee. Not exactly work attire... Although, I guess if he was the only one in the office.

He straightens when he sees me and clears his throat, turning into the kitchen area. "Hey."

"Hey…" I watch him, wondering if he's avoiding me. "I tried to call."

"Oh, yeah?" He lifts his phone and his eyebrows quirk.

"Are you okay?" Closing the space between us, I catch his arm. "What's going on? Where did you go?"

"It's not your business."

"I think it is." My voice is sharper than I intend. I'm struggling with residual fear mixed with frustration mixed with this ache in my chest.

He's agitated, suddenly frustrated, and pulls his hand away. "I didn't ask you to come here, Noel. Just the opposite, in fact."

I'm stunned by his words. They feel like a stab in the chest after last night. Or I guess after the few hours we spent together last night. Now that I think about it, after I fell asleep, I don't know what he did.

"I was worried about you. Sawyer said you were hurt. Something's clearly wrong."

"I was hurt." His eyes flash, and I realize I've never seen him angry. It's scary. "I'm always in pain now. Do you know what that's like? Every move radiating agony through your body?"

His voice is a knife, and my eyes heat. I blink quickly. "No… I don't. What can I do? Let me help you."

"You can't help me. No one can." His jaw clenches, and I see a sheen of perspiration on his lip. "You need to go home."

Another flash of anguish spreads through my chest. I'm having trouble breathing. "Would you at least tell me what happened? The last time we talked, you were going for Marley, then—"

"Then everything changed." He leans forward and grips the table. The blood drains from his cheeks, and I can see he's hurting.

"Taron—"

Inhaling sharply he leaves the room, going into the bathroom and shutting the door. I wait, listening as he opens the medicine cabinet. I hear the noise of pills shaking in a bottle, water running, then silence. My insides are so tight. My eyes are damp. My heart is breaking.

After several minutes, the door opens, and he's calmer. His muscles seem relaxed. He's more like he was last night, only with a dark shadow following him. "We can't be together, Noel. I'm not the same man I was before. This is my life now."

"What?" My voice cracks higher. "What is your life now? Tell me!"

"Pain…" He growls, moving slowly across the room to the sofa and lowering himself carefully. "Pain. And drugs."

Blue-green eyes flash to mine, as if he's daring me to judge him.

I collapse to my knees at his feet, holding him, begging. "Taron, just let me try—"

"No!" He shouts, cutting me off. His eyes close, and the muscle in his jaw flexes as he inhales slowly, exhales and stares straight into my eyes, jaw clenched. "I want you to go home, Noel. I want you to leave."

My insides crumble. "I can't do that…" My voice breaks on my tears, but he grips my upper arms hard, dragging me to my feet.

"Yes. You. Can."

"You're hurting me." Tears stream down my cheeks, and I see the break in his eyes. "Why are you doing this?"

"When I get back. I want you gone." He releases me with a little shove. His brow lowers, and he turns away, going to the door. "Find someone who deserves you. It's not me."

"It is—"

"NO." He's in my face, his hot breath on my closed eyes. "I don't want you here." Every word is a stinging lash to my already bleeding heart. "It's over, Noel. Go. Home."

Sitting by the window on the airplane, I look out across the gray clouds obscuring the horizon. My small carry-on is overhead, and on the outside, I appear like any other traveler. But in my heart, a tornado has touched down, and it's spinning and demolishing everything. With the speed of sound, his voice digs deeper, ripping trees from the ground, tangling its fingers around my soul and pulling by the roots…

My brother puts his arm around me and drives me home from the airport. My vision is clouded by the storm raging in my chest. It won't stop until everything is destroyed.

The house is dark. My brother speaks, but I can't hear the words. I go to my room and shut the door.

Aftershocks

Noel

SIT IN THE CHAIR FACING MY WINDOW. AKELA PUTS HER HEAD ON MY LAP, but I don't lift my hand. Inside the tornado has passed, but it's silent.

No survivors.

So she drops down to the floor at my feet, waiting like a sphynx, her eyes fixed on the window where he'd come, guarding me as if she knows I'm not here.

Inside my chest, the path of destruction is miles wide, splintered throughout, written in his hand, with his words. I can't feel my heart beat. I only feel sharp stabs of broken wreckage. A wasteland where my dreams once grew green and thriving.

Empty.

Ravaged and torn.

The sun still rises, shining through my windows as if I don't exist, as if the world has forgotten what once flowered here. I'm left to fade away like a house covered in vines and shadows, better things to think about, happier things to see.

Inside is silence.

My brother comes to me. His face is worried as he sits beside me and holds my hand. He knows I'm not the same. Does he know my heart is missing?

I think it stopped beating.

I think it was destroyed.

Souls, bones…

"You've got to get up, Noel. You've got to keep going." Sawyer's voice is quiet, strained.

Do I? Why?

More time passes, I don't know how much. I lose count of the times the sun appears in my window, the indifferent sun. The hateful day. The cold night.

My best friend comes. She talks to me. She helps me in the shower and waits as I move my hands and arms, washing away the invisible dirt.

She brushes my hair and talks to me about school and the holidays. She talks about going out and football games and the old lady I used to visit.

I've grown old. On the outside I look the same, but inside is old and dried out. Gray wood, brittle to touch and covered in cobwebs.

Akela stays at my feet watching the window. Waiting.

Leon brings me food. He talks to me about the weather. He says when it's not so cold, he'll take me outside. The warm air, the sun will help me feel better. He's afraid.

"You need to get up now." Leon stands in front of me, angry in a way I've never seen. "This isn't who you are."

It's not?

My father lived for love. I lived for this love.

I waited for it to come, and when it did, I gave it everything.

Now it's gone.

Leon leaves angry.

My eyes go to the window and pain claws at my empty chest. This empty shell still has the ability to feel.

Rising to my feet, I go to the glass and slide it open. Akela follows at my side as I step through the opening like a portal to the past.

Walking along the porch in my bare feet, I go down to the yard and walk out to the hill with the trees stretching up to the sky. Open palms, grasping fingers.

The sweet scent is gone, and the air is cold and dry.

I stand looking down on my daddy's house. What is left when you lose something so precious? Something irreplaceable?

A quiet breeze moves through the trees, sliding my hair off my shoulders. Akela sits at my feet and waits. I strain my eyes to find the answer, to see the bend in the road ahead.

All I see is black.

"Daddy?" I squint into the darkness.

I want to go to him. I want to be free of this pain crushing my bones to powder. No one warned me pain could be this deep. No one told me not to give myself completely to another.

Going farther into the trees, the cold settles against my skin. I find the biggest one to sit against, my back against the wood, and let it pull me closer.

My daddy's presence is with me here, and I close my eyes. His sadness matches mine. He understands my loss. I want to take his hand and go with him to a place of peace. I want to be released from this misery.

"Noel?" My brother's face is stricken, panicked.

He lifts me off my feet like a doll lost in the woods. My bare feet dangle over his arms, bouncing with every step. He goes quickly to my room and tucks me into my bed, pushing the blankets tight around my sides.

He calls someone, and I expect my friend to return. Instead it's Mrs. Jenny.

Her dark head is over mine, her dark eyes stern. She takes me into the bathroom and puts me in the shower, and while I go through the motions, she digs in the cabinets.

"How long has it been?"

I'm confused as she holds up a box of tampons. *How should I know? Time has passed?* She leaves, and I return to my chair, my dog returns to my feet watching.

More time passes… I think.

I was with my daddy. He was going to tell me something. What was it?

Mrs. Jenny is back. Worried faces. She takes my arm and leads me into the bathroom, turning me and holding a plastic stick at my face.

"Pee on this end."

I do as she says even if it makes no sense. Doesn't she know? Everything inside me has died. He tore it all out by the roots and put salt on the earth. Nothing will ever grow here.

Back in my bedroom, I'm staring at my daddy across from me. He understands.

He gives me permission…

"Noel Aveline?" Mrs. Jenny is back at my side, her voice strong and commanding. "You are going to be a mother. You have to stop this. You hear me?"

My brow furrows, and I blink once, twice. I turn my head slowly to look at her, and something nudges at my empty chest.

"Get up and stand on your feet. Your life has a bigger purpose now."

A mother?

My daddy's image fades. Slowly, slowly he drifts into the silence and my mother's scent is here.

On the gentlest of wings, soft as a butterfly, love drifts down, like a sigh from heaven.

Where the tornado ravaged, leaving death and destruction, where the bodies lay strewn across the ground, where nothing was left standing, now the smallest flutter of life pushes through the soil.

The storm clouds begin to break, and I blink through the haze. A tiny dove carrying peace settles in my upturned soul, and for the first time in a long time, I step into the light. Morning breaks.

I blink several times and meet Mrs. Jenny's worried eyes.

She waits, and I look around. "What day is it?"

Present Day

CHAPTER
Twenty

Taron

"Y**OU'RE SURE IT WAS HEROIN?**" T**HE WOMAN SITS ACROSS FROM ME** in her small office, gray hair like spider webs threading the part of her severe, brown bob.

It's quiet as she waits for my answer, the only sound a trickling fountain behind her desk. I've been coming here a long time—once I accepted I was going to die if I didn't change my behavior.

Once I decided I didn't want to die.

"I know what it was."

"And you had no desire to take it?" She shifts in her seat, smoothing her hand down the front of her blazer.

My jaw tightens, and shame is a knot in my throat. "I considered it. For a whole minute, I let myself remember what it was like not to feel, to completely disconnect from the pain."

"And?" Dr. Curtis's dark eyes zero in on me over her heavy, brown reading glasses. The withering glare of Dr. Charlotte Curtis, daring me to lie to her.

"I walked out the door." I shift in my chair, cautiously allowing a moment of pride. "Seeing my friend in that state, knowing it's the end, the ultimate outcome... I think it helped me. Or at least it put it in perspective."

"Don't downplay this achievement." Her tone is clinical, but knowing how stingy she is with compliments, I do a mental victory lap. "You've come far, Taron. Do you know how hard it is to kick an opioid addiction?"

"I'm not planning to relax just yet." The shame of how far I'd sunk six years ago never leaves my mind.

If I ever try to let myself off the hook, I only have to remember Noel's face. Her tears, her shattered expression. The things I said, the way I shouted at her, hurt her... Again, I shift in my chair, trying to escape what I can never forgive.

"Is the acupuncture helping with your back?" Dr. Curtis reads from her computer screen, not smiling.

"I think it is."

Her eyes flicker to mine. "I don't want you self-medicating with alcohol. More than six drinks a week is heavy drinking. Give your liver a break."

My lips tighten, and I nod. "I'm thinking of leaving town."

"Is that so?" She leans back in her chair, steepling her fingers in front of her lips. "Any particular reason?"

Noel...

"I haven't been happy here in a while. I've made more money than I can ever spend in one lifetime. Patton doesn't need me anymore."

Despite what he thinks... Why he thinks he needs me, I'll never know. I owe him more than I'll ever be able to repay. He's a slave to his sense of guilt over what happened to us, but it's so unwarranted.

"I'm concerned you still aren't seeing anyone. You're a handsome man."

"Dr. Curtis, are you flirting with me?" I give her a grin, and she shakes her head.

"Don't charm me, Taron Rhodes. I'm too old." She rocks back again. "Love, companionship, these things are important parts of the human experience. They're important to your continued recovery."

Inhaling slowly, I stand, walking to her window that faces the smoky mountains. They rise, hazy blue in the distance. "A long time ago, I spent a summer on a farm. Sorry, an *orchard*." I remember a young Noel correcting me, so sassy and sweet. "It was the happiest time of my life."

She's quiet, and when I glance back, she gives me a smile. "What's her name?"

Shaking my head, I study the lines on the carpet. "It was a long time ago. I'm sure she's married with kids…"

Sawyer and I email occasionally. We chat about our lives, and I purposely don't ask about her. I don't want to know if she followed my orders. I don't want to know some other man is loving her.

I'm a selfish bastard, I know.

"I think a change of scenery would do you good. I'm comfortable releasing you. You have my number if you need to talk."

"Thanks, Doc. For everything."

She rises, and I take her outstretched hand, shaking it. I feel like I'm graduating again, like I should get a certificate or something I can put in a frame.

We slowly cross her pristine office to the door. "We didn't talk about the dream. Still have it?"

My shoulders tense. Nightmare is more like it. A Mexican girl lying dead on the floor of a shack, green eyes staring vacant at nothing, my bullet through her chest.

No amount of drugs could ever kill that pain. It's a sin for which I'll never find absolution.

"Sometimes… Occasionally."

Her stern eyes go from scientific to kind—it's something you don't get often from Charlotte Curtis. "Forgiveness is a gift you give yourself, Taron."

"I know." I'm pretty sure I've said those words to Patton before. I should get them tattooed across my chest.

As it stands, the only tattoo I have I got in the throes of a bender, a week when all I could do was lie on my back in my bed and ache for Noel. Her name is inked above my heart, where she will always be.

I broke my heart just as surely as I broke hers.

"You might find this book helpful." She steps to her desk, quickly scribbling on a tablet and ripping off the top sheet. As she hands it to me, she presses it into my palm. "It wasn't your fault, Taron. Terrible things happen in the line of duty."

I give her a tight smile. "Right."

No one who says that has ever lived it. I'm pretty sure I'll have the memory of that girl with me for the rest of my life.

In the meantime, I'm driving back to the office. Patton's not going to like what I have to say, but I've done everything I could do to help establish Fletcher International. We took it to the next level. It's a multi-billion-dollar corporation. He kept his promise and made us all filthy rich. Now I want to see if there's something more for me besides making money.

"I have to say I'm surprised to hear from you." Sawyer's voice is unmistakable. He sounds happy. "Everything okay in Nashville?"

"We hit some rough waters, but I think we're coming out of it."

"Right." His tone drops. "Patton told me. I was sorry to hear about that."

"He's going to be okay."

"And you?"

A knot forms in my throat. Shame, my constant companion rears his ugly head. "I'm good. I've been clean for a few years now."

"I'm glad to hear it." His voice is grave, but that's not why I called.

"We've hired some new people here. I'm thinking about taking a break from Fletcher International."

"From what I hear, you've got the money to do it."

"Yeah," I manage a laugh. "We tried to get you in on the ground floor. Remember?"

"That life's not for me."

My stomach is tight. I don't know why this feels hard to say. "It's actually why I called... I don't think it's the life for me either. Not anymore."

"I was wondering when you'd call to tell me that. I guess you had your reasons for waiting."

I'm not sure what he means. "Yeah, well, I've been thinking about that summer in Harristown..." *I've been thinking about Noel.* "It was..." *The best summer of my life?*

"Hot... grueling." He's hassling me, and I laugh.

"It wasn't all bad."

"I've got a lot of work coming up in the next year. It's time to rotate the trees."

The welcome in his tone boosts my confidence. "What does that mean?"

"Means I need help. Peach trees produce a maximum twenty years if you're lucky. We're on year fifteen of these. I've got to start planting new ones and phase the old out. It's a lot of work."

"I'm not afraid of hard work." My stomach is tight with anticipation. "The foreman's cottage still vacant?"

He chuckles, "I'll have it ready for you."

"Give me a few days to settle up here, and I'll drive down."

I want to ask about her, but I don't. I say goodbye and we disconnect. Seeing Noel again is like imagining a dream. I try to think of what I'll say... My heart beats faster. What is she like now? I want to leave today, but I have to talk to Patton.

I quickly send him an email setting up a time to meet, then I head to my penthouse to start packing.

CHAPTER
Twenty-One

Noel

SEVEN YEARS.

It's been seven years since Miss Jessica gave me this old shed, and I'm finally opening the front door.

I got pregnant, dropped out of business school for a year to have a baby, went back to business school, graduated, and got my master's degree.

Now I'm finally going to have a physical store.

As soon as I clean out the rats.

Akela's right beside me, ears at attention. Her shoulders bristle like she senses the teeming rodent hoards lurking just beyond the rickety door...

I grit my teeth, squinting my eyes and raise the broom higher. My heart thunders in my chest, and it's now or never. Placing my boot squarely in the center of the door, I give it a hard shove as I shout. "No rats!"

Like that'll make a difference.

I jump back, and the door barely moves an inch.

All is quiet.

My shoulders drop with my exhale, but I summon my courage once more. "Okay, girl. This time we're getting in."

Akela dances side to side, and I pat her head. I step forward ready to kick, and she resumes attack stance.

Boot against the wood, I shove harder, screaming once more, "Please, Jesus! No rats!"

The door flies open, bouncing off the wall… and I jump back.

Again, nothing happens.

The inside is silent.

"Darcy Hayes said it doesn't matter how talented you are. She said the judges only care about your dress and your hair… and how you smile. And how you walk." Three and a half feet of golden-haired happy trots up behind me, not even pausing for a breath.

"Tara Dove." My voice is quietly on guard. "I told you to stay at the house."

"I have to sell sponsorships, Mamma! Darcy Hayes said her uncle Digger bought three full-page ads from her already!"

I step forward carefully, shining my giant flashlight along the wooden floors of the old shed. They're covered in a layer of dust so thick, they look gray instead of brown.

"Digger Hayes has always been a show-off." I walk to a large cardboard box in the middle of the room.

My daughter's small voice goes whiney. "She's gonna win with that kind of head start, and she can't even sing *You Are My Sunshine!*"

"Dove." I pause to face her. "That pageant is a year away. You've got plenty of time to sell sh… stuff."

She blinks up at me with blue-green eyes that will never stop looking like her daddy's, and her rosebud lips are pouty. "Darcy said you hate Princess Peach because you didn't win it."

"Of all the…" Shaking my head, I give the box a nudge with my boot. "I don't like pageants because they're just a bunch of opinions. They're not reality."

Or in the case of Princess Peach, one person's bank account.

I give the heavy box a harder nudge, waiting to see what happens next. So far, it seems the stories of rats in this shed were greatly exaggerated.

"Why are you in here, Mamma?" Dove walks to an old desk moldering away against the wall. "Uncle Sawyer said he'd clean the shed for you."

Feeling around the walls, my fingers land on a light switch. I flip it up and down, but nothing happens. "Uncle Sawyer's got enough on his plate with planting all those peach trees. I'm perfectly capable of—ahh!"

A little white mouse streaks across the floor, and I squeal, hopping onto the desk. Akela charges after it, skidding to a stop at the crack in the floor and dancing around it.

"A mouse, Mamma! A mouse!" Dove shrieks loud enough to break glass, and I hop down and scoop her onto my hip, grabbing the flashlight again and heading for the door. "It was Angelina Ballerina!"

"I think we'll let Sawyer come set some traps this evening."

My daughter twists in my arms, looking back with round eyes. "If Uncle Sawyer catches the mouse, can I keep it in my room?"

"Mice shouldn't live in houses."

"That one does."

Sliding her down my hip, I hold her hand as we walk up the hill to the farm house. Akela jogs along beside us. We only take a few steps before Dove starts to skip.

I glance down at her shiny blonde curls bouncing and smile. "What's got you thinking about the pageant already?"

"They handed out sponsorship forms in class today. Mrs. Jenny said we all need to participate. It's tradition."

"I'm not sure about that." Lifting her under the arms, I help her hop up the back steps to the kitchen, one by one.

"She said my grandma won every pageant she ever thought about. Is that true?"

"It's true."

"Do I look like her?"

I wasn't expecting that question. "A little."

"Woo hoo!" She pumps her little fist over her head as she bolts through the door. A quick detour, and she runs straight to my brother standing at the bar. "Leon's home!"

She flings her arms around his legs, and he swoops her up onto his hip. "Hey, bird brain. What's three times three?"

"I'm not a bird brain!" she cries. "Nine!"

"What's four times five?"

"Twenty!"

"What's six times…" His eyes slide side to side, and hers go wide. "Seven?"

Dove closes her eyes and shouts, "Forty-two!"

"Yeah," he laughs. "Who says girls can't do math?"

"Nobody!" Dove holds his neck as he gives her a bounce. I give him a quick peck on the cheek. Leon makes her so hyper.

"Hey, weirdo. How was your day?"

"Fine. When's dinner? I'm starving."

"You are always starving." Going to the refrigerator, I take out a plastic bag with three marinating steaks inside. "I'm giving you a worm treatment."

"Uncle Leon has worms?" Dove crinkles her nose at him, and he puts her down.

"I'll worm you."

"Ew!" She squeals and runs into the other room. I cut up carrots and celery, asparagus and red potatoes and start them in the cast iron skillet on top of the stove. It's the same old recipe I've been making for years, but I try to mix it up a little bit.

"Where's Sawyer?"

"He's talking to Deacon about buying trees and shit."

"Leon!" I hiss but the music of a harp and flutes playing the *Angelina Ballerina* theme is loud in the living room.

"She's not listening to us."

"Still. Watch your mouth." I give him a pinch and return to the stove, moving everything into the oven.

Deacon Dring has become our financial adviser since returning from Dallas again. Mindy's the only one who knows the whole story on the handsome man who keeps coming back to our town. I only know he gives sound financial advice. He's guided me a few times on my own business.

"I need him to set some traps down at the feed shed."

"You finally getting back to your dream?" His hazel eyes soften, and as much as I try to keep Leon as a kid in my head, I know he's a twenty-two-year-old man.

"I never gave up on it. I had to put a comma there. Take care of more important matters before I could come back to it."

"A comma." He nods, a hint of a grin in his voice. "Some comma."

We look in the catalog at the peach tree varieties and how long it'll take for them to be shipped, whether they'll be bare root or in burlap.

"We can pretty much plant these any time, but I think he wants to prep the soil for now and wait for April first."

I'm about to mention the store when my older brother comes through the door. "Smells good in here."

"Oh!" I step back to the stove, taking the skillet of sizzling meat, potatoes, and vegetables out of the oven. "Supper's ready when you are."

We sit down to eat, and Dove splits my steak with me. "Mamma saw a mouse in the old shed and she screamed real loud. Akela tried to eat it!"

Sawyer grins at her warmly then glances up at me. "I'll set some traps before I go to bed tonight."

I want to say he doesn't have to... but I decide to let him this time.

After we've eaten, Dove helps Leon clean the dishes and load the dishwasher. Sawyer steps out onto the porch, and I follow him, looking out over the hills of peach trees, our family land.

I know this job is heavy on his mind. It's going to require a huge initial investment, and establishing a new crop of trees has its own set of risks and problems. Not to mention the need for additional hands.

"Did Deacon find a full-time salary in our books?"

He glances up at me and puts a strong arm around my shoulders. "It's interesting how things come together, timing and all. Sometimes it feels like providence."

This surprises me. My brother has never been particularly spiritual. "What do you mean?"

"I found someone who'll work for room and board."

My chin pulls back. "Who?"

The screen door opens and my little whirlwind runs out onto the porch. "Mamma! I brushed my teeth—it's bedtime!"

She grabs my brother's hand and gives it a tug. He lifts her easily, and she hugs him around the neck. "Night, Uncle Sawyer."

"Night, baby girl." Sawyer's big hand smooths her little back, and warmth fills my chest. His eyes meet mine. "We can talk about it tomorrow. Get some sleep."

Stepping forward, I kiss his scruffy cheek and take my girl from his arms. She wiggles down and leads me into the house, where we curl up like always with an Angelina Ballerina board book and her stuffed Alice mouse.

Dove snuggles lower into the blankets at my side, and I rest my head on my arm, tracing my finger along a golden curl. As always, I'm amazed by her. She changed my life so much... She saved my life.

When my heart was torn apart, she came and brought me peace. She calmed the storm and brought back the sunshine.

It's like all the happiness and love we found that summer is enclosed in her little body. Even with those blue-green eyes that twist the ache in my chest at times, she brings me so much joy.

My eyes drift shut and the sounds of her breathing carries us to sleep.

CHAPTER
Twenty-Two

Taron

PATTON'S OFFICE IS MY LAST STOP BEFORE HEADING OUT OF TOWN THIS afternoon.

He sits behind his massive mahogany desk in Armani with his dark brow lowered, dark eyes leveled, growing more irritated with my every word. I've actually seen men older than me sweat under the intimidating gaze of Patton Fletcher.

I'm not sweating.

I give him the good news first. "The Dubai contract came in overnight. Sandra's scanning the signed documents into the system."

Our office manager Sandra already knows what's coming. She predicted an earthquake, but Patton and I have known each other way too long for that.

"Why do I feel like there's more coming?" He leans back, crossing an ankle over his knee.

"Because you're good at what you do." I shift in the leather chair, trying to keep the mood light. "It's my last day, Patton. I talked to Sawyer, and I'm resigning as of—"

He's on his feet. "You're not going anywhere. I don't accept your resignation."

Standing, I exhale slowly. "It's done, Patton. I can't do this anymore. Not physically, not mentally…"

"Is this about your back? We'll get you the best physical therapy, a standing desk, whatever you need. Charge it to the firm."

"It's not about that." Going to the window, I pick up a framed photo of the four of us in Mexico. We look so fucking young. "You don't need me, brother. And I've got to see if there's any chance…"

"Is this about Noel?"

I glance over my shoulder, and I don't have to tell him yes. Setting the photo down again, I reach out to shake his hand. "I'm sorry, Patton."

Several seconds pass. His frown-game is solid, but I guess he sees something in my eyes—the truth. I'm already gone.

With a deep exhale, he begrudgingly shakes my hand, and I know he's going to be fine. Raquel is sharp as a tack, and she cares way more about this job than I ever did.

Before I leave, I consider trading in my Tahoe for a pickup, but I don't want to lose any more time. I'm four hours into the drive, somewhere between Memphis and Little Rock when my phone rings in the car.

Remington Key appears on the dash, and I tap the answer button on my steering wheel. "Remi, what's up?"

"What's this I hear about you leaving Fletcher?" The friendly voice of our young investment partner fills the cab.

Remi and I got to be friends after he and his partner Stephen Hastings put up the seed money to take Patton's company global. He's a Navy guy, and we clicked. We're both far more laid-back than our no-nonsense business partners.

"I'm headed south. Going to see if there's more to life than the grind."

"And leaving me alone with Stephen and Patton. They might kill each other. Or spontaneously combust."

I chuckle at the thought. "I bet they work it out—and you'll like Raquel. She'll keep Patton on his toes."

"Already met her. Already like her. Now tell me what's behind this desertion?"

He's got me on the spot. I've only thought about this in my head, and saying it out loud makes me feel self-conscious.

"I've made too many bad memories in Nashville." My eyes travel along the road ahead, and my mind fills with images of soft arms, silky hair, pillow kisses, all the things I had that summer. "I'm hoping there's still something better for me down here."

It's a fucking longshot, but I'm taking it.

"Down on the farm?"

"It's an orchard, but yeah."

He's quiet a beat. Still, Remi's easy. "Can't say I blame you. It's beautiful there."

"I didn't know you knew the place."

"Patton showed me some investment property on Lake D'Arbonne. While we were there, we stopped in to see your Marine buddy."

"Sawyer. He's a good man."

"He is, and his little niece is a show stopper. I was homesick for my girls, but she kept me busy."

"Niece?" My stomach tightens. "I don't know her…"

"His sister Noel's little girl? She must be six now."

My chest is on fire, and I notice I've accelerated to ninety. Easing off the gas, I realize I'm not even listening to my friend as my mind races through all the possibilities. Digger? The thought makes want to pull over and retch. Or punch the lights out of somebody.

I tune in and realize Remi's signing off. "…wish you the best, my friend."

"Thanks, man. I'll be in touch."

We disconnect, and my fists tighten on the steering wheel.

The remaining four hours of the drive are like moving through molasses. It's like I've passed through a fucking wormhole and time has slowed to a crawl. I'm tormented by images of Digger with his arms around my girl. If she's married to him... If they have a baby...

It's after midnight when I finally turn onto the long dirt road that runs the length of the hundred-acre orchard up to the house. My SUV doesn't make a sound as I pull in behind the foreman's cottage.

The door is unlocked, and as promised, Sawyer has left the place ready for me. Stepping inside, the smell of old books and peach lotion brings the memories rushing back. The chair is in front of the small flat screen television... It's all the same.

Light from the post across the yard shines through the window onto the double bed, and I can still see Noel there, beautiful as the sunset, her dark hair hanging long and silky over her small breasts. Whiskey eyes would look up at me full of so much love... Pain twists in my chest.

Turning, I pause before I close the door and look up toward the house. Her bedroom window is dark, and I realize she probably doesn't live here anymore. I actually believed nothing would change in almost seven years? What the fuck is wrong with me?

Shutting the door, I go to the bed and sit. "What the hell am I doing here?"

Toeing off my boots and slipping out of my clothes, I crawl between the blankets and drift into a troubled sleep.

My eyes open with the sun streaming through the window, and the delicious scent of breakfast is in the air. Whatever else has changed, it still smells like it did that summer...

Sitting up in the bed, my back aches, and I can tell I drove eight hours yesterday. I wonder if I'm even up to the work I promised to do for Sawyer. Moving around the small cottage, I pull on my jeans and a long-sleeved tee, step into my boots. My hair's longer now, and I use my fingers to slide it back, sticking a ball cap on my head.

In Nashville, coming back seemed like a dream. In reality, it feels like utter foolishness. I thought she'd still be waiting? After what I did?

A cold burst of air hits me outside. "Shit." I step back and grab my denim jacket.

When I finally reach the back door, I hear their voices. I pause, looking inside before opening it. Noel is the first thing my eyes go to…

She's in faded burgundy sweatpants that hang on her small waist, and she's still so fucking gorgeous. Again, she's reaching too far over her head for a platter, and the long-sleeved white tee she's wearing rises, giving me a glimpse of her midriff. My breath stills at the sight of her olive skin. I remember putting my mouth on it. I remember the day she fell into my arms like an angel out of heaven.

Leon stops behind her and takes down the bowl and platter.

"Thanks." She turns to the stove, her hair in a high ponytail with the ends grazing her shoulders.

A little voice I guess is Sawyer's niece breaks the scene. "I want to ice skate. Uncle Leon, will you take me to ice skate?"

Leon's voice is deeper than I remember. "I wonder if that old pond on the Hayes property ever freezes?"

"It does if it gets cold enough." Sawyer is at the table looking at his phone. "The reservoir would, but the current is stronger in the winter."

"I'm surprised it's not frozen year-round. My nuts almost fell off the last time I went in there."

"I want nuts! Pecans please!" The little girl raises her hand, and I chuckle.

"Different nuts, baby." Noel smacks the back of Leon's head, and he ducks.

"Ow! Hands off, woman!"

"I'll check and see if they're planning to do an ice-skating rink at the coliseum in Shreveport." Noel's voice is a touch lower, still with that slight rasp that makes it so sexy.

The memory of that freezing as shit reservoir and the day I threw her in drifts to my mind, and my stomach tightens. My heart beats in my chest as I reach for the door. This is either the best or the worst decision I've ever made.

"Taron?" Sawyer sees me first. "When did you get in?"

He stands out of his chair and circles the table to greet me.

"Late. After midnight. Thanks for having the place ready—"

A hollow *Crash!* cuts me off.

"Oh, shit..." Noel squats beside the bar cleaning up broken eggs all over the floor. The cardboard carton is on top of them.

"Mamma! You dropped all the eggs and you said a bad word..." The little girl stands in her chair, putting her head at the level of my chest.

"Dove, stay there." Noel doesn't face me, but the little girl does.

"Hi!" She smiles up at me.

I turn to her, and my throat knots.

All the air seems to be sucked out of the room as I look at her looking back at me with round, blue-green eyes impossible not to recognize. They're fringed in thick lashes, and her hair is golden blonde... just like my mother's.

Reaching out, I hold the wall, trying to stop the onslaught of emotion. This little girl... Remi's words are in my head... *She must be six now.*

Six years...

My eyes cut back to Noel, and she's standing, the messy carton in her hands, her amber eyes wide.

"Is she..." My voice breaks on the sentence.

Her full lips part as if she'll speak. Instead, her chin dips slightly in a nod.

I step back, catching the door handle and charging down the steps. I need to catch my breath. I need to process this.

Images of the night she came to me all those years ago slam to the front of my brain. I was so broken, so fucked up and high all the time. Oxy was the only thing keeping the nonstop pain at bay, the only thing drowning the memories of a dead girl…

I was addicted as hell. I'd written Noel some probably incoherent letter telling her it was over between us. I couldn't stand the thought of her seeing me that way, loving me when I had fallen so far from what I wanted to be for her.

Still, she showed up at my door. I should have known she would.

One kiss, and all the months of longing for her, needing her, dreaming of her came rushing back. I couldn't stop myself. Pain was consumed by desire. We made love… Once? Twice? Her body was so beautiful. It was the briefest light shining in all that darkness.

Stopping at a tree I reach out to hold the trunk as the waves of emotion sucker-punch me in the gut. *A daughter?*

I try to imagine Noel so young, so beautiful carrying my baby. I try to imagine what it must have been like for her to be alone… I try to imagine a world where everything didn't fall to pieces…

Leon's voice cuts through my spiraling. "I owe you an ass-kicking."

Lifting my chin, I see the kid I liked so much has grown into a man. A man with anger burning in his eyes at me from under a lowered brow.

"Leon…" My voice is ragged.

"I told you if you hurt my sister, I'd kick your ass, and you hurt her. Bad."

I wince at his words, hating the fact of them. "I won't fight you, Leon."

"I know you have specialized Marine moves or whatever, but I can hold my own."

I do, but what he wants is not happening. "I'm sorry I let you down. I'd give anything to go back and change the past."

"I've never seen my sister like that. I didn't think she was going to come out of it… until Dove." *The little girl… My daughter.* "I won't let you hurt her again."

"I won't hurt her again." My voice is certain, and my eyes meet his.

"You're right. You won't."

Broad shoulders stretch the sweatshirt he's wearing, and while he's not as tall as I am, he's clearly in good shape. He lunges, slamming into my side with his shoulder, arms around my waist. I barely have time to brace for the hit, and a grunt pushes from my lungs as I catch him.

Pain blasts from my old injury, nearly blinding me. "Leon…" I grind out, doing my best to hold him.

"Stop!" Sawyer's voice is loud at my side. "Leon, get off him!"

He grabs his brother around the arms, pulling him away from me.

"Let me go, Sawyer. I'm going to wipe the ground with his sorry ass."

"I said stop!" Sawyer turns, shoving Leon in the opposite direction from me. "Go back to the house and cool off."

We're all breathing hard, and Leon shouts at his brother. "You're going to let him come back here after what he did?"

I'm holding my side, leaning my back against the tree, trying to breathe through the pain.

"You don't know the whole story, Leon." Sawyer stands between us, blocking my view.

"I know enough. I know what he did to Noel."

"There's more to it than that. A lot more. Things I hope you never have to understand… or experience." Sawyer's voice is grave, but Leon makes a disgusted noise before turning and stomping down the hill.

Dropping my face, I rub my forehead with my fingers. "He's right. I shouldn't have come back here."

"I'll talk to him." Sawyer steps over and takes my arm. "You okay?"

"I will be."

"You were right to come here. You need to know your daughter. She needs to know her dad."

"You don't want to kick my ass, too?" I'm only partly joking.

The fury coming off Leon was powerful, confirming my worst fears. Everything I remember about that last night with Noel is true. I was so fucked up. I hurt her so badly.

"The demons we fought were strong. Almost too strong." Our eyes meet, and he gives my shoulder a squeeze. "But you were tougher than them. You beat them, and you're here."

"I lost what matters most."

"Maybe not."

We slowly start down the hill for the house, the pain in my back beginning to ease, but I have a slight limp. "I'd give anything for you to be right."

He pauses, looking up the road ahead. "Everybody deserves a second chance."

Dove is still in the kitchen when I return to the house. She's standing in a chair, leaning over the table coloring with a brown, stuffed mouse in a green dress beside her. For a minute I watch her so focused on her project.

Her brow is furrowed, and her nose turns up right at the end. I can't get over her blonde hair. She's perfect.

I step closer, and the floor creaks. She sits down in the chair and studies me.

"Mamma says if you see somebody who needs a smile, you

should give 'em one of yours." She smiles at me, and a little dimple appears just below her mouth—just like her mother's.

And just that fast, she steals my heart. "Do I need a smile?"

"You did." She's still grinning, her little-girl teeth showing. "What's your name?"

"Taron."

"That's like my name." She stands in the chair and starts coloring again. "Do you like to color?"

"Sure." I sit beside her and pick up the blue crayon and start on the coat of a mouse wearing glasses. "What's your name?"

"Tara Dove Noel LaGrange." She says it like she's reading a script, nodding her chin at every word.

"That's a pretty name. I like Tara."

"It's for my daddy. Mamma said he's a handsome prince. She said that's why I have blue eyes when hers are brown."

A flash of emotion tightens my chest. "Where's your mamma now?"

"Down at her new store." The little girl's nose wrinkles. "It's not really new. It's really old, but Mamma says it's going to be the best thing I've ever seen when she's finished with it. I told her I've seen a lot."

"Have you?" I want to laugh. I want to pull her to me and hug her. I want Noel to be here so I can hold them both in my arms. It's a dream I don't deserve to have, and I ache for it in my bones.

"Are you a prince?"

"No. I've never been a prince." *Despite what her mother used to say.*

"I can't wait to meet my daddy."

A flash of emotion tightens my stomach, and I'm not sure what to do about this part. How do we tell this beautiful little girl the truth?

I watch her filling in a pink tutu on the page. "What if your mamma was just pretending and your daddy isn't a prince?"

"Oh, he is." Her eyebrows rise, and her expression is certain.

I put the blue crayon down and pick up a brown one, starting on the trunk of a tree. "What if he's just a regular man—like your Uncle Sawyer?"

She stops coloring and presses her cute little mouth into a pout, thinking. "Is he a hero? Mamma says Uncle Sawyer's a hero."

My dream of earning Noel's love, of being good enough to deserve her permeates my mind, tightening my throat. "He wanted to be a hero... but bad stuff happened. He went to a really dark place."

"Like Prince Phillip?"

"I don't know him."

Her eyes grow serious. "He was trapped in a dark dungeon but Merryweather the fairy helped him to escape. Then he had to cut through big thorny bushes and fight a dragon before he could get to Sleeping Beauty and save her from the evil spell."

"That's pretty dark." I consider the metaphorical aspects of her story and figure I can work with this. "He had to do something like that... but he's still not a prince."

Her head tilts to the side. "Is he a good man?"

I put the crayon down and pat her little back as I stand. I want to explain everything to her. I want to tell her even though we've just met, I'd cut through thorn bushes and fight a dragon for her. I want to tell her I'm her dad and I love her.

"He's a better man."

She nods, returning to her picture. "I think that's okay."

CHAPTER
Twenty-Three

Noel

THERE SHOULD BE A TORNADO SIREN BEFORE TARON RHODES IS allowed to appear in my kitchen that way.

Any kind of heads up would've been nice.

Instead he walked right through the door like some sexy version of the Ghost of Christmas Past and stopped my heart all over again.

And broke all the eggs.

My face flashed hot and cold, and for a moment, I thought I might follow the eggs to the floor. I did not faint. Somehow, I remained standing.

Then he took one look at our daughter... No need for a paternity test to know whose child Dove is. She has looked like a pinch off her daddy since the day she made her newborn appearance.

When he looked at me again, the question in his eyes wasn't really a question. I silently answered, and his expression... At least two of us got the wind knocked out of us this morning.

He staggered out the door with my little brother hot on his heels. Leon took off like a house on fire, but Sawyer hesitated, watching them through the window.

"You knew he was coming?" My hands shook, but I kept my voice steady.

"Who is he?" Dove studied me, but I managed to smile.

"He's... an old friend of Uncle Sawyer's." *How could I tell her about her daddy just like that?*

She was temporarily satisfied and returned to coloring Angelina Ballerina.

I returned to my brother. "You didn't think this was something you should've told me?"

"He got here earlier than I expected." Sawyer stood and went to the door. "I'd better check on them."

I put a biscuit on a plate and ladled grits into a bowl for Dove. "Here, baby. Eat your breakfast now. I'm going to work on my store."

"Aren't you eating breakfast?" Her brow furrowed.

"I'll eat in a few minutes. You stay at the house."

Grabbing a few items of food out the fridge, I took off—needing to get away, to decide what to do about this.

More than an hour later I've swept the floor, the walls, the mantle over the small fireplace... Cobwebs are everywhere, and it's almost symbolic.

I sweep and sweep and sweep. My insides are trembling and fragile. I thought I'd moved past this, but tears stream down my cheeks, coating my face in saltwater. I use my shirtsleeve to wipe them away. I've probably got dirt all over my face as a result.

Akela is right with me, sitting at the door and watching my every move.

I half expected her to run after him. She always loved Taron, but no, my faithful dog remains at my side, standing guard just like always.

"Figures he'd just show up without a word or a warning." My voice shakes as I talk. I don't know if it's from how vigorously I'm cleaning or from how hard I'm shaking inside... or both. "What do you think he wants?"

Akela's head tilts to the side, and I wonder what she would say.

My broom hits something loud and metal. Another dead rat in a trap.

I look at the brown, limp carcass. "I know the feeling, bud."

Using the broom, I scoot him out the back door onto the small pile in the grass. Akela watches, not going near the mouse mass grave. I should get a cat.

With a shiver, I go back inside to where a bucket of wood soap and a mop, sponges, sanders, and knee pads are waiting for me. I plan to spend the whole day scrubbing this place top to bottom.

I'm just stepping into my knee pads when the hollow thump of boots on the wood floors draws my attention. Sawyer enters the room, his brows pulled together. "What the hell, Noel?"

His tone takes me aback. I straighten, putting my hands on my hips. "What the hell yourself."

"I thought he knew about Dove."

My shoulders drop. "Are you kidding me right now? That's what you're worried about?"

"You said you told him."

"I said I was *going* to tell him."

"So what happened?"

I exhale a frustrated breath. "Life? You act like I was just sitting around intentionally not telling him. I had to drop out of school because of him... Then Dove came, and I had to take care of her. Then I had to get back in school so I could take care of her, and the whole time my store was blowing up. I had to keep up with all the orders... Hell, it's still a challenge sometimes..."

He shakes his dark head. "If that were me—"

"If it were *me*, I would've told my sister the father of her child was about to show up!"

"I was about to tell you last night. I told you, he got here early. Anyway, I thought you were in contact with him."

"I haven't spoken to him since…" Shaking my head, I fight the mist filling my eyes again. "He kicked me out, Sawyer. He told me to leave and never come back. His exact words were 'Find somebody else.'"

"He was messed up. You of all people should have seen that."

"No." I will not let him cast me this way. "I went to him. I would've done anything to help him. I begged… and he kicked me out. Strike that. He didn't kick me out, he screamed in my face to get out."

My brother's jaw clenches. I see the muscle move back and forth… then just as fast, his shoulders fall. His eyes meet mine, and he closes the space between us, pulling me into a tight hug. It takes half a second for me to relax and wrap my arms around his waist, hugging him back.

"I'm sorry, sis." The crack in his voice tightens my chest. "I know what you went through. I also know what he went through… what we all went through. You need to come together and deal with your past. For Dove."

We hold each other a few beats longer before stepping apart. He clears his throat, and I wipe my sleeve across my damp eyes again.

This man never left my side as I grieved, then he stepped right up to help raise my daughter. He has never let me down.

"So about those rats…" I point to the back door.

"Where are they?"

It's late when I finally decide to call it a day.

I only took a break to eat the food I'd grabbed on my way out the door, and I texted the guys—*lunch is on your own*.

Dove ran up the hill a few times with Akela to watch me on my hands and knees scrubbing "like Cinderella with the singing bubbles"—her words.

She pretended to sweep while actually dancing with the

broom to her version of the *Angelina Ballerina* opening theme, and when she got bored, Akela ran with her back down the hill to the house.

Sawyer had disposed of the rodent carcasses before my little princess had a chance to see them. Then, when it finally got too dark to see, I dragged my exhausted body the quarter-mile back to the house, weary from a full day of cleaning.

A full day of avoiding the giant elephant in the orchard.

The shed actually looks pretty good since I removed the decades of dirt. The floors are a pretty yellow pine with dark lines of character in them. The walls need a coat of paint, and that huge box needs to be sorted. It seems to be mostly old letters and family things, and I need to take it to Miss Jessica.

Dove is in my bed with Alice the mouse cuddled at her side when I emerge from the shower. My hair is damp and wrapped in a towel, and I'm in sweatpants and an oversized shirt that falls off one shoulder.

Going to where she sleeps, I trace my finger along her little hand curled into a loose fist at her cheek. Sawyer's accusation this morning is heavy in my chest. *Why didn't I just tell him? How do I tell her now?*

A solid day of cleaning and avoidance didn't clear my head. I still have no idea what to do about this, the man or the perfect gift we've been given.

One thing I know for certain: I will *not* fall in love with Taron Rhodes again.

I will not let him destroy me like he almost did…

I'm rubbing the towel in the length of my hair when a tap on my window makes me jump. Akela lifts her head off her paws, where she's lying at Dove's feet, and when she sees him outside the glass, her ears lie back and she seems to smile.

My silly heart tries to beat faster—the same heart he ripped out of my chest.

Stop being a sadist, heart. He killed you once, remember?

I buried those feelings and paved a road on top of them, but clearly they had tree roots, so deep you can never get the last one. His blue-green eyes hold mine through the glass and everything inside me heats right up. Old feelings break through my defenses like baby trees growing in concrete.

I go slowly to where he waits, lifting the glass so he can swing his legs into the room. I almost expect him to catch me by the waist and pull me to him, cover my mouth with his and kiss me senseless.

"Hey." His voice is low, warm, sexy. His hair's longer, and a piece has fallen over one eye, daring me to thread my fingers in it… Crossing my arms over my chest, I feel very exposed in only my sweats, fresh out of the shower, with my hair wet.

"Sorry to bother you. I thought we needed to talk."

"Okay." I'm cautious, guarded. He might still have the power to shake me, but I stopped being impulsive a long time ago. "What do you want to talk about?"

"Seriously?" His sexy grin lights his hypnotic eyes, and my stomach tightens. His eyes never change, even if he does.

When I went to Nashville, he was thin, weak, and wounded. He was haunted, and darkness hovered around him like a cloud.

Not anymore.

Now he's his old self again—but more. His forearms are lined, and his shoulders stretch out his shirt. I'm sure under his clothes he's the same physically, and I can tell inside he's more confident, more relaxed, surer than he's ever been before.

"I heard you made a lot of money in Nashville." *Is being rich the difference?*

He looks down, almost as if he's embarrassed. "Patton had this idea for his dad's company. He wanted to make it the Air BnB of commercial real estate. It was actually pretty brilliant."

"I guess that's why I never heard from you again?" Yeah, it's a jab. It jumped right out of my mouth.

He scratches the side of his beard with his thumb and cuts those eyes up at me from under his brow. I wonder if he knows how fucking hot he is—especially when he looks at me that way. "I didn't trust myself with you."

My eyes narrow. Whatever that means.

He stands, taking a step into my room, and at six-foot-two, muscular and healthy, he completely fills my space. "We have a daughter."

That old magnetic energy between us is in his eyes when he looks at me, and I feel it in my core, in my hardening nipples. Even if I try to fight, my body remembers everything.

His voice is tender as he steps over to watch Dove sleeping in my bed. "She's so beautiful."

"She looks like her daddy."

He winces, then cuts his eyes at me. "Why didn't you tell me?"

My heart beats faster, and I do my best to fight my tears, to summon the strength he's always taken so easily. "We are not doing this right now."

"I had a right to know."

"And I was going to tell you…" My hands tremble, and all the emotions I struggled with so long ago are right at the surface, like they never left. "I started a letter a hundred different times… I-I guess I didn't know what to say after the way you left things." *The way you screamed in my face and threw me out.*

"You could've called me."

"No." It's a barely controlled snap. "Not after the way you left it."

Going to my closet, I climb inside to where a box sits in the very back… A box filled with one letter wishing me happy birthday, a wooden Día de los Muertos mask, a pillowcase I slept with every night, and a box holding a turquoise ring I promised I'd never take off.

Moving these mementos aside, I dig out the crumpled sheets of paper.

I don't even read them.

I don't have to.

Climbing out of the closet, I return to where he stands and push the sheets of paper against his chest. "Here."

Tears threaten, but I will not cry in front of him. "I wasn't trying to hide her from you. I really didn't know what to say. I didn't want you to think I was trying to trap you with a baby."

His large hands close over mine, taking the sheets of loose-leaf paper from me.

"That's not what I meant." His voice is quiet. "I never thought that."

"What did you think?"

"My dad was never there when I was a kid... I'm not sure if he even knew I existed. I never wanted to be that guy."

Pain like shards of glass slices through my insides. I lift my watery eyes to his and tell him the truth. "You hurt me, Taron. You hurt me more than I've ever been hurt in my life... You made me stop believing in love. You almost made me stop believing in anything." A wobbly inhale helps me to finish. "Then she was born. She brought me back... She gave me hope. She gave me peace. It's why I named her Dove."

"Noel, I—"

"Mama?" Our daughter's sleepy voice makes us both take a step back.

She tucks her little chin, and her fist clenches, sliding around the bed where I should be lying beside her. "Mamma? What's happening?"

Taron looks at me like he's not sure what to do.

"Just go," I say before climbing into the bed and sliding down beside her.

I scoot her closer to my chest as I hear him quietly slipping out my window. Tucking my chin, I kiss the top of her head, curling my body around hers and letting the tears stream silently down my cheeks.

I tell myself I'm not doing this again. I remind myself how far I've come…

I don't need him to be happy. I don't belong to him anymore.

It takes more effort this time, but I calm my breathing. I put him aside once more, put him back in the box where he belongs and fall asleep.

CHAPTER
Twenty-Four

Taron

SITTING ON THE FLOOR, MY BACK AGAINST THE DOUBLE BED, I READ and reread the words she'd written, erased, rewritten, scratched out...

Never sent.

Every word twists a knife of pain deeper in my gut.

Dear Taron,
I still love you...

Dear Taron,
Is there a time-limit on forgiveness? If there is, I haven't reached it...

Dear Taron,
I should have told you this a long time ago...

When did she write them? Why did she never send them? Scrubbing my forehead with my fingers, I wonder if she might possibly still have any of these feelings...

How could she after what I did?

My eyes squeeze shut. Remembering myself back in those

days is like pouring acid on an open wound. I was so fucked up for so long. Sometimes I wasn't sure if I'd live to see another day. Sometimes I wasn't sure I deserved to.

I sure as hell didn't deserve Noel Aveline LaGrange.

An email from Sawyer actually gave me the push I needed to drag my ass to get help. He probably doesn't even remember it. Looking back, it was one of those random messages we'd send on occasion, just letting each other know we were still alive, still hanging in there.

Another harvest has ended, and I'm tired but happy. It's hard work, and in the past, before it all, I would've taken something like this for granted.

Now I realize another day is the best we get, another chance to try again...

He'd included a photo of the hills covered in trees with the sun going down, and I realized he did see them. That morning we'd driven together, I'd wondered if he'd ever even looked at the beauty around him. Maybe he didn't then, but he does now.

I knew then this was the only place I would find what I needed. I decided if I could get myself clean, I'd come back here. If I could stay clean long enough to know I wouldn't hurt her again, I'd try one more time to deserve her.

Tracking her on the Internet became an obsession. Her products would sell out on her website, and I'd wait for her to announce a restock, picturing her working, wondering if she was in her bedroom or in the kitchen.

Closing my eyes at night, I'd see Akela at the foot of the bed. I'd see Noel sitting on the floor in front of the laptop watching a how-to video or making notes. Some nights, if I was lucky, I'd feel her in my arms.

It was the hardest battle I'd ever fought. Physically, I thought I was dying. Mentally, I didn't believe I would succeed.

Now, looking at her swirly handwriting on these sheets of

paper, I wonder if they would have made a difference. I wonder if knowing she still loved me, that she might forgive me, would have made it harder or easier.

I wonder what I would have done if I'd known about Dove…

Lying on my back in the bed, I know I can't rewrite the past. I can only start where I am and try to make the future better.

I'm here now. I'm in this place, and I've got to try.

Before the alarm even sounds, I'm out of bed, pulling on my jeans, shoving my feet into my boots, and slipping the shirt over my head. I give my teeth a quick brush. It's not as cool this morning, but Thanksgiving's coming, then Christmas… Noel's birthday.

Akela greets me halfway to the house, lifting her front legs and doing a happy hop. I give her head a quick rub before stopping at the back steps.

Watching Noel through the door before she even knows I'm here has always been my favorite part of the morning. She's in gray sweats and a long-sleeved tee, and her pretty dark hair hangs in waves down her back.

Our pint-sized pixie sits on the counter beside her. "Why don't you like pageants, Mamma?" Dove frowns, seeming very focused on stirring whatever's in the bowl she holds.

"It's not that I don't like them. I just think they're silly." My eyes are drawn to Noel's cute little ass as she bends forward into the refrigerator, standing with a fresh carton of eggs in her hand. I wait until she puts them down this time, feeling a hint of a grin as I remember what happened last time she saw me.

"It's like sticking a blue ribbon on one of those pigs at the state fair." She finishes, breaking eggs one after another into a bowl.

"I'm not a pig." Dove's nose scrunches.

"No, you're not." Her mother taps that nose. "You're my little dove. Now give me that batter. You've stirred it enough."

She shifts on the counter, turning her back to me. "But I want to be Princess Peach."

It appears safe, so I open the door. "Morning, ladies."

Noel's eyes fly to mine, and she blinks away quickly, turning to face the stove. "Morning."

"Need some help?" My voice is quiet, and I enter slowly, as if I'm approaching a wounded animal.

"Taron!" Dove scoots around to face me, and I catch a small frown on Noel's lips. I told Dove to call me Taron... I didn't know what else to do—yet. "Mamma says pageants are like putting ribbons on pigs, but I want to be Princess Peach. What do you think?"

She blinks those bright eyes up at me expectantly, and I'm stumped. "Ah... Well. You're very pretty." That makes her smile. "What will you do for talent?"

I'm guessing they have talent. Don't all pageants have talent?

"Dance like Angelina Ballerina." She wobbles her little head at me like *Duh*. "Do you watch *Angelina Ballerina*?"

"I can't say I have—"

"Come on." She picks up the brown stuffed mouse lying on the bar beside her and scoots into my arms. Sitting on my hip, she points to the living room. "We can watch the one with Mr. Operatski while Mamma makes us breakfast."

I hold her. I really like having her so comfortable in my arms, but I wonder what I've gotten myself into with this pageant thing.

Noel saves me. "Dove, Taron needs to help with the hoe-cakes. You can watch Angelina while we talk."

Her little shoulders droop, but she wiggles out of my arms. "Okay." She huffs, prancing through the door and into the other room.

I hear the sound of harps and flutes, and I watch for a second as she swings her arms side to side and twirls, kicking her leg straight out behind her.

"Angelina Ballerina?" I step up to where Noel is spooning batter into the hot pan.

"It's a cartoon. A dancing mouse." She passes me the bowl and takes a step back, putting her hand on her hip. "She calls you Taron?"

"I didn't know what to tell her. *Mr.* sounds wrong, and I thought it was probably too soon for her to call me—"

"It's too soon." Noel's voice is short, but she seems more protective than angry.

I watch the batter frying in the pan as I think about what I want to say. I think about last night and how standing next to her right now, making breakfast like we used to pricks a longing so deep, I've got to fight pulling her against my chest.

I want my family.

"I kept track of you while I was in Nashville." I give her a smile. "Your business really took off."

"So you're a stalker?" Amber eyes cut up at me, and I shrug, flipping the four cakes quickly.

"Did you ever stalk me?"

"No." She answers fast, then adds quietly. "I didn't dare."

Another slice of pain. I give the four cakes a beat longer before scooping them onto a plate. Setting the bowl aside, I face her straight on.

"I don't want to hurt you, Noel."

"You've said that before."

"I don't want to fight with you either. That's not why I came back."

She pours the scrambled egg mixture into the large skillet and as it starts to bubble, she looks up at me. "Why did you come back?"

For you... We're interrupted by Sawyer and Leon entering the room. "Smells good in here." Sawyer reaches out to clasp my hand before going to the table.

Leon doesn't even look at me. He takes down five plates and goes to the table, putting one at each seat.

They're both wearing blazers and khaki slacks. "What's the occasion?" I step over to where Sawyer's pouring coffee from a carafe.

"Church." Noel steps past me putting the bowl of eggs and the plate of hoecakes on the table. "Dove, come eat breakfast."

Church? Reading my face, Sawyer answers my silent question. "We've been going more regular since Dove came along."

"Dove, breakfast." Noel opens a drawer and pulls out forks and knives then glances up at me. "You don't have to go."

"No, I'm glad to go, I just..." I look down at the jeans and long-sleeved Henley I'm wearing. "I need to change clothes."

Be the fountain and not the drain is out on the sign in front of the small, brick building. I have no idea what that means, but I guess I'll find out.

Inside, I'm surprised to see so many faces I recognize. Noel takes Dove to another part of the building where she says she's going to Sunday school. Sawyer steps over to talk to a man I'm pretty sure is Ed Daniels, and Leon leaves us to sit with a pretty girl I don't know. I wonder whatever happened to Betsy.

"My goodness, is this Taron?" A wobbly voice draws my attention, and I look down to see a birdlike old woman with thin gray hair styled in a little bun at the nape of her neck.

She's neatly dressed in a smock that has little flowers all over it. It's been a long, long time, but I recognize her at once.

"Miss Jessica?" Taking her outstretched hand, I carefully hug her fragile body, and she laughs.

"You have a good memory."

I remember everything about those days, even her smiling face appearing on my phone during one of my many calls. "I couldn't forget you."

"Still as charming as ever." She pats my hand roughly, and I notice a woman with a name tag standing off to the side watching her. "How long have you been back?"

"I got here late Friday night."

"I take it you've met your daughter?"

"Yes, ma'am."

"She's a beauty. And sweet as her mamma." She slides her hand into the crook of my arm and helps me escort her down the middle aisle to a row where she stops. "How long are you planning to stay?"

Glancing to where Noel is just returning to the small sanctuary, I lower my voice. "Hopefully, a long time."

That lights her gray eyes. "I'm so glad. This is a good thing."

She lowers herself slowly into the pew, and I glance up to catch a pair of dark eyes slicing into me. Mindy sits in the pew beside her mother, and from the look on the woman's face, Mrs. Jenny does not think me being here is a good thing.

Chords sound out from the organ at the front of the room, and I quickly join Sawyer and Noel in a pew across the aisle. Sawyer is on the end with Noel between the two of us. A slim man wearing glasses stands in the pulpit at the front of the room and holds out his hands to welcome us.

Then the organist is joined by a piano playing "A Mighty Fortress is our God," and I hold the maroon songbook for Noel and me. She seems surprised I know the tune, but I grew up in Nashville, not Nepal.

A few more hymns and we take a moment to shake hands. Mindy appears at Noel's side, smiling up at me. Her green eyes are wide, and she's tied her kinky-curly brown hair back in a ponytail.

"Taron Rhodes? What a surprise this is!" Her eyes go to her friend's. "When did this happen?"

"Yesterday." Noel hugs her and I can't make out what she says in Mindy's ear.

Mindy leans back, looking straight in her eyes. "You'd better."

Her mother is behind her, giving Sawyer a hug then turning to Noel. "You feeling okay, honey?"

"I'm fine." Noel's voice is flustered, and the woman faces me.

"So you're back." It's not a question, and she's not smiling.

"Yes, ma'am." I reach out to shake her hand. She does not shake mine, so I lower it, wiping it down my dark jeans. "I hope that's not a problem."

"I do too."

The pastor takes his place at the podium, and we all take our seats. He starts talking about ways we can be fountains, refreshing, life giving, rather than draining away the happiness from others around us.

I look around the room as he continues speaking, remembering what Noel told me about the people here stepping in to take care of them after her parents died. Mrs. Jenny's stern eyes meet mine, and I guess I deserve her disapproval. I guess to her I'm a massive drain.

Not anymore.

The pastor says for us to bow our heads and as I'm turning, I catch a frown I had not expected. Digger Hayes is glaring at me from the front of the room.

Bastard.

The final Amen is said, and the organ bursts into the Doxology. Noel stands beside me, and Sawyer says he'll get Dove. I touch her arm lightly, but she moves it out of my grasp.

"You never said why you came back." Even pissed at me, she's still so beautiful.

She's wearing a chunky burnt-orange sweater that makes her amber eyes glow and black pants that hug her curves down to the black ankle boots on her feet.

Her dark hair hangs over one shoulder in smooth waves to her breast. I remember her in her bedroom last night in only that thin shirt and sweats, her hair damp from the shower. She's still so fucking beautiful... and so defensive.

She's a woman now, the mother of my child. I want her to be the mother of all my children. I came back because my life will never be complete without her in it, but it's too soon to say all of that. I have to earn it first.

Instead, I hold out my hand, escorting her to the back of the room. "Maybe we should take it slow."

"You can take it however you want. I'm not going anywhere with you."

We stop for Noel to hug Miss Jessica at the back door. She tells me to come by and see her, and I hug her again before the nurse leads her out to a waiting van.

I hold the door for Noel to exit the sanctuary. "Can we try to be friends? For Dove's sake?"

Our daughter comes up the walk skipping. Sawyer holds one of her hands and in the other she has a handful of papers.

"I would do anything for her." Noel's voice is quiet.

It's not exactly what I had in mind, but I can work with it.

"Taron Rhodes. Didn't expect to see you here again." Digger's voice makes my skin bristle, and we stop, turning to face him.

A little girl with mousey brown hair in perfectly formed sausage curls stands at his side. I don't miss her scowling at my daughter, and I think the Hayes family must have a lot of bad eggs in it.

"I didn't come back to see you." My voice is level. We're at church, so I don't plan to engage with him.

"If history's our guide, you'll be gone as soon as you get what you want."

Dove slips her small hand in mine, and my jaw clenches. "I left to serve my country as you well know."

"Uncle Digger donated two thousand dollars to make a Dixie Gem office space at the civic center." The little girl's voice is as snide as her uncle's.

Dove inhales a little gasp, and her eyes flash to mine. I'm caught off guard by her turning to me, and a surge of protectiveness floods my chest.

"This your niece, Hayes?" I nod toward the little girl who's wearing a matching leopard print coat and knit hat with black boots and leggings.

"She is indeed." He smiles proudly at the little girl, who is currently smirking at my daughter.

I have a sadistic urge to pull her knit cap down over her face.

Noel speaks up, her voice annoyed. "Unusual timing for a donation of that size, Digger."

"Darcy, what have I told you about discussing family business in public?"

She looks up at him, fake remorse in her eyes. "I'm sorry, Uncle Digger." Then she sticks out at her tongue at my daughter... *Little—*

"Good morning, brothers, sisters." The pastor walks up, preventing me from grabbing Digger by the collar. "I see we have a visitor today. I'm Pastor Sinclair."

"Pastor, this is Taron Rhodes." Noel's voice is smooth, but I'm not ready to let this go. "Taron was in the service with my brother."

"Well, thank you for your service." The older man shakes my hand, and I break my staring war with Digger. "And welcome to First Methodist. I hope we see you again."

"Thank you, sir. I'll be back."

"He's staying in the cottage!" Dove skips beside me smiling and holding my hand. "He's helping Uncle Sawyer with the new trees."

"Is that so?" The man bends down to smile at my daughter,

holding his Bible into his side. "That's a big job. I'll be praying God protects and gives you good weather."

Noel smiles, placing her hand on Dove's shoulder. "Thank you, Pastor. I guess we should all get some lunch now."

"Very interesting sermon, Pastor." Digger's tone is haughty. "I'd never heard that expression before, but I was edified by your elaboration on the topic."

Oh, brother.

"I thank you for that…"

They continue talking, but Noel catches Dove's hand, guiding us away quickly. Once we're at Sawyer's old Silverado, which she's now driving, she lets out an exasperated noise.

"Same here."

Dove looks up at us with worried eyes. "Darcy's sure going to win Princess Peach now."

Noel's lips tighten, and she shakes her head. "That's not how it works, honey… At least, that's not how it's supposed to work."

A note of worry is in her voice, and I decide to meet Digger head-on with this pageant nonsense. He's not the only one with a bankroll.

CHAPTER
Twenty-Five

Noel

DOVE IS INFATUATED WITH TARON, AND TO HIS CREDIT, HE'S TAKING the time, getting to know her. Every morning, he's up with us at breakfast, talking to her and letting her help him make hoecakes.

She sits on his hip watching as he spoons the batter into the pan, and they wait, having little conversations about her favorite foods, her friend Boo, Angelina Ballerina, and of course, Princess Peach.

"That one's ready." Her head is on his shoulder, and she points to a cake in the back right corner. "That one's ready, too."

He flips them, balancing her on his arm. "Good eye."

His muscle flexes, he kisses her head, and I can't stop a swoon…

At night she snuggles up with him on the couch while he reads whatever Angelina Ballerina book she's chosen. I peek through a crack in the door to watch, snorting as he does the different voices.

He's so big and she's so little, but they look so much alike. I'm surprised my brilliant little girl hasn't figured it out yet.

"You can be Mr. Operatski." Dove points to a picture in the book.

Taron makes a face. "I don't like him. He's a big grouch all the time."

Her little lips press together and she thinks. "Mr. Mouseling?"

"He's Angelina's dad?"

She nods, and the way he looks at her, the tenderness in his voice, melts my heart. "Okay."

"He runs the *Mouseland Gazette*, but he builds stuff, too, like the Royal Theater for Angelina to play with."

He might be taking it slow, but my heart is off to the races. It's like a puppy on a leash, straining and jumping all around for the thing it wants.

The thing that isn't good for it.

The thing that almost killed it.

During the days he works with my brother, preparing the soil for planting, going into town and meeting with the growers, stacking the new trees as they arrive, their roots wrapped in burlap sacks.

Sometimes, on my way to prepping my store, I'll slow my pace to watch him work, to let my eyes run down his strong body, watching the flex of his muscles, the deepening of the lines in his arms, and the pull of the fabric across his shoulders.

Of course, he busts me, and his grin is as powerful as ever, even more now that his hair falls over his eyes. He pushes it back with a large hand, and my memories of those hands on my body flood my mind.

Blinking away, I focus on the store and my future—cleaning, arranging, making the products I need to sell.

Time passes.

Thanksgiving is in a few days, and I'm sitting at the table going through the paperwork Deacon prepared to register Miss Jessica's old shed as a place of business when he bustles through the door with Dove chattering beside him, home from school.

She skips to the table where I'm sitting and climbs into a

chair. "I told Ms. Moody we're making presents for Miss Jessica's friends at Pine Hills. She said we're doing community service."

I slide the papers together and drop them in a folder before moving them out of her way. "Why were you telling her about that?"

Dove's eyes are wide, and she tilts her head to the side. "Darcy said she and Mr. Digger were volunteering at the food bank in town on Thanksgiving Day."

The rivalry between my daughter and Digger's niece frustrates me. Darcy Hayes is a little brat, and I want Dove to be better than that. At the same time, I'm not about to let a her have an edge on my daughter.

"I have an idea." Sliding my work away, I take down a roll of newspaper. "Let's make a sample kit for Ms. Moody to show her what we're giving them."

"We can give her Miss Jessica's favorite lip balm!" My daughter's voice goes loud with excitement.

Taron stops behind her. "Is that the same lip balm you made for me?"

"It is." Turning quickly to the pantry, I fight the memory of that first night... when I ran my finger across his full lips, and he kissed me.

Hell, every time I'm in this pantry, I fight with the memory of him at my back doing very dirty things. A shuffling at the door causes the little hairs to rise on my skin.

"Can I help with anything?" His voice is quiet, and I wonder if he remembers what happened in this pantry as well as I do.

Reaching up, I grab the shea butter, sweet almond oil, and raw coconut off the shelf, trying to hurry from this small space and its big memories. I'm moving too fast, and when I turn, I slam right into his hard chest.

Large hands catch my upper arms. "Easy."

Lifting my chin, I meet his eyes, warm and dark.

"I'm sorry… thanks." His lips are so close, his breath is a whisper across my cheek. The space between my thighs heats, but I'm stronger than that. "You can let me go now."

He doesn't let me go right away. He holds me a minute longer, and his eyes move from mine down to my lips. My heart beats so hard it's painful.

"I ran out of that lip balm a long time ago. Would you make some for me?" His eyes blink up to mine again, and I can't move.

I'm a deer caught in the spell of dying for him to kiss me, dying for the feel of his lips on mine, on my body, rough, hungry… and knowing if I let it happen, I wouldn't be able to stop. Am I ready for that? Do I trust him not to hurt me? My heart says *yes, yes!* But my mind remembers…

"Sure." The word escapes on a weak sigh.

His grip on my arms squeezes and relaxes, and it takes a breath for me to realize I can step back, step away from the fire that burned me beyond recognition once.

Turning on my heel, I hurry to the table, where Dove has put on the special pink apron I got for her.

She frowns at me. "Mamma, why is your face all red?"

Jesus, little kids. "Is it? I think I stood up too fast. Here… Spread out the newspaper."

Taron's boots thud on the floor behind me, and I set everything on the counter, hurrying into the pantry again for the ingredients to make the lotion. I move faster this time. I can't be alone in here with him again.

When I return to the table, they've spread the newspaper, and she hops down, reaching to take Sawyer's grilling apron off the door.

"You can wear this." He takes it from her slipping it over his head. "If you get any of this oil on your clothes, it will not wash out."

Pressing my lips together, I grin at her authoritative little voice. She sounds just like me.

Taron smiles, and the love in his eyes for her almost completely nukes the barriers I've built around my heart.

"You're really good at this." He sits in a chair across from where Dove stands beside me.

"I've been doing it since I was five." She nods at him, like she's not only six and a half.

We spend the next few hours measuring out lotions and scents, putting balms in glass pots and sticking labels on the outsides. When we have enough set to the side, I pat my daughter's back.

"We'll put them in gift bags later. It's time for you to get some sleep."

She turns and hugs me then holds out her arms to Taron. He slips the apron over his head then picks her up and carries her to my bedroom where she'll take her bath before they read their nightly story.

I'm almost finished cleaning up when he returns. "She might look like me, but she acts just like her mamma."

"I hope that's a compliment." I arch an eyebrow at him, and he gives me that panty-melting grin.

"It's a compliment." The ripple in his voice is too much.

"I'm pretty tired tonight myself. I'm heading to bed now, too. Thanks for helping." I've got to get out of here before I do something foolish like kiss him silly.

"Thanks for this." He holds up the small pot of lip balm.

I do a little wave. "It's your payment for helping."

"I was thinking…" He pauses, sliding a hand in the front pocket of his jeans. "Maybe it's time to tell her the truth?"

My stomach tightens, and I don't know why the thought of telling Dove Taron's her father makes me nervous. "Okay."

He exhales a laugh. "I'm glad I'm not the only one who feels a little terrified at the prospect."

"No!" Shaking my head, I try to fake confidence. "She's going to be thrilled to know you're her dad."

"I'm already Mr. Mouseling, I guess."

Stepping forward, I put my hand on his chest and look up into his pretty eyes. "You're so good with her. She knows you love her. She loves you. It'll be fine."

"I guess the real question is when?"

Chewing my lip, I look up at the clock. "No time like the present?"

He holds out a hand, and I lead the way, going through the kitchen into the living room all the way back to my bedroom. The bathroom light is still on, but it's quiet.

"Dove?" I peek in the bathroom, but she's not in the tub. The water is run, but I don't see her. "Where is she?"

Turning, I start to feel nervous, when I look up and see a little golden head on my pillow. Taron turns on the lamp at the side of my bed then laughs. Dove is sound asleep with Alice clutched to her side.

He squeezes her little foot gently. "Making cosmetics is hard work."

"You should know."

"I do know. I sat in this room with you many nights watching you do it."

We're standing at my door facing each other. The light from my bedside lamp is dim yellow. The house is quiet. Sawyer goes to bed early, and Leon hasn't come home yet. It's just the two of us, caught in this moment with our daughter asleep a few feet away.

"You've done a really good job with her. She's so sweet and funny… and really smart."

"Leon is partly responsible for that. He's been testing how much she can learn since she started talking."

His expression changes, and he looks toward the window. "He's a good kid."

I reach out and slide my hand into his. "We've all been through a lot."

Closing his fingers around mine, he looks into my eyes. "I wish I could change what happened... I only want good things for you."

My chest tightens, and I search his gaze. "I believe you."

Lifting my hand, he presses his lips to the backs of my fingers. My eyes are fixed on the place where we touch, and so many emotions rush to the surface... self-preservation being one of them.

"We'd better get some sleep. I have to take those kits to Pine Hills tomorrow, and Dove has her Thanksgiving party at school."

He nods, a touch of sadness in his eyes. "Goodnight, Noel."

Miss Jessica is wearing a smock covered in turkeys when I arrive at the nursing home. Pure bliss lights up her eyes as she takes out each product from her gift bag.

"Oh, this is my favorite eye cream." She turns it over in her hand, examining the label. I help her remove the cap and she gives it a sniff. "I love that scent."

She goes through the exclusive foot cream I only make for her and me now, a cinnamon-peach candle, lip balm, and my signature scent body lotion, which again, I only make for us.

"Dove is so sad she couldn't be here to help pass out the presents, but she's a pilgrim in the school play."

"I'm sure she's amazing in it."

"She actually just gets off the boat at Plymouth Rock. I think she carries a Bible and a corn stalk." Miss Jessica laughs, and I wrap my arms around her thin shoulders. "I am so thankful I met you that Christmas."

"I'm thankful for you and Dove. You keep me young." She's so happy. It's hard to believe she's eighty-six now. "And how are things going with Taron? I tell you, he is such a handsome young man. Every time I see him at church, I have to fan myself."

My lips tighten. I want to avoid this topic, but she reads it all over my face. "It seems like he's trying very hard."

"He is." I nod, holding her freckled hand. "I'm just so afraid. He was my first love. I loved him without caution, without care… and he almost killed me."

Her face grows serious, and she blinks down at our clasped hands. "I know, honey. I remember."

"I know we're supposed to forgive people… But how can I forget that?"

She only nods. "Only time can answer that question. I know you'll do what's right. You always do."

Gratitude overwhelms me and again, I hug her closer. For a moment we sit in a silent embrace. "The store is so cute. I painted the walls a light peach shade with green trim. The floors are such a pretty pine, and I'm installing shelves and cases…"

"Oh, I wish I could see it." Her voice has such longing, I know we can do it.

"I'll talk to Mindy about driving you out there. If you're able to go to church, I don't see why you can't come to see your old investment property."

"My schedule's wide open." She's teasing, but it makes me remember.

"I found a box of old papers, letters and things. I need to bring it for you to go through."

She just shakes her head. "I didn't keep anything of value in that old shed. I'm sure it's just old receipts and accounting ledgers."

"Still… I'll probably look through them anyway to be safe." I give her one last hug. "I'm headed to the school, but I'll let you know. Maybe Taron can help us."

I'm about to leave when her grip on my hand tightens. "Remember it's the darkest nights that produce the brightest stars. If he's showing you his true colors, believe him."

"But how do I know which are the true ones?"

"You'll know."

CHAPTER
Twenty-Six

Taron

'M SURE EVERY PARENT FEELS THIS WAY, BUT SEEING MY DAUGHTER LAND on Plymouth Rock with the rest of the first-grade Pilgrims makes me proud to be an American.

A little boy speaks his lines about establishing a new country where all men can be free, but my entire focus is on the little blonde pilgrim in the back holding a Bible and a corn husk.

They sing "This Land is Your Land," and when it's all over, the whole room erupts into cheers. I whistle loudly, and Noel pulls on my arm.

"What?" I look down at her, and she just shakes her pretty head.

Ms. Moody steps to the mic as the children file off the stage. "Thank you, parents for coming. The children are heading to their classrooms to prepare our Thanksgiving meal for you all."

We start moving toward the doors, but she isn't finished. "Before you disperse, I'd like to say a special thank you to Mr. Taron Rhodes, Dove's father, for his generous contribution to the playground improvement campaign. His ten-thousand-dollar donation not only exceeds our fundraising goal, but it will allow us to secure the latest in safety sod and even include the special-needs enhancements on our wish list. Mr. Rhodes is truly an asset to Harristown Elementary, and we are so grateful for your generosity."

The room is silent a split second then bursts into applause. Parents make their way to where I'm standing to shake my hand and say thank you.

Noel steps back, but her eyebrows rise, and her lips part. "What did you do?"

Moving closer to her, I put my arm around her shoulders. "I talked to the principal last week. Patton sent me an email with our year-end numbers. I want Dove to have a safe playground."

We're moving toward the door when I catch Digger's narrowed eyes. He turns quickly and disappears into the crowd headed to the classrooms, and I bite back a big laugh. *In your face, Hayes.*

Noel doesn't miss a beat. "Dove's safety is your primary concern?"

"Always." Satisfaction tightens my chest, and I put my hand on her waist, leaning closer to her ear. "And Digger's little niece can stick that in her knit cap and wear it."

"Taron. She's only six."

Our eyes meet, and her lips press together, fighting a laugh. It doesn't work. We swap a low-five before making our way to the classroom for elementary Thanksgiving Dinner.

Mindy meets us at the door of the classroom. "That's some gift, teacher's pet." A twinkle is in her eye, and she pushes a lock of curly brown hair behind her ear. "I didn't know you cared so much about playground equipment."

"Kids play rough. It's good they're safe."

"Well, I think it's great. Merry Christmas to us all." She pokes me with her elbow. "And if it helps her win Princess Peach, you got my vote."

"I don't know what you mean... Is that a thing?"

She grins and narrows her green eyes before going to help her niece who's sitting beside Dove. Noel squats beside our daughter, and Boo is making her banana in a pilgrim hat and googly eyes talk. It's all lively and hilarious, but Dove is quiet.

Her elbow is propped on the table, and she pokes at her Rice Krispie Treat turkey with a pretzel stick.

My satisfaction turns to concern, but Noel doesn't seem to notice. She chats with Mindy, while I stay with the rest of the dads, observing from the perimeter.

Digger stands behind his niece's chair not smiling, and even Darcy is flicking her cheese cubes around on her plate with her fingernail and studying my daughter across the table.

When the kids have finished eating, they go outside and run around the old playground a while. Noel helps the mothers clean and pack the leftovers, and she gives Ms. Moody a small gift.

Standing by the fence, I'm watching Dove sit on top of a dome-shaped climbing area when Digger stalks up beside me. "Well played, Rhodes. I guess you think you got me."

"I don't know what you're talking about. I had a good year, and I want the kids to be safe."

"We all do." He smiles insincerely. "Will you attempt to buy Noel while you're buying the rest of the town?"

Anger tightens my chest, and I take a step closer. "Still after my girl, Hayes? When are you going to get it through your head she's mine?"

"I don't see a ring, and clearly you can afford one. Perhaps Noel has finally come to her senses and seen you for what you are. Money won't change that."

"You should know better than anyone."

"I know some people better than anyone."

My fist clenches, but Noel's voice cuts through the tension. "Everything okay over here?"

Her soft hand covers my fist, and I glance down at her. The

red sweater she's wearing makes her cheeks glow, and her lips are stained with a pretty red lipstick. She's so fucking gorgeous, and that asshole Digger has my number.

I've been working my tail off to prove to her I've changed, but no amount of money can make up for the hurt I caused her. She'll have to decide if she's ever going to forgive me, and so far, it hasn't happened.

"Just chatting. Happy Thanksgiving, Noel."

Her eyes glide between him and me, but she accepts Digger's explanation. "Happy Thanksgiving to you."

"Ready to head back?" She looks up at me, and I don't know if it's what Digger said or my wishful thinking, but something seems different.

Mindy leads the girls to the truck and Dove climbs inside quietly. Noel gives Mindy a hug, and she invites us over for Thanksgiving dinner. We're all quiet on the drive back to the house. Dove falls asleep in her booster chair, and I carry her upstairs to the bedroom she never uses, tucking her beneath the pink ballerina blanket.

Noel leans on the bar, reading a thick book, her hands around a mug of coffee when I re-enter the kitchen.

"Does she seem okay to you?"

Her eyes flicker up from what I see is a recipe book. "Why?"

"She's always talking about something. I've never seen her be this quiet before."

"Does she have a fever?" Noel puts her mug down and starts for the door.

I'm right behind her feeling foolish. Why didn't I think of that?

Noel goes straight to her bedside and puts her hand on our little girl's forehead, moving it down to her neck. Then she leans over and puts her lips on her head. Dove exhales a sigh and rolls over, still asleep.

"She feels fine to me. Probably just exhausted from all the excitement." We're back out in the hall, and Noel pulls the door almost closed. "You were really great today. That gift was…" She shakes her head. "Unexpected."

We walk slowly down the short hall then descend the stairs with her leading the way. I think about her and Dove and warm pride swells in my chest. Fuck Digger. These girls are mine. I just have to show them I'm here for the long haul.

"It felt like a good place to start. I can do more…"

At the bottom of the stairs she stops and smiles up at me. I take the last step, which puts me right in front of her. Her pretty head is at the level of my chest, and I want to pull her close. I want to bury my face in her hair and kiss her neck. She still wears the scented lotion we made together.

"Like what?" Her voice is soft, her eyes fixed on mine.

It's the closest to an invitation I've had since I got back, and I lean closer. She doesn't pull away. "I'd like to kiss you."

Amber eyes blink to my mouth, and her tongue slips out to touch her bottom lip. Heat surges below my belt, and I slide my hands up her arms, ready to pull her to me. My throat is tight, and I quickly realize Dove is asleep, the house is otherwise empty.

I can still taste the warmth of her mouth. I want to taste her everywhere. She exhales a soft noise, a quiet yes, and a loud knock on the door makes her jump.

We step completely apart when the kitchen door opens. "Noel? You around?"

"Deacon." She shakes her head. "I asked him to come over and look at the books for me."

She hurries into the kitchen, and I fall forward, leaning my forehead against the wall and sliding my hand over the bulge in the front of my jeans. *So close…*

Noel spends the afternoon discussing finances with Deacon, and I'm impressed by the numbers I hear them throwing around.

I realize Noel doesn't need to stay in this house with her brothers. She's here because she wants to be, because they're family.

My girl is an incredibly successful businesswoman, and it makes me proud. She doesn't need me to save her or Dove, and it makes me want to earn her kiss even more.

I remember what Leon said long ago about her being serious-minded. He still hasn't forgiven me. Sawyer had a conversation with him, but the most I get is a passing greeting from him. He still watches me like a hawk or ignores me completely—like all through dinner.

My little mouseling remains unusually subdued through the meal. Her mother says she's not sick, but by story time, I'm ready to get to the bottom of what's going on.

She sits beside me on the couch instead of her usual climbing into my lap, and I hold the book a second before scooting around to face her.

"Is everything okay?"

Her blue eyes are on her hands, and she nods.

I'm not a child psychologist, and I've only known Dove a few weeks. Still, I'm pretty sure that's a no disguised as a yes.

"I thought you were really great in your play today. I didn't know pilgrims could sing so well."

A slight smile curls her lips, but it's gone just as fast. I hesitate a moment, but I open the book to the first page, where Mr. Mouseling is working on a story for the *Mouseland Gazette*. I start to read when Dove interrupts me.

"Angelina looks just like Mr. Mouseling. Except for his glasses." She puts her little finger on his face, and my throat tightens.

"It's true. They look alike, except Angelina's a girl."

Her round eyes meet mine. "Ms. Moody called you my daddy, but Mamma said you're Uncle Sawyer's Marine friend."

Closing the book, I shift in my seat, doing my best to swallow the hard lump in my throat. "It's true."

She blinks a few times as if waiting for me to say more. Only, I'm not sure what to say. I want to call her mom to come help, but I don't want to lose her trust.

"Uncle Sawyer was always here."

She doesn't say it, but I feel her question. *Where was I?*

I push my hair back and lean forward, getting closer to her level. "Remember that time when we were talking about princes and pretending?"

"Prince Phillip?" Her brow furrows, and she looks up at me. "Were you trapped in a dungeon?"

Sliding my hand over my mouth, I think about the right thing to say. "Not exactly… I was really sick for a long time. I got hurt when I was with your Uncle Sawyer, and I didn't take care of myself."

"Is that why you limp sometimes?"

My eyebrows rise. "Yeah. I didn't know you knew that."

She nods, her round eyes solemn. "When are you going away again?"

"Who said I was going away?"

"Uncle Leon asked Uncle Sawyer. He wanted to know what happened when you left again."

Pain twists in my chest, and I realize she's been thinking about this all day. Sitting up, I inhale deeply. "Is it okay if I hold you?"

The corners of her mouth turn down, but she nods. I pick her up and hug her to my chest. Her little face presses into my neck, and I feel her breath hiccup. Something inside me breaks, and my eyes heat.

"I didn't know you were here when I came to help your Uncle Sawyer." Clearing my throat, I smooth my hand up and down her back. "Now that I've met you, I'd really like to stay with you."

She puts a hand on my shoulder and sits back. When our

eyes meet mine, hers are pooling with tears. "Will you stay in the cottage?"

"I will for now. If that's okay?"

Her lips press together and she nods quickly. "And we can make hoecakes and read bedtime stories?"

"As long as you want."

"I think that would be okay." She looks up at me, and the corners of her lips slowly start to rise.

I can't resist asking. "You don't mind that I'm not a prince?"

She tilts her head to the side and thinks about it, and I'm almost sorry I asked. "You said you were a hero?"

A slight wince, and I confess the truth. "I wanted to be a hero."

Settling into my side, she picks up the book and opens it again. "You've got time."

"I've got time." I give her a little poke in the ribs and she squeals a laugh.

The sound of her laughter is the best thing I've heard all day. She bounces around and throws her arms around my neck, her little face in my ear.

"I love you, Daddy."

It's the sweetest whisper, and my heart melts completely in her hand.

CHAPTER
Twenty-Seven

Noel

MRS. JENNY'S THANKSGIVING TABLE IS A GLORIOUS SIGHT. AN enormous turkey is in the center surrounded by bowls of mashed potatoes, stuffing, dressing, fresh cranberries, sweet potatoes, green-bean casserole, glasses of red wine…

And a plate with a tin-can imprinted pillar of cranberry sauce.

"So gross," I mutter under my breath.

"Don't hate!" Mindy cries. "I have to have my Ocean's Spray or it's not Thanksgiving."

I shake my head and look around at my family. Mrs. Jenny is at one end with Sawyer at the other. Mindy's daddy passed away years ago, so my oldest brother took his place at the head of the table.

To Sawyer's right is Leon and next to Leon is Deacon with Mindy beside him. Taron is across from Mindy and Dove sits between us, ending with me beside Sawyer.

We all join hands and Sawyer says a brief prayer, then the table erupts into the happy noise of everyone passing plates and forks hitting china. Mrs. Jenny pre-cut the turkey in the kitchen before bringing it out, and this year she skips the retelling of how she put Sawyer on the spot that first year by asking him to cut it.

She probably doesn't want to embarrass him in front of his Marine buddy. She's come around some as Taron showers Dove with affection. Watching him with his daughter is enough to bring anybody around.

Dove has been stuck to him like glue ever since Ms. Moody's big reveal, and she seems to find any chance to call him at the top of her lungs.

"Daddy! There are pecans mixed in those little cabbages!"

"They're brussels sprouts." Taron's voice is low and so calm. "Want to try one?"

Her nose wrinkles. "Nuh uh!" Then she points again. "There are marshmallows on top of the sweet potatoes. I don't like sweet potatoes. Do you like sweet potatoes, Daddy?"

Taron grins, unaffected by her calling him *Daddy* for the eleventy-millionth time this morning. If their bonding weren't so adorable, I'd make her stop. She's totally his mini-me, and he clearly adores her.

When our bellies hurt from eating all the food, Mindy and I flop on the couch in the formal sitting room, glasses of red wine in our hands, while the guys camp out in front of the television to watch SEC football. All except Taron, who is too busy being *Daddy*.

"Those boys are racing a little car down the sidewalk. Can we go see, Daddy?" Dove grabs his large hand and drags him to the door.

Mindy gives me wide eyes from the other end of the couch, and I fall to the side, my head in her lap. "Stop! Don't make me laugh. I might throw up."

"Don't barf on me, glutton." My best friend shoves my shoulder.

"Your mom's dressing is too delicious. I have to be sure none's wasted." I'm holding my stomach as she combs her fingers through my hair.

"So how are you doing with all this *Daddy*?" The way she says it makes me laugh a little more.

"It's like she's been waiting to call him that since the day they met." Lifting up, I look out at them, and she's propped on his hip, pointing at where she wants him to take her next.

Seeing her this happy fills me with a joy I've never known. It's like a kaleidoscope of butterflies is in my stomach, and every time she calls him and he picks her up, holds her and adores her, they swirl around inside me.

"She always loved Sawyer and Leon, but this is next level."

Mindy looks out the window at them. "I can't really blame her. I'd want a hot as hell man-slave at my beck and call, too. But what about you? How are you feeling?"

Pulling my feet under me I release a sigh. "He's trying so hard. He seems so sincere…"

"But?"

"I don't know." I laugh softly. "I'm glad he's here for her. I'm glad he loves her so much…" An old ache squeezes my chest. "He hurt me really bad, Min."

"I know. I remember."

"At the same time, he was wrestling with some major league shit."

"Have you talked about any of this?"

"Not really. We've really been focused on her and letting him get to know her so it wouldn't be such a shock when she found out."

"That girl is not shocked." Her eyebrows are up, and she points out the window. "She is in heaven."

Deacon walks out the door to where Taron is standing with Dove, and it's my turn to give her arm a shove. "And what kind of spell have you cast on Deacon Dring to keep him coming back for more? Just when I think he's gone, here he is again. Not that I'm complaining. He's the best financial adviser I know."

"He's the only financial adviser you know." She tries to play it off, but I'm not letting her.

"Spill. I thought you two had parted ways."

"I don't know what you mean. We've never really dated." She shakes her head and turns her back to the window where our tall, handsome former classmate is chatting with Taron.

"You are so full of shit."

"I'm not! We only dated a few times. Deacon is not here for me, whatever you think. He's looking for some family history or something."

"What in the world?" Now I'm intrigued.

"He was raised by his great aunt. She's one of those old Dallas wild-cat wives who has more money than God. She's pressuring him to settle down and get married. She wants him to have kids or she'll write him out of her will."

"You have got to be kidding me." I hop onto my knees. "That's crazy! Why didn't you ever tell me this? It's like a Disney story. Is he looking for a princess to marry?"

"Hell, no!" Her brow furrows. "And don't repeat any of this!"

"Who am I going to tell?"

"Anyway, he's looking for some Harristown relative or something to get her off his case. I don't know. I kind of stopped listening halfway through."

"You stopped listening or you started making out?"

Her lips curl in a smile, and we both start laughing. "I'm not one to kiss and tell."

"Sounds like you're the one with the magic stringing him along all these years."

"I'm not stringing him along. He just happens to be in town, and we just happen to get along well…"

Her voice trails off, and I chew my bottom lip. "It's time you found someone of your own, you know."

She shakes her pretty head. "I'm trying. It's just…"

"I know." First loves can be hard to shake.

We sit for a few minutes in silence, watching the men talk. Dove's head is on her daddy's shoulder, and her little fingers rise and fall, patting his back.

He doesn't even seem to notice, and my insides warm. The ice melts and mist fills my eyes. They're so perfect...

Mindy's phone buzzes, and she looks down. "Tamara said they just got back from her in-laws. She says Boo is whining for Dove to spend the night tonight. Yes?"

"Sure... If she can tear her away from her dad."

"That's a real consideration. I'll let her know."

Making cookies and *Christmas in Mouseland* manage to pry my daughter out of her father's arms. Leon heads out to hang with friends, and Sawyer has his own truck, leaving Taron and me alone for the first time since that afternoon after the school Thanksgiving party.

"Feel like you're missing a limb?" I can't help teasing as I drive us along the dark country road to the house.

"Yeah." He exhales a laugh, shifting in his seat. I wonder if his back is aching. He never complains about it. "The day she found out, I wasn't sure how she was going to respond. I was nervous."

"I'm sorry I wasn't there with you. I had no idea she'd overheard Charlene make that announcement."

"No good deed, right?" He glances at me in the darkness, and the light in his eyes heats my entire body. They widen, and he grips the dash. "Shit! Watch out!"

Slamming on the breaks, I turn the wheel hard right, narrowly avoiding a doe dashing across the road. I turn the wheel left again to avoid flipping, and the truck shimmies before skidding and straightening with a jerk.

"Holy shit," I gasp, holding the truck straight with trembling hands. My whole insides are shaken.

"That was some badass deer dodging you did just then," Taron quips.

Adrenaline surges in my veins, making me laugh. We both do, and he reaches over to squeeze my shoulder as we turn in at the orchard road. A little farther, and I park the truck in the drive between the house and the cottage.

He hops out, coming around to help me out of the cab. "You okay?" He stands in front of me, his hands on my waist, searching my face.

His clean, masculine scent is all around me, and I want to snuggle closer in the cold night air. I want him to hold me. I want to thread my fingers in his hair and kiss him like I used to.

"I'm okay now." My voice is quiet.

"We have to let those Fast and Furious guys know they're missing a stunt driver."

"I don't now about that."

We stand a moment longer, his hands still on me, my hands on his forearms. My breath is shallow, and looking in his eyes sends energy snaking through my lower stomach. That old pull between us is stronger than ever, fueled by our past, by our present, and the little girl binding us together.

"Deacon seems like a nice guy." His hands slip off me, and he steps back.

I'm confused and frustrated by this unexpected shift. "Yeah?"

"He was kind of a cock-blocker the other day, but I listened to the two of you talking. You've been really successful. I'm proud of you." He slides a hand in the side of his hair, pushing it back and looking up at me. "You don't need me, but I want to be a part of Dove's life. I want to take care of her... and you."

His voice softens on the last part, and if he didn't already have the family advantage, with those words, he reclaims ownership of my heart.

"A long time ago, you caught me when I fell." My voice is a high contrast to his. "You said you'd save me if I ever needed saving."

"You said you'd save me right back."

Stepping closer, I put my hands on his arms. "I wasn't able to save you before…"

"I didn't really let you." Regret fills his tone.

I've heard it so many times. I know it so well. Dolly would say *storms make trees take deeper roots*…

"Maybe we can try again?" Our eyes lock, and the words are barely out of my mouth when his arms circle my waist, pulling me firm against his body.

He's moving fast, like he's been waiting, covering my mouth with his, pushing my lips apart. I chase to keep up with him, and a soft groan escapes from my throat. His kiss is eager, hungry, sweeping his tongue inside to mine. I grasp at his shoulders, and his scent intoxicates me. The firmness of his body against mine is a drug.

My hands are on his scruffy cheeks, moving higher, threading into his soft hair. His lips pull mine, nipping and tugging. He lifts me off my feet, and my legs immediately circle his waist.

Boots scuff on the wooden porch of the cottage, and he fumbles to open the door. His lips break from mine, and I moan, leaning forward, kissing his neck, higher to his ear. I feel his erection between my legs, and my core aches for him to fill me.

Lowering me to my feet, he holds me in front of him. We're breathing fast. "Is this what you want?"

Nodding, I lift my chin and close my eyes for another kiss, but he catches my chin.

"Noel, I want to make love to you. I want to be with you all night—"

"I wish you'd stop talking about it, then."

He grins, and we're back. Mouths sealed together, desperate, hungry. It curls my toes.

We're in the cottage, and he gives me an order. "Lie back on the bed."

I don't even hesitate.

CHAPTER
Twenty-Eight

Taron

NOEL IS SPREAD OUT BEFORE ME, HER BACK ARCHED AND HER TAUT nipples pointing to the ceiling. The light of the moon streams through the open window, coating her naked body in silver light. She's a goddess, and I have my mouth all over her, kissing her, tasting her, drinking in the sounds of her moans.

Her legs tremble as she comes, my tongue circling her clit until she's gripping my hair, pulling, and begging me to be inside her.

I quickly shove my jeans down, turning her onto her stomach and catching her by the hips. She moves to all fours and looks at me over her shoulder, her amber eyes hot with lust and her dark hair, wavy over her shoulders.

My cock is an iron rod. Her ass is a heart tipped up at me, and I slide my dick up and down her wetness before slamming balls deep into her luscious pussy. She drops to her elbows and lets out a loud moan, and I have to hold a moment as the sensation of being completely inside her blanks my mind.

My hips move, thrusting in and out, chasing the orgasm that's just within reach. She came hard only moments before, and I feel her clenching, squeezing around me. It's so good, I groan low and loud as I feel the tension rising in my dick, tightening my ass and centering on the place where we're connected.

Reaching around, I circle my fingers over her clit, and she breaks into another cascade of orgasm, clenching and moaning. It's the final push I need to fly over the edge, pulsing and filling her, reaching forward to brace the wall in front of us, scooting her farther onto the bed as I hold deep, riding out the final waves of orgasm, the soul-deep satisfaction I never thought I'd have with her again.

We're breathing hard, and I move us around, turning her and pulling her to me. It's cold, and I quickly whip the blankets back, sliding between the soft threads with her beside me.

Noel Aveline is in my arms. Her body is flush against mine, chest to stomach to thighs to toes. Her hands hold my shoulder blades, and her cheek is tucked against my heart. My heart that only beats for her. My heart with her name inked above it. Our breathing slows, and I smooth my hand down the length of her hair. I press my lips to her temple.

"How do you feel?" My voice is rough, husky from the emotions surging in my chest.

"Good." I feel her cheeks rise with her smile, and I love this woman so much. "What's this?" She lifts her face, her eyes on my tattoo.

"Something you own."

Her chin lowers, and she presses her forehead against my skin. I slide my hand down her soft hair. She doesn't speak, but it's okay. I know we've taken a big step.

Do I deserve this? A twinge of darkness lurks at the corner of my mind. That old anxiety tries to raise its head, but I won't let it in tonight.

Placing my hand on her cheek, I lift her mouth to mine again. Her kisses are like a sip of water in the desert, soul-deep and satisfying. With my knee, I part her thighs, moving above her and sinking into her core.

Her moans are the melody I dreamed of so many nights when I'd lie alone, in the pit of hell, believing if I could survive one more night, I might make it back to her again. Her fingers thread in my hair and we slowly rock together, fire molding us into one.

When she comes, I lift my head and look deeply into her eyes. They glisten as I let go, filling her and kissing her tears away. Her hands move to my neck, holding us close, and I press my lips to her shoulder, silently promising to never let her cry alone.

Never again.

I hold her, listening as her breath slows, as she sleeps in my arms.

Tonight I have my one dream in my mind: Noel and me... and the beautiful little girl we created sharing a life together, building a family.

The next morning, I wake to find cold sheets beside me. *Not cool.*

I step into my jeans, jerk them over my hips quickly followed by my boots and a dark green Henley. A brush of my teeth, ball cap on my head, and I cross the yard with Akela hopping along beside me. I swear she's smiling.

I stop at the back door, love expanding in my chest as I watch my girl moving around the kitchen, her hair up in a messy bun on her head.

"Is anybody still hungry after the dinner we had yesterday?" I close the space between us, pulling her firmly against my chest.

"Leon is always hungry." She smiles up at me and I kiss her lightly.

Then I think better of it, and I give her another, longer kiss, parting her lips, curling our tongues together. She tastes like sunshine and fresh orange juice, and forever, and when I pull back, the light in her eyes fills me with so much gratitude.

"Let me go now. I've got to make breakfast." She smiles, and that little dimple appears below her mouth.

I step back, admiring that ass as she turns to dig in the refrigerator. "Maybe you should get something from the pantry."

She straightens fast, pink flushing her cheeks. "Taron! Shh!" She looks over her shoulder. "Sawyer's right in the living room."

As much as I know she loves being here, I'm beginning to see some drawbacks to living with her brothers.

"When does my baby get home?"

"You're not enjoying your break?" Noel arches an eyebrow at me over her shoulder as she breaks eggs into the bowl.

"No." I exhale a chuckle. "I miss her."

I've gotten used to her sweet little voice calling me every two seconds, holding her on my hip, and hearing her thoughts about everything. She's a chatterbox, and I love it.

"Ask and you shall receive." Noel smiles at me, and I hear commotion in the other room.

Sawyer greets them coming through the door, and two little girls run into the kitchen, both in pink and purple glitter tutus, and start dancing around.

"Daddy! Look what Mrs. Tamara got us!" She twirls, jumping and kicking her leg behind her.

Her friend Beverly "Boo," a little girl with dark hair cut in a bob at her ears, does the same. Mindy's sister enters, carrying a small bag and placing it on the counter.

"They were up past midnight watching movies. I couldn't get them to sleep." She steps over and Noel kisses her cheek.

"Don't worry about it. They've got til Monday to get straight."

"They talked nonstop about ice skating. Bill said he'd check to see if the coliseum is doing anything. I'll let you know."

Tamara corrals Beverly and the girls hug and kiss goodbye before they head out the back door. Dove skips over and holds her arms up to me. I lift her onto my hip so she can wave to her bestie until they're out of sight. Then she wiggles out of my arms and dances into the living room to watch her favorite show.

Noel has her back to me. Hot biscuits are on a plate, and she quickly cuts little pats of butter and slips them into each one. I put my hands on her waist and lean down to kiss the back of her neck, just below her ear, inhaling the scent of her, coconut, peaches, a touch of rose... I'm feeling happy, like I'm finally home, surrounded by my people.

I slide my hand forward to cup her breast, and she inhales sharply. "Taron."

She drops the knife on the counter, turning in my arms.

Looking down, I smile, sliding my thumb along her chin. "Sorry."

"You're not sorry." Her lips press into a smile, and she blinks up. Our eyes meet, and it's electric.

"You're right. I'm not. I'd like to take you into that pantry and..." I want to slip my hand down her pants, but she slides her fingers around my wrists.

"I think we need to slow it down a little."

I don't care for this. "Any particular reason?"

She shrugs, picking up the knife again. "I don't want Dove to think we're together until... unless we're sure."

"I'm sure." My stomach is tight, but I gentle my voice. "You're not?"

She blinks quickly, putting the last pat of butter in the last biscuit. "I'm not *not* sure... I guess I just want to be completely sure."

The knife is on the counter, and I stop her. Catching her chin, I lift her face so our gaze meets.

"I get that, and I deserve it." Amber eyes flicker away, settling on my chest, right over my heart where her name is inked. "I will prove myself to you, Noel. I won't let you down again."

A quiet whisper. "I'm trying."

Lifting her hand, I kiss her palm. Our eyes meet, and I hope she can see the depth of my commitment. I hope she can see my heart. "I'll wait for you."

It's a hard thing to do. It's excruciating to be so close, to have held her in my arms all night and still have her put a hand up, but it's my fault. She needs time.

Time… I won't lie and say I like it, but she's important to me. Dove is important to me. They're why I'm here, and I'm prepared to earn her back.

After breakfast, I want to work. I want to be alone and work my muscles. I want to sweat.

Sawyer says we need to be sure the roots on the new trees are well covered. The temperature is dropping, a bitter front is moving through, and forecasts are calling for ice, possibly snow.

Dove falls asleep on the sofa in front of the television, and I head outside to get started. I've just finished checking the canvas on the first row of trees when I notice Leon standing with his hands in his pockets looking down at the concrete loading dock.

"Hey." I go to where he's waiting.

"Hey." He looks up at me. His anger has cooled, and I've been waiting to have this conversation. "I've been pretty pissed at you for a while now."

"I know."

"Sawyer said you were injured, but I don't understand what kind of injury makes you forget your promises."

My throat knots, and it's like he's slammed me in the side again. I feel like I'm back at Square One, trying to come out of the hole I've fallen into.

"I started on pain meds…" Shame flashes hot in my chest. I hate this weakness. I hate admitting how far I fell. Still, I know from every time I tried to run, denial only leads to darkness. "The force of that addiction is something I'll never forget."

He studies me, brow furrowed. Leon is smart—I can see him thinking about this. "So you're over it now?"

"I'll never be over it… but I've learned to fight it. I've learned when to walk away. When to get help." I look down at my scuffed boots.

We're quiet a moment. A bird chirps in the top corner of the shed, and I wish Akela would put her head under my hand.

Lifting my eyes, I meet his. "I'm sorry I let you down, Leon."

He straightens and his jaw flexes. Then he nods. "You're really sweet to Dove. She loves you a lot."

"I love her. She's something to fight for… and Noel." I mean these words with all my heart. "You're a great uncle. I appreciate you taking care of her when I couldn't."

He shifts from one foot to the other, and I glance up to see his expression has eased. "She's my family."

My lips tighten, and I nod. *Of course*. If I've learned anything about Sawyer, Noel, and Leon, it's that family comes first.

After what they've survived, I get it.

"I thought you might be my family once." He slants an eye up at me.

"I'd like that. More than anything—it's why I'm here now."

"Sawyer said sometimes good people get hit hard. We have to forgive them because we never know when it might be our turn to need forgiveness."

Swallowing the knot in my throat, I nod. "Your brother's a smart guy."

"He's usually right about people."

Glancing up, I see Leon's holding out a hand to me. I step forward and take it, shaking his hand and putting my other on top.

A smile curls his lips, and he steps forward into a brief hug. "We've got you."

CHAPTER
Twenty-Nine

Noel

TELLING TARON I NEED SPACE IS THE HARDEST THING I'VE EVER DONE. Being in his arms was like going home. He might have torn my heart out by the roots seven years ago, but he also planted the seed of forgiveness when he gave me Dove.

Coming back, loving her, being so amazing… It's all gone a long way to mending the damage done so long ago.

Still, it's like my brain threw a leash around my chest and pulled it tight. I can feel the restraints binding against my ribcage. He has my name inked on his skin. Tears fill my eyes, and my heart wants to fly… But my mind says *not so fast*.

Standing in the doorway, I watch him with Dove in the living room. She's chewing gum, which is new, and she's making him help her learn the opening dance for *Angelina Ballerina*.

"It's my talent for Princess Peach," she explains like we should have already figured that part out. "Hold out your arm, Daddy."

Taron is on one knee, and she jumps, switching her feet beneath her like the cartoon mouse. I'm pretty sure this move is called a *changement*, and it's pretty basic. Still, Taron is her biggest fan.

"That's good. Have you taken dance?"

"Nuh-uh." She shakes her head and does a *sissionne*, which is basically the same move, going to the side.

The one year of ballet I took in high school has given me that much info.

"What's happening in here?" Leon walks into the room and flops on the couch. "Dude. She has you doing ballet now?"

I sit on the arm of the chair beside him, watching their progress. "Taron is filling in for Freddie," I tease, referencing Angelina's dance partner in the books.

"Lift me up, Daddy." She puts his hands on her little waist, and when he lifts her, she points one leg out. "*Grand jeté!*"

It's so cute, I clap and laugh. "That's good!"

Taron turns her in the air and props her on his shoulder, and they both hold an arm out. Even Leon claps at their silly antics, and I wonder what's wrong with my stubborn brain. This big, strong, alpha man allowing his little daughter to wrap him around her finger like he does should be enough to heal any wounds.

He puts her down, and she walks over to the small trash in the corner and spits her gum into it.

"Goodness, Dove," I scold. "From the penthouse to the outhouse! Use a napkin next time. You look like a trucker."

"I'm Uncle Leon." She puts her hands on her hips and saunters back to where Taron is now sitting on the couch.

We both look at my younger brother, who's making a *shut up* face at my daughter.

"What does that mean?"

"I don't know what she's talking about."

"Are you chewing tobacco again?" Stepping up, I smack his arm. "You want all your teeth to fall out?"

"Woman!" he barks. "Stop abusing me!"

I do a little growl. "Disgusting habit."

Still, I'm happy. We're coming so close. I feel sure it's only a matter of time before I'm able to give Taron everything, no uncertainty or fear.

Dove is curled up asleep in my bed, and I'm putting clothes away in my closet when a tapping on my window makes me jump. I look around the door to see Taron smoldering outside the glass.

Akela doesn't even lift her head anymore. Crossing the room, I slide it open, and he sits, swinging his legs inside and pulling me between them.

"It's cold... Here." I close the window behind him, checking over my shoulder to be sure Dove is still quietly snoring with Alice clutched to her side.

I surrender to his kiss. He covers my mouth with his, pushing my lips apart and finding my tongue, making me hot and slippery.

My heart beats so hard, it aches in my chest. Being in his bed, making love with him was the satisfaction of a year's-long need, and I want him holding me down again, turning me over, pushing inside, and claiming what's his.

Lifting my chin I can barely catch my breath as his hands go under my shirt, lightly cupping my breasts.

"Taron..." I drop my forehead to his, dragging my fingernails through his beard. "What are you doing in here?"

"Missing you." His head dips, and his beard scuffs my skin as his mouth closes over a hardened nipple.

"Oh..." I gasp as he gives it a firm suck, and my knees are liquid. I bite back a moan, and he straightens, catching my cheeks.

"I want you in my bed. Now."

Electricity is in my veins, and I want to say yes. "It's risky... If she wakes up and I'm not here, she'll come looking."

His eyes go to our baby, and the struggle is real. "That little girl." He sighs, and his hands move around to my back, warm palms pressing me against his chest.

I feel his heartbeat through his shirt, and I don't want to let him go. I consider putting him in my bed, but I don't think we're strong enough for that.

"Grab a coat and come with me." He steps out the window again, and I grab my thick, fluffy coat, wrapping it over my thin tee and sweats.

"It's freezing out here." I pull up my wooly socks and snuggle closer into him on the porch swing. "Here."

I open my coat and straddle his lap as he slips his arms around me and we rock. For a little bit we're quiet, letting our bodies heat each other's.

When he speaks, his tone has changed. It's quiet, solemn. "Every second of the mission to rescue Marley, I thought about you. I worried about you. I dreamed about you. It was the longest we'd ever gone without speaking since we'd met."

My heart beats faster at his words, but I go still. We need to have this talk.

"Sawyer was able to call you because they considered him the head of your household… and it was possible we could've been killed on the mission."

I tuck my chin, putting my damp eyes against his shoulder. I remember those days clear as a bell.

He continues, his voice neutral, his muscles tense. "We eventually found him. He was deep in the jungle, in an old, abandoned shack… I was the first one through the door." A pause. A breath. I feel him swallow the thickness in his throat. "He was messed up bad. I didn't secure the interior like I should have. I didn't check for anyone else. I went straight to him and started cutting off the ropes. He was bleeding and barely conscious. I was so relieved we'd found him, but I was also thinking of you, finally being able to get back to you."

Turning my face, I press my lips to his skin.

"I didn't see her in the corner. I didn't see her until it was too late, and she was swinging a machete at our heads. I did the only thing I knew to do. I pulled out my gun and I shot…"

My throat goes tight, and I sit up, searching for his eyes.

They're downcast, not meeting mine. Placing my palm on his cheek, I'm not sure I understand.

"What—?"

"I killed her. She was just a kid, probably a kidnap victim herself. I don't know. We had to leave her behind… I'll never know."

My heart aches at the pain in his voice. "Was this the thing…"

"I fell on the way out and was injured. Back injuries are pretty much an automatic medical leave. They gave me a purple heart and sent me home. But I knew what I'd done. I could never… I can never forget her lying alone in that hut in the jungle."

"Oh, Taron." Tears spill onto my cheeks, and I wrap my arms around his shoulders, hugging him with all my heart, wishing I could take this pain away.

We're quiet for a little bit, swaying slowly in the swing, sharing this terrible memory. My hands slide up and down his broad shoulders, and I calm my tears. Sitting up, I dry my eyes, placing my hands on his neck. He's been strong enough to tell me this. I'm strong enough to hear it.

"I'm so sorry that happened to you."

His beautiful eyes meet mine, and they're like the sea, blue-green and glistening. "Can you forgive me?"

"Of course!" I lean forward kissing his lips and pressing my cheek to his. "It wasn't your fault."

His brow furrows, and he shakes his head as if he can't accept what I'm saying. "Our daughter wants me to be a hero. I don't know how to tell her that's something I'll never be."

My insides tremble, and I can't let him believe this. I don't know how to make him hear me, and I can see this burden is so heavy, it almost took him from me completely.

"Our daughter will love you no matter what. Because you love her unconditionally."

He exhales a heavy sigh. "I'll never be her hero."

"Never is a long time."

CHAPTER
Thirty

Taron

"**Y**OU HAVE TO GO TO THE COTILLION. IT'S TO RAISE MONEY FOR the parish library!" Mindy leans on the bar, but Noel is shaking her head and stirring a saucepan of pralines.

"Christmas orders are through the roof. I've got to finish shopping, and everybody's coming here for dinner. I don't have time to find a dress, get my hair done—"

I give my daughter a little nudge from inside the living room, and she springs into action. "Mamma, look at me! Look at me!"

Dove twirls into the kitchen in that pink and purple tutu, only now she's wearing a headband with white mouse ears and carrying a stick with a ribbon attached to the end. She does the steps we've been learning by pausing and rewinding the opening to her favorite show, and I know she's mine, but she's really adorable.

I'd name her Princess Peach today.

"Oh, my goodness!" Noel puts her hand on her chest and kneels briefly. "It's Angelina Ballerina!"

Dove continues hopping side to side, tapping her heels together in the air, and swirling her wand with the ribbon over her head, and I laugh, clapping as I enter the room. She runs to me, and I do the lift, holding her up as she extends her arms and legs briefly before sitting on my hip.

"That does it." Mindy claps, shaking her head and laughing. "I want you to be my dad, too."

Noel's voice is teasing. "You already have a daddy."

"Who's Miss Mindy's daddy?" Dove's brow furrows, and she looks curiously at her mother's friend.

Noel arches a brow. "Mr. Deacon."

"You have got to stop with that." Mindy shoves her friend's arm.

Dove frowns at me. "He's not her daddy!"

I frown right back. "This is getting weird."

Noel lets out a little yip. "Shoot! It's time…" She moves the pot off the fire. "Quick! Hand me that pan."

Mindy grabs a large, metal cookie sheet, and we watch as she spoons little clumps of the caramel-brown pecan and butter mixture onto it.

"I almost burned the pralines."

"Serves you right." Mindy turns to me. "Tell her she has to go to the cotillion."

"What do you say, babe?" I look over at my girl dressed in jeans that hug her sexy ass and a chunky white sweater. She slides the band out of her dark hair and shakes it out over her shoulder. It makes me want to invent an excuse to get her alone.

"I've got to get these over to Pine Hills." Noel walks to where I'm standing, holding our little girl, who's twirling her ribbon wand. "You're still helping me bring Miss Jessica to the store, right?"

"I'm ready when you are."

She takes Dove out of my arms. "Go get changed."

My daughter sulks out of the kitchen, and I catch Noel's cheek, giving her a quick kiss. "How's that for talent?"

Her nose crinkles and she smiles up at me. "I think she's going to win it."

The last two weeks, ever since that night on the swing, we've grown steadily closer. What happened in Mexico was the last thing I held back, and I felt if I were going to prove to her I'm all in, I had to put it all out on the table.

Everything between us shifted after that conversation, and while we still aren't spending the night together, we've found ways around our daughter's sleeping habits—most of which involve sudden errands the both of us need to run together.

I'm pretty sure Sawyer's onto us, especially since most of these errands take place while Dove is at school.

"Just think…" Mindy is still going on about the fundraiser. "Evening gowns, tuxes, fancy music, dancing… your *birthday*. It's going to be so romantic."

"What if I just make a big donation like Taron did?"

Mindy's brows shoot up. "You can do that?"

"Maybe not every year, but I can this year."

"No." Mindy shakes her head. "Even if you're as rich as Beyoncé, I want you to come. It'll be fun! Taron, can't you help me?"

Amber eyes meet mine, and Noel gives me a smile I've come to love. It's calm and confident, like she knows something she's ready to tell me.

I want to hear it.

"I'll talk to her."

"This is so nice." Miss Jessica is in the front seat of my Tahoe, and she runs her hand along the leather arm rest. "I don't think I've ever been in such a large, nice vehicle."

"It's just a truck." I pat her thin hand.

"I feel like a queen going to see my old shed in all its glory."

"I hope you like it," Noel calls from the second row. "I hope people come to shop when it's open."

Her elderly friend looks in the rearview mirror. "It's going to be a hit. You'll see!"

Dove is oblivious to our concerns. "Boo said her daddy took her ice skating in Monroe last week. I want to go ice skating, Daddy!"

I meet her eyes in the mirror. "I'll ask him about it, sweet pea."

"Uncle Leon said the cold, cold reservoir should get ice on it. I bet I could ice skate there." She looks out the window at the lowering sun, and I make a mental note to get that girl to an ice-skating rink.

She's been asking for weeks.

"That reservoir has always been as cold as Valley Forge." Miss Jessica laughs. "It's not too far from the feed shed, or I should say your new store... We'd go down there after working all day in the hot sun. It was always a dare to see who'd take a chance going in those waters."

"Your daddy threw me in on our first date." Noel winks at me in the mirror.

"Daddy!" Dove cries.

"Your mamma shoved me off a flatbed trailer. Nearly broke all my ribs."

"I did not!" Noel's voice goes high, and I laugh.

Miss Jessica laughs more, and we're pulling up in front of the cutest little cottage.

"My goodness!" She clasps her hands in front of her mouth. "Is this it? What a change. This is amazing."

I put the truck in park, and Noel hops out quickly, opening the passenger's side door. I jog around to help her ease the lady to her feet. She's light as a twig, and her excitement is infectious.

"Taron painted the exterior." Noel takes her hand, and while I'm in front of her, Miss Jessica gives me a firm hug.

I lean down to hug her back, grateful for this sweet old

person. She's always treated me with warmth and acceptance, even after I came back.

"Such a good man," she says, patting my cheek.

"He is." Noel states emphatically, and my chest tightens.

"Daddy! Get me!" Dove is out of her booster chair standing in the middle of the seats.

I reach in and help her to the ground, and she takes off running to the store with Akela bounding right beside her.

"That little girl has more energy than a jack rabbit!" Miss Jessica laughs, and Noel holds her hand, walking slowly over the uneven ground to the sidewalk we added.

Dove goes through the door, leaving it open. We're close behind, and when Miss Jessica sees the inside, she gasps.

The walls are painted a peachy gold, and the floors are sanded and waxed so the warm yellow pine is soft and inviting. Noel's hands are clasped in front of her lips, and she watches her friend inspect the place. I'm pretty sure she's holding her breath, wanting her to be proud of it. I put my arms around her shoulders. I'm proud.

With the setting sun coming through the new windows, the place looks absolutely golden.

"I have to get an electrician out here so we can get some light and heat." Noel holds her hands out. "Otherwise…"

"I love it." Miss Jessica's eyes are teary. "It is truly Autumn's Bounty."

"Uncle Leon's home!" Dove bounces on her toes in front of the window at the sound of a truck driving past.

Leon does a little honk, and we wave. Dove takes off running out the door with the dog right behind her. "It's starting to snow!"

Noel shouts after her. "Go straight to the house. It's getting dark."

I watch her golden head skipping down the hill, and a flicker of hesitation moves through my chest. "Think she's okay by her-self…"

But Noel's distracted showing her friend the glass cases and built-in shelves. I stand back while they discuss where to put ev-erything. Fat clumps of snow fall from the sky, and I know it won't last. It's cold, but we don't get real snow this far south.

The sun is gone by the time we finish dropping Miss Jessica off at Pine Hills and getting her settled.

"We need another batch of pralines, Noel!" The nurse greets us at the door, taking Miss Jessica's hand.

"Already!"

"They were gone in five minutes."

Miss Jessica's jaw drops. "I didn't even get one!"

Noel gives her a hug, speaking quietly in her ear. "I'll bring a special batch just for you next week."

That satisfies her, and we're on the road to the house when Noel reaches over and takes my hand. "This was a good day."

My hand closes over hers, and I want to tell her what's in my heart. I want to make her and Dove my family once and for all. I decide tonight, after everyone's in bed. I'll go to her window…

She hops out the cab when we reach the house and jogs up the back steps. "I'm sure Leon's going to be fussing for his supper."

Pulling the door open, she calls. "Dove, Leon, we're back."

I'm halfway through the door when I hear the panic hit Noel. "What do you mean, she isn't here?"

"I thought she was with you guys…" Leon is on his feet, Sawyer right beside him.

Our eyes meet, and ice shoots through my veins. "What's happening?"

"Dove never came back to the house." Noel's voice rises an octave. She spins on her heel and bolts out the back door, yelling, "Dove! Dove!" She screams her names again, louder, and I'm right behind her—we all are.

"Dove!" Sawyer's deep voice projects across the hill. He catches Noel's arm. "How long ago did you see her? Where was she?"

Roaring is in my ears. I can still see her little blonde head skipping away from me down the hill, Akela right behind her.

"About an hour? Maybe less?" Adrenaline spikes in my veins. "It was right after Leon passed us. She wanted to come back here to see him."

Leon takes off running up the hill toward the store. "I'll check the road."

"Snowing..." Noel trembles, and tears are on her cheeks. "She said it was snowing."

"Think!" Sawyer orders us. "Where could she have gone?"

We grab coats and flashlights. The air is freezing with snow clumps still falling to the ground.

"It's so cold. Oh, God, it's so cold." Noel's voice trembles.

I'm internally panicking, but trying to stay focused. "Akela's with her."

Noel takes off running in the direction her brother went, and I'm right behind her, flashlights shining along the road.

My stomach cramps. A million horrible images crowd together in my mind, but I shove them all out. If she fell, we'll find her. If she got distracted and wanted to build a snowman, we'll find her. If she decided to wander into the woods...

Why would she do that?

We meet Leon jogging back in our direction. "I didn't see any sign of her."

"Oh, Jesus!" Noel collapses, but I catch her. "You don't think somebody—"

"No." Sawyer cuts her off sharply. "We'd have seen someone or traces of someone."

"She doesn't just wander off by herself!" Noel's voice rises to a shout. Her entire body is trembling.

She's crying, but not entirely broken down, and I'm trying to force my brain to focus.

"Akela is with her..." Sawyer's voice is strained. He's thinking, but I can tell he's like me—close to the edge. "Where would she—"

The realization hits us both at the same time. "The reservoir!" He turns to his little brother. "Get help."

Leon sprints to the peach shed, while the rest of us charge in the opposite direction toward the small thicket of trees in the distance. Noel's hand is clasped in mine. Her brother is ahead of us, and our feet make damp, swishing sounds in the snowy slush.

"Oh, God, please..." Noel's voice is low, strained.

My insides are wracked with terror. My little girl, my sidekick, my mouseling. She has to be okay. I summon my military training, strategic thinking, focus under pressure as we get closer to the small body of water, a frigid holding pond between two rivers. In the summer, it's relatively calm, but as Noel's brother pointed out, the current grows faster in the winter.

Ice is in the pit of my stomach the closer we get. It's too quiet. *God, no...* I just hear the first whine of a dog when the loud noise of the three-wheeler breaks the silence.

Leon races over the hill, joining us fast, and Sawyer shines his light over the surface. Two lines cutting through the snowy face show us where she ventured out. He shines his light farther up, and it hits the yellow reflection of Akela's eyes thirty yards away. She's in the water, her front paws clawing the ice.

Noel lets out a scream. "Dove!"

Leon kills the engine, and we hear Akela's whines, the click of her claws as she struggles to climb out of the rushing water.

Sawyer catches Noel around the waist before she can charge out onto the thin ice. Leon has a yellow, nylon rope he's tying around the cage on the back of the ATV. It all feels like it's taking too long, but we're moving as fast as we can.

"It's the best I could find." His voice is ragged, and I wrap it several times around my arms as I start for the water.

Sawyer passes his sister to Leon. "Hold Noel."

"No!" she screams, trying to break free.

"Let's go." I leave Sawyer behind, carefully walking as far as I can before dropping down to my belly to avoid breaking through.

My eyes blink rapidly and my heart is hammering in my chest. I see the dog, but it's too dark. I can't see if she's there…

"Shine a light out here!" My voice is ragged with fear.

Straining my eyes, I look closer and see her little hand clutching Akela's collar. Her face is pressed into the back of the dog's fur, and Akela fights to hold onto the edge of the ice. Her nails scratch, and her voice is weak, failing.

"Good girl, Akela… Good girl." I have to stay calm. "Dove, can you hear me? Dove!"

Her head doesn't move, and I turn, sliding backward toward them. I'm almost to the edge. I can't break this ice or we'll all go under, we could lose them both.

The water hits my legs and it cuts like a knife it's so cold. I know from training to stay calm when the cold hits, but hypothermia is my bigger fear. I don't know how long they've been out here. Sliding to the side, my hand makes contact with Akela's paw.

"I've got you. I've got you, girl." My voice is controlled panic, calm with an edge. "Almost there."

"Tie the rope around her!" Sawyer yells from halfway back.

He's staying back, knowing too much weight could cause the whole surface to give. There's no way Leon and Noel could get us all out of here. With the temperature of this water, we'd freeze to death in minutes, which has me terrified now.

As I'm looking, I see her small hand lose its grip on the dog. "Dove!" I shout louder. "Hang on to Akela, Dove, Daddy's coming!"

I lunge in panic, and it's a critical error. The ice breaks. My large hand closes around her small one when it all goes, and we're hit like a freight train with the full force of the frozen water.

The last thing I hear is Noel's scream.

CHAPTER
Thirty-One

Noel

I T SOUNDS LIKE A TREE LIMB BREAKING IN TWO, OR A GUNSHOT AT CLOSE range.

The entire surface of the reservoir cracks open, and Sawyer hits his stomach, still holding the rope. Taron disappears into the black along with my daughter and my dog. I drop to my knees screaming.

The tornado touches down in my chest again, spiraling and ripping through my insides. It's tearing my heart out, and I don't have time to take shelter.

Leon releases me, dashing to help his brother.

"Do you have them?" His voice is more of a scream.

"I don't know!" Sawyer scrambles to his feet, grabbing the rope again.

Akela's head is the first above the water. She dog-paddles against the current, but she's losing the race. She's a cold-climate dog, but we don't know how long she's been in this stream.

Taron's head comes up next, and he clutches Dove against his chest. "Hu-hurry!" It's a loud noise like a cough or a growl. Splashes behind him, and I can see he's kicking his legs.

Leon runs to the three-wheeler and shoves the starter down,

then he starts to move it forward slowly. The rope goes taut, and Sawyer puts it under his arm, carefully guiding it, pulling them out.

Taron's upper body rises higher. I see the rope wrapped multiple times around his forearm, and he's holding our daughter against his chest, doing his best to keep her out of the water.

I'm on all fours, clutching my hands together and praying. Every muscle in my body is tense as I watch them fight the icy currents.

Horns honk behind us, and the noise of a siren seems far away. My vision is tunneled as my entire life plays out before me.

"God, please!" I pray again, my voice a screaming cry. "Help us!"

It all goes into slow motion when it happens. The knot slips or Taron's grip slips.

"Leon! Stop!" Sawyer yells at my younger brother when the yellow rope goes slack.

The siren is loud now, cutting across the field as EMS races to the scene. A swarm of workers surrounds me. A large man grabs me, wrapping a blanket around my body and pulling me back.

"No!" I try to struggle and fight him, but my arms are pinned beneath the canvas.

"We have to move fast!" A woman yells, and they carry yellow body boards out onto the ice. "How many are there?"

"Two and a dog!" Sawyer shouts.

Lights flash, blinding me. I can't see what's happening. I'm shoved into a cop car, and a woman puts a plastic thermos in my hand. "Drink this."

"Let me out... It's my daughter!" I'm frantic, trying to get back to them.

"They're going to be okay. We're getting them out. We'll get them to the hospital. Please stay calm."

I can't see what's happening. Tears blind my eyes, and I strain, trying to see what they're doing through all the commotion. So many people are here… they're all working fast, and I hear something that sounds like a motor. Men shouting.

Panic constricts my lungs, and I want to help. I want to know what's going on. I need to see my daughter, Taron.

"Help, please—" I barely have the words out when three doors slam.

The ambulance shoots off into the night, and we follow in a caravan of lights.

"We came as soon as we heard." Mrs. Jenny and Mindy run up the narrow hallway to where I'm standing outside the doors of the Emergency Room with my brothers.

"What's happening?" My best friend takes my hand.

"Don't know yet." Sawyer's arm is around me, but I haven't stopped shaking since we left the house. "Dove is unconscious. They think she's suffering from cold water shock. Taron was with us all the way until the last break. I think the ice hit him…"

"Lord, no." Mrs. Jenny steps forward, pulling me into a hug.

Up to now I've been completely numb, as if I'd fallen into the icy waters, but with the breakdown of my long-time pillar of strength, I feel my insides collapse. The weight of this is more than I can bear.

"I can't lose them." My voice is a broken whisper.

She clears her throat, clutching my shoulders and holding me straight. "You're not going to. The Lord said he wouldn't give us more than we can bear."

My eyes are wide and dry. I've run out of tears, but it doesn't mean I'm not dying inside. The hospital door opens, and a young man in blue scrubs strides out.

"LaGrange?"

"That's us." Sawyer steps forward quickly.

"Which one of you is the mother."

Everyone puts their hands on me, and I step up. "That's me."

He looks at the five of us huddled in a group—Sawyer, Leon, Mrs. Jenny, Mindy, and me. "I take it you're all family?"

Mrs. Jenny extends a pleading hand. "Yes, please tell us what's happening."

"She's stable. Her vitals are strong…"

"Oh, thank you, Jesus." We collectively exhale.

"But she's in a state of posttraumatic unconsciousness. We're monitoring her, but I'm concerned she suffered a lack of oxygen to the brain while she was in the water."

My chest feels hollowed out. I start to fall forward, but my older brother holds me. "What does that mean?" Sawyer's voice is grave.

The doctor's lips press together. "It could mean anything. We won't know until she regains consciousness."

I'm having trouble breathing. My throat is tight. Mrs. Jenny pulls me into a hug while my brother talks to the doctor.

"How long will she be like this?"

"I don't know, but we're moving her to a room. Hopefully hearing her mother's voice, talking to her will bring her around. It's a waiting game now. I'll have the nurse show you back."

"Thank you, doctor." Leon's voice calls after him.

My brother helps my friend lower me into a blue vinyl chair. "We'll sit with her. We'll talk to her, and she's going to wake up." Mrs. Jenny's voice is confident. "You know how chatty she is. She'll want to join the conversation."

I don't know what I know. My shoulders ache, and I feel all hope slipping away from me. "What about Taron?" I sound hoarse. "Did they tell us anything about him?"

"Last I heard, he was being treated for a head wound—"

"I officially have a hard head." His low, rich voice is like a balm to my aching insides.

My hand trembles as I reach out, and he's with me, in front

of me, holding me in his strong embrace. "Taron." I can barely speak. "You're okay."

He leans back and catches my eyes. A small bandage is above his left temple and an ugly purple bruise is on his left cheek, but he's warm and alive. He slides his hand under my arm and helps me stand. "I had her with me the whole time. I don't know what happened when the ice broke… I lost consciousness briefly."

"You saved your daughter's life." Mrs. Jenny reaches out to pull him into a firm hug. "I always knew you were a good man. You proved it tonight."

"LaGrange family?" Our circle opens for a young nurse in khaki scrubs. "I can take two of you back to see Dove. Are her parents here?"

"That's us." Taron holds my hand, and we follow her down the quiet corridor, past doors decorated with paper balloons and animals.

I don't want to think about the torture of being forced to stay here indefinitely waiting. I can't let my mind go to what that would ultimately mean.

"Here we are." The nurse leads us into a dark room where my baby lies on a large bed surrounded by beeping machines and a ventilator.

"Oh, no." I whisper, but Taron keeps me standing.

We're left alone, and I go to her bedside. Her golden hair is around her face in damp waves, but her beautiful eyes are shut. A clear tube is in her nose, and her little chest is moving.

"She's not on the ventilator." Taron stands behind me, speaking softly. "That has to be a good sign. It's like she's sleeping."

"Dove?" My voice is louder. "Mamma's here. Please wake up."

Silence is my only reply.

Silence and the noise of beeping machines.

I blink worried eyes up to her father, and his face is solemn.

He's watching her little body, waiting as helpless as me for any sign she's still in there. Any indication she's going to come back.

The doctor says the first twenty-four hours are critical. He tells us if she's unconscious longer than that, the risk of brain damage increases dramatically.

My heart can't unclench. It's tight as a fist in my chest, and as much as I want to believe Mrs. Jenny's words, I have to get up and walk around.

Taron is the opposite. He's at her side, his large hand under her small one, watching her little face and waiting.

"Hey, baby girl. Time to wake up." The smallest crack enters his voice and splinters my heart.

"Oh, Taron." I put my hands on his shoulders as the tears heat my eyes.

He doesn't take his eyes off her. He only waits, holding her hand.

CHAPTER
Thirty-Two

Taron

SLEEPING BEAUTY. OUR FIRST CONVERSATION WAS ABOUT THE STORY OF that prince. He was in a dungeon and then he had to fight through thorns and slay a dragon…

I said I'd cut through thorns and slay a dragon for her.

"Wake up, Dove. It's Daddy. We need to practice your dance for Princess Peach."

Silence…

I've been in combat.

I've gone up against drug lords.

Hell, I survived Marine boot camp, but nothing like this.

Her pretty little face is so still and calm. It's like she's only sleeping, but she won't open her eyes. She's somewhere we can't reach her, and the helplessness is overwhelming.

After twenty-four hours, they'll have to intubate her. It's like the point of no return, throwing in the towel, and waiting for the end to come.

My chest aches. I can still see the moment she walked away from me in the store. It's so clear in my mind. My heart said to stop her.

Why did I let her go?

Noel can't sit still. She's nervous and panicky, and her hands won't stop shaking. I try to hold her, and she lets me for a little while. Then she has to move again.

I want to give her my strength, but I feel it draining out of me just as fast.

It's like being on watch. I study her dark lashes lightly touching her soft cheeks. My ears strain for the sound of her breathing. I want to hear her voice again.

She said my name at least a thousand times, but still it wasn't enough. I haven't had enough time with her. *Please, God... Don't let this be my punishment...*

"I think I'll go to the chapel." Noel touches my arm. "Maybe if I pray..."

I lift her hand and kiss the top of it. "Sounds like a good idea."

I can't leave her side. If she opens her eyes, I have to be here. When I was in the water, I had her in my arms. I felt the life in her... I think I heard her say my name, and I was sure I'd get her out alive.

The ice broke, and I lost my hold.

Another hour slips past.

"Angelina, it's Mr. Mouseling. Wake up so we can build a sled."

Silence...

Another hour slips past.

Warm hands grasp my shoulders. "How are you doing?"

I look up to see Mindy's mother standing over me, smiling kindly. "I'll be a lot better when she wakes up. Where's Noel?"

"She's talking to Pastor Sinclair." She puts her hand on Dove's. "Come on, baby girl. Time to wake up."

She seems so certain. I want to have that kind of faith, but I don't.

"Noel has been through so much." She gazes at my daughter while she speaks. "What she's had to survive, the Lord gave her strength to survive. He won't ask more of her than she can stand."

Guilt weighs on me like a boulder. "I shouldn't have come here."

"What are you saying?" Her dark eyes meet mine.

"I've done things... bad things. Noel shouldn't have to suffer because of me."

Her hands are on my shoulders again, grasping me sure and strong. "It doesn't work that way. You put yourself in chains holding onto the past. Let your mistakes go and forgive yourself."

I start to answer, but she stops me. "The darkest hour is just before dawn." Then she goes to the door and leaves us.

Looking back at my little girl, I think about her words. I think about the dungeon I've kept myself in since Mexico. Is it possible Mindy's mom has given me the keys to set myself free?

My hand is on Dove's, and I lower my forehead to my arm. It's so quiet, I'm not sure if I doze. I only know time passes, and Noel comes back. She sits beside me and puts her head on my arm. I move and pull her against my chest.

"I love you." It's the only thing I can say. I'm at the end of my ability to fix this.

She lifts her head, giving me a sad smile. "I love you."

Reaching for her cheek, I pull her lips to mine and kiss her, softly, gently. Our eyes meet, and I would do anything to take away her pain.

Tucking her head into my chest again, I close my eyes and say a silent prayer. She's in my arms, secure in my embrace. I have to believe it's going to be okay.

"Daddy..." A sleepy little voice startles us. "Were you kissing Mamma?"

My head snaps around. "Dove?"

Her pretty eyes blink round, and her mother dives forward. "Dove? You're awake!" Noel kisses her cheek. She kisses her other cheek and her neck and the side of her hand. "Oh, my baby… my sweet, angel baby…"

I step back, giving her room as happiness, relief, gratitude, joy surge in my chest. Going to the head of the bed, I reach down to stroke her soft hair.

"How are you feeling, sweet pea?"

"My head hurts." Her voice sounds tired. "I was so cold. I held onto Akela. She was warm. She tried to get me out…" She looks up at me, and her little eyes go round. "I'm sorry I didn't go home like you said."

"It's okay… You're not in trouble…." I don't know how to say this. "Don't ever do that again, okay?"

She nods, solemnly. "Is Akela okay?"

Noel gathers her up for a kiss as the nurse enters the room and starts moving quickly, making notes and checking her vitals.

Dove's blue-green eyes never leave us. "Is Mamma your princess now?"

I only smile, so thankful for a second chance. "We'll talk about everything when we get home."

CHAPTER
Thirty-Three

Noel

"**F**IVE TIMES FOUR?" LEON LEANS ON THE BAR WITH DOVE PERCHED right in front of him.

"Twenty!" She shouts, doing a little jump.

"Two times two?"

Her head cocks to the side. "Too easy... Four."

"Okay, try this. Seven times..." His voice trails, and her eyes widen. "Nine!"

Her little lips part, and she thinks a moment. "Sixty-three?"

"Yes!" Leon holds up his hands and she high fives both of them hard. "Baby genius for the win!"

That gets him an instant frown. "I'm not a baby!"

Taron laughs from where he stands, leaning against the opposite bar as he watches them. He is so damn sexy in a black tux with his hair pushed behind his ears and his ocean eyes full of love.

I linger a moment letting the sight of them flood my veins with joy. I'm not sure it's possible for me to be happier than I am right now.

As if agreeing with my thoughts, the best dog in the world trots up to my side and puts her head under my hand. I squat down to give Akela a good head scratching, and she licks me right in the face.

"Oh!" I laugh. "Easy on the makeup, girl."

Leon declared Akela a hero.

Dove declared her daddy a hero.

Sawyer and I say they're both right... Taron, of course, says he just did what any good dad would do. I'm sure Akela would say for a Siberian Huskey, a dunk in a freezing lake and helping save the life of a little girl is all part of the job. I love them all.

Standing, I smooth my hands down the front of the floor-length evening gown I'm wearing. It's sleeveless, made of thick navy silk with a full skirt and a beautiful floral print near the bottom. I went back and forth over wearing my hair up or down and finally went with down, over one shoulder.

Taking a nervous breath, excitement tightening my throat, I make my grand entrance.

"Mamma!" Dove gasps, holding her cheeks. "You're a princess!"

"Dang, sis," is the best I get from Leon.

Taron's expression squeezes my chest. He straightens, taking his hand out of his pocket, and he appears stunned, like he's seeing the sunrise for the first time. "You are so beautiful."

Heat floods my cheeks. My heart beats faster, and I look down, letting a dark wave fall across my cheek. He slides it away with his fingers and pulls me into a hug.

Closing my eyes, I take a deep inhale of his scent. I feel the strength in his body, and the reins binding my heart are finally loosened. The fear is gone, and I'm free to love this man completely, with my head and all my heart.

"I'm really glad you decided to go tonight." His voice is low, but I feel his arm moving.

Looking around, I see our daughter tugging on his sleeve. "Me too, Daddy..."

He grins and picks her up, holding her on his hip. She puts her arm around my neck, pulling all three of us together in a hug, and I kiss her hair.

A moment passes, and my brother piles into my side. I start to laugh, lifting my arm and pulling Leon into our group hug. Next thing we know, Akela shoves her nose into the middle, and Dove starts to wiggle.

Taron lets her down, and she hugs Akela before skipping into the living room, our dog following behind her.

"Y'all have fun." Leon follows after her, and I turn to my date.

"Shall we do this?"

He holds out an elbow, and I slip my hand in it.

We're back in the civic center, and it's about the same as it was the night of the Peach Ball. Looking around, I see the familiar faces of our friends smiling at us. The whole town knows about what happened to Dove… and how we all saved her, but mostly her daddy.

"So glad you guys could make it." Ed Daniels stops us at the door, shaking Taron's hand and giving me a hug.

Sawyer is in the back talking to Jeff Priddy, and when our eyes catch, his brows rise. He gives me a little thumbs-up, and I shake my head with a grin.

Mindy swirls up with a guy I don't know right behind her. She's in a gorgeous butter-yellow gown, and her date is in a well-tailored lavender suit. It's clear they're not together in a romantic way.

"Gorgeous." She steps forward to kiss both my cheeks. "You look like a supermodel."

"Thanks." I hug her back, speaking close to her ear. "I expected you to be with Deacon."

"He's in Dallas." She motions to her escort. "Noel, Taron,

this is William. We met in art school, and he's looking for a new roommate."

"Nice to meet you, William." Taron shakes his hand, and William's eyebrows shoot up.

"Is this the hero I've been hearing about? You are wearing that suit, sir. *Bravo*."

"Ahh... Thanks, I guess." Taron pats his shoulder, and Mindy laughs.

"You have to learn to take a compliment, T."

"Wait..." My brow furrows. "What's all this roommate business? You're moving out?"

"I'm thinking of moving to Dallas. I've got a job offer at a design firm, and well... I think it's time for a change."

"Nooo..." I hold her arm, but she pushes me.

"It is your birthday. Dallas is not that far away, and you can come see me any time. We'll talk about it later." She puts her hand in William's arm and blows me a kiss. "Happy birthday. Have a ball!"

They sweep away, and I look up at my gorgeous man.

He looks down at me, and smiles, taking my breath away. "Shall we dance?"

The band plays a slow Christmas song about driving home for Christmas, and Taron pulls me close, placing his hand against my lower back and holding my other to his chest.

We sway side to side, and I'm lost in a magical place with his arms around me, the yellow twinkle lights glancing off his hypnotic eyes, and the heat rising from our bodies pressed together.

"I've been trying to decide what to get you for your birthday." His mouth is at my ear, and the whisper of his breath across my skin gives me chills.

"You saved our daughter from drowning. That's the only gift I'll ever need."

"That wasn't your gift." He kisses my cheek. "Saving Dove was for all of us. It's why we all did it."

My heart squeezes, and it's so true.

"So I had a few things in mind. I think I've decided which it'll be."

Lifting my chin, I smile up at him. "It's fun listening to you decide right in front of me."

He tweaks my chin and pulls me off the dance floor. "Come with me."

Our hands are clasped as he leads me quickly to the door. My lip goes between my teeth, and I'm proud and a little self-conscious following his sexy swagger through the room, I notice heads turning as he passes, and I think of the first time I ever saw Taron Rhodes. I thought he was a god. Now I know he's all that and more.

We step out into the night, and the cold air hits me. "It's freezing out here!"

He pauses to remove his tuxedo coat, putting it around my shoulders. I slide my arms in the sleeves, and he leads me a little farther to where a white gazebo is elevated in the middle of the park.

Christmas decorations light up the scenery in pretty shades of red, gold, and green. I've never minded being born on Christmas Day. The whole world is beautifully decorated, the songs are amazing, and it's really hard not to feel the love in our small town.

Taron faces me, pulling me closer again. "I've wanted to talk to you about this for a while, but things keep happening."

"Talk to me? Is something happening?"

"I hope so." He reaches to his chest then stops, exhaling a laugh. "My bad."

Reaching forward, he feels into the breast pocket of his coat, which is way too big for me. "I talked to Sawyer about this a while back…" He takes a step back and goes down on one knee.

"Oh my God, Taron… What are you—"

"Noel Aveline, I don't deserve you. I never have. I went away to try and prove I could be good enough for you, but I fucked that all up…"

"Taron, no! You didn't—"

"This isn't really a birthday present for you, because if you say yes, you'll be giving me the greatest gift I could ever ask for." He takes out a beautiful ring. It has white-gold branches wrapping delicately around a glowing white stone. "It's a moonstone. It represents new beginnings, success and good fortune. You're the only fortune I ever want. You're the love of my life. You're the mother of my children. You're the half of me I can't live without. Will you marry me?"

My throat is so tight, I can hardly speak. Tears flood my eyes, and I can only nod quickly as I hold a hand over my nose, not wanting him to see me ugly cry.

"Oh, Taron… Yes! Of course, I will. I love you."

He rises, slipping the beautiful ring on the third finger of my left hand. "I know it's not traditional—"

Reaching up, I put my hand on his cheek, smiling so big. "Nothing about us is."

Leaning down, he covers my mouth with his, kissing me slow, curling his tongue against mine. "Let's go tell everybody."

"What?"

Clasping my hand, he takes off jogging toward the civic center. I hold the lapels of his jacket closed doing my best to keep up, and when we get back to the crowded ballroom, he bursts through the doors and shouts, "She said yes!"

The entire room erupts into cheers. People shoot off poppers, and streams of confetti fly all around us. Champagne corks explode, and the band launches into "All I Want for Christmas is You."

"Yaasss, girl!" Mindy runs up and grabs me around the waist. "Congratulations, you two."

Sawyer comes over and shakes Taron's hand then hugs me. "So happy for you, sis."

My eyes heat at his words, and I look up at Taron, who's looking down at me with so much pride in his eyes.

"You did all this?"

He nods, grinning in that way that makes me want to rip all his clothes off. "I'm glad you said yes, or I'd have been embarrassed."

"As if I would ever say anything else." I reach up to hug him, and he lifts me off my feet.

Everyone cheers again as he spins in a slow circle, holding me in his arms. I laugh, and he puts me down. We're surrounded by so many friends, our family. I can only think of one thing left…

"We have to tell Dove and Leon."

"Well, Leon already knows. At least, he knows I was planning to ask you."

We dance a little longer, shaking friends' hands and hugging necks, until I can't stand it any longer. Then we wave and head out the door, back to the house.

Dove is sitting on the couch between Leon and Akela when we arrive. Leon stands, giving Taron a hand clasp and squeezing my arm.

"Welcome to the family."

His words clearly mean a lot to Taron, but I'm focused on the little lady watching us so curiously. Going to her, I sit down and take her hand in mind.

"Is it okay if we talk for a minute?"

She shifts around, furrowing her brow. "Am I in trouble?"

"No!" Taron laughs. "Not at all, baby. We just wanted to talk to you about something… See how you feel about it."

"Okay." She nods, looking up at us like a little adult.

Clearing my throat, I take the lead. "Dove, you love Daddy, right?" She nods emphatically, and I keep going. "I love Daddy, too. So we were thinking, well, we decided…" I hesitate, and Taron steps in.

"Mommy said she would marry me. She's going to be my wife, and we're all going to live together like a family. Is that okay?"

She doesn't immediately react, and my nerves kick in. "Dove? Is that okay?"

Her bright eyes blink quickly, and her little chin quivers. Taron and I both react at once. "Honey, what's wrong?" I take her hand, putting my other on her shoulder.

"Does this mean Daddy's going to take us away? I'll never get to see Uncle Sawyer or Uncle Leon or Boo or Akela anymore?"

"No!" A lump is in my throat and I almost cry. "No, baby, it doesn't mean any of that!"

"Dove," Taron's voice is gentle. "I love it here. I would never take you away from your family."

"Daddy's becoming a part of our family now. For real."

As we speak her expression changes. She starts to smile, and even though a little tear escapes, she jumps up on the couch and waves her hands. "It's going to be a wedding! Just like at the end of *The Little Mermaid*, and we'll have rainbows and music, and can I wear a fancy dress like yours, Mamma?"

Sniffing back my tears, I start to laugh, pulling her into a hug. "Of course, you can."

Taron surrounds us both with his strong arms, but we can only hold our little munchkin a second before she's off the couch and dancing around the room.

"A wedding! And nothing's going to change!" She hops, lifting her leg behind her and doing her Angelina dance moves.

"Well, one thing will have to change." Taron's low voice makes us both pause. We look at him with wide eyes, wondering. "You're going to have to start sleeping in your bedroom upstairs."

My lips press together, fighting a grin, and Dove frowns. "You don't want to sleep with me?"

"Only on special occasions. We need our special time, too."

I'm surprised how worried I am about her reaction. Her big eyes move to the side, and she seems to think. "Can Akela sleep with me?"

"Yes!" Her dad and I both answer at once.

"Woo hoo!" Her hands go up, and she starts dancing again with Akela on the couch watching. I'm pretty sure she's smiling.

Later that night, when the party clothes are off, and Dove is sound asleep in my bed, I slip out the window and run down to the cottage. Taron is at the door when I get there.

"I was just coming to see you." He grins, looking down at me.

I step forward and put my arms around him. Just as fast, he wraps me in his strong arms. We hold each other a long moment, and I listen to his breath moving in and out. I listen to his heart beating. I feel the strength of his body against mine.

"Thank you for coming back."

He leans up, sliding his thumbs across my cheeks. "Thank you for waiting for me."

"Thank you for loving me."

His arms tighten, and he tucks my head under his chin. "I'll never stop."

Lifting my chin, I seek out his lips. He covers my mouth with his, and it doesn't take much for us to be in his bed. He's between my legs, and we take the time to be completely united, bodies covered in sweat, breathing heavily when we're done.

His arms are around me, and I'm so grateful for the roots that were too deep to be destroyed. I think about our future and the road ahead. I know it won't be without its bumps and valleys, but after all we've been through, I'm confident we can face whatever challenges might come.

I've learned love is a tornado, destructive and fierce and powerful. It's also a butterfly, soft, gentle, beautiful. But to get to the butterfly, you must go through the tornado. Love has to change you. You have to grow, and it's difficult and life-altering and scary and lonely… but coming out on the other side, we've spread our wings.

We traded the pain and the loss for something far more beautiful and valuable and lasting. We've created something original and new.

Walking across the yard to the house, I look up at the moon, and I think about the ring on my finger. New beginnings, healing, the start of good fortune and blessing. Pausing, I listen for the sounds of my mother. I even listen for my dad.

Family doesn't stop going just because you can't see it. Family is something that is unbreakable, forever. It's in the trees, stretching up to the heavens. It's tradition and laughter and love. My final thanks is to them.

We're starting a new family, and this family isn't afraid of the tornado.

This family can fly.

Epilogue

Taron

NOEL AND I WERE MARRIED IN THE SPRING WHEN THE TREES WERE blooming and the crocuses were bursting through the soil.

She wanted to wait until the fall, plan a big event to be held after harvest, but I couldn't wait. We'd been apart so long and worked so hard to get back together. Even four months felt like too long to wait.

We were married in the orchard in April, as soon as the weather turned warm enough for Noel to wear the dress she'd chosen.

I'm sure every husband thinks this, but Noel was the most beautiful bride I'd ever seen. She wore her sexy hair in two braids right at the top of her head with peach blossoms woven into the crown. The rest hung in waves around her shoulders. I'm a big fan of her hair, but her dress took my breath away.

The top was sheer lace with a type of bra top covering her breasts, then it was long in a mermaid design. She looked like something out of the sea with her hair and her dress. I simply stood at the front in my tux with Sawyer, Leon, Patton, and Marley, trying to convince myself this wasn't all a dream.

The guys were blown away by Dove... and Noel. Of course,

they were, and my little sidekick asked if she could sing a song in our wedding. I can't get over how she loves to perform. She told me dancing wasn't a good enough talent for the pageant, so she wanted to try singing. Like I was going to tell her no.

At our spring wedding, she made her public debut with "Love is Like a Butterfly," and while I don't really like that song (*I know, I'm wrong.*)—when I heard my little girl's sweet voice singing it to her mother and me while we stood under peach trees covered in pink blossoms... it became my favorite "Aunt Dolly" number.

A gentle wind carried the fresh scent around us as we swore to love each other, honor and cherish each other as long as we live.

They're words I've promised to her every night since I came back. They're words I dreamed of saying to her every night we were apart, and sealing them with our little girl singing to us was more than I could have imagined.

What else I couldn't have imagined was my mother showing up at the wedding. Noel insisted we invite her, even though I said she wouldn't come. Guess who lost that bet?

Lucille Rhodes showed up in all her Tennessee Mountain glory, wearing a cream top and a peach skirt, her white-blonde hair styled long over one shoulder, and Dove was immediately in love with her. The feeling appeared to be mutual.

"You look like Aunt Dolly!" My daughter said the minute they met.

My mother wrapped her fringed, embroidered silk shawl tighter around her slim shoulders and evaluated the six-year-old. "You look like me. What's your name?"

"Tara Dove Noel LaGrange Rhodes. What's yours?"

That was enough to make them fast friends. Anybody with that many names, no matter how old she was impressed my mom. By the end of the wedding they were making plans for Dove to go and stay with her in Tennessee and visit "Aunt" Dolly's amusement park.

Fast forward two months, and we were busting our asses, sweating it out in the harvest. My injury held me back some, but I was able to get in there and do everything but haul palettes. We had another successful season, and the new trees put out shoots and sent deep roots.

Just like our family.

Noel planned the grand opening for her store to coincide with the start of the Peach Festival. She was terrified, first that no one would show up and then that everyone would show up and she would sell out of everything and have to close the store and everyone who came later would be mad at her.

I think my beautiful new wife can be a little nutty at times, and I love her for it.

"Baby, you're just going to have to close your eyes and jump." I slid my fingers through her beautiful hair as she laid her cheek against my bare chest.

"I've dreamed of this for so long..." Her voice was terrified, and I just kissed her and held her, doing my best to comfort her.

She didn't sleep the whole night.

She let me know—she was awake for my snoring, for Dove's nightly arrival around 2 a.m.... Our baby is having a tough time staying in her own bed, even with Akela there. I wake up every morning with a little girl's foot in my face and our daughter sleeping upside down between me and her mamma.

Sometimes Akela is also at the foot of the bed. I'm not sure how the four of us fit in Noel's queen-sized bed, but we manage.

We still get our "alone time" every night until we fall asleep. As for spontaneity, we figured that out before we got married.

Do I have to tell you Noel's store was a massive success? She did sell out of her most popular items, but most people were excited for the new business in town. They were excited to sign up for her mailing list, and she even recruited some of the local craftsmen, cooks, beekeepers, and peach condiment makers to stock her shelves.

"It's what I always dreamed of doing!" Her arms were around my neck, and I got the benefit of her excitement in hugs and kisses and some really hot sex.

Which brings us to tonight...

The Princess Peach pageant.

I didn't believe my wife when she described this experience to me before. I always thought of pageants as kind of silly, women's shit.

Now I'm wishing I'd never encouraged Dove to follow her dream of being Princess Peach. I wish I'd encouraged her to focus on her math skills, which apparently count for nothing in this realm.

We're halfway through.

The lights rise, and it's time for the talent portion to begin. I'm standing in the back of the room with the other dads, but my chest is painfully tight as I wait for Dove to take the stage.

"I can't believe we're doing this." Noel paces at my side with her hands clasped in front of her lips.

I've also learned this about my wife: when she's nervous or scared or worried, she can't be still.

"She's going to be great." I cross my arms over my chest like the other dads, and I realize it's a defensive move.

This is scary as shit.

"And now we have Miss Dove LaGrange-Rhodes singing 'Over the Rainbow.'" The jackass MC from Shreveport introduces her in his gameshow voice. You'd think she was about to be the next contestant on *Wheel of Fortune*.

Dove walks out in a blue and white checked dress, a bright red wig on her head styled in two ponytails, a little basket, and Akela by her side. The room chuckles at the dog-switch, and she launches into her song with a confidence that impresses me.

She's more like a sixteen-year-old than a six, and I'm not just being her dad when I say she has a really good voice. It's sweet and clear, and she can carry a tune. It's not Broadway caliber, but it's good.

She walks slowly, singing about birds and wishing on a star and longing, all while wistfully looking overhead with Akela at her side. My eyes go to the five "celebrity" guest judges, and they don't smile. They look down at their desk, some making notes. All I know is those assholes had better decide she's the best singer they've ever heard.

"I get it now." I lean over to whisper to my wife.

Noel looks up at me. "What?"

"Pageants suck."

Dove finishes, and the room erupts into applause, looking around, I see a few women wiping their eyes, and I clap louder, doing a Taxi whistle with my fingers. Noel shakes her head, but I don't care. My baby killed it.

Making my way to the dressing room area, I pass a woman in a sable coat, and I pause.

"Head up!" she whispers, watching the girl out on the stage now. "Smile."

I lean to the side, peeking around the wings, and I see Darcy is on the stage singing "Good Morning, Baltimore."

My brow furrows as I look from the girl onstage to the woman in the wings frowning and moving her arms as if the little girl isn't doing a good job. I mean, okay, Darcy is a piece of work, but she's doing a decent job speak-singing the song.

I feel a tugging at my waist, and I see my little Dorothy-Dove in front of me. Smiling, I sweep her onto my hip and give her a hug. "You were amazing."

She pushes back, giving me a worried look and nodding at the stage mom losing her shit behind me.

"No!" The woman hisses. "Smile, Darcy! Chin up!"

Dove looks out toward the stage, and her brow is still furrowed. I follow her gaze to where Darcy is waving her hands, performing hard in her little bouffant wig and fifties outfit.

She finishes and the room bursts into applause, Digger on the front row standing and clapping his hands high. Darcy returns to the backstage, and the woman jerks on her collar.

"That was terrible. You might as well have sleep-walked through the whole thing."

Darcy's chin is tucked, and I'm about to say something to the woman.

"Sorry, Mamma."

She takes the little girl's hand and drags her farther backstage, and I look at Dove.

My daughter doesn't say a word, but her blue eyes are big and thoughtful.

She leans forward and kisses my cheek. "I gotta go back there, Daddy."

I put her down and she goes to wait with the other little girls while the judges confer and make their decision. I return to where Noel is pacing the back of the civic center chewing her nails.

"How does she seem?" She looks up at me, her amber eyes as big as her daughter's.

"Good. She's pretty cool about the whole thing."

Mr. MC calls out the names, bringing the final five little girls up to the stage just like a real Miss America contest.

He goes down them one by one. Boo made it to fourth runner-up, and we clap loudly, giving Tamara a hug.

"At least she did that well," she laughs. We all got a kick out of Boo playing the crystal glasses as her talent.

"It's all Bill knew to teach her," Tamara explained. "My talent is sewing, and you can't sew a dress for a pageant."

We're down to the top two, and Darcy and Dove are the only little girls on the stage. My heart is beating so hard, it can't be healthy. Noel buries her head into my chest, and I hold the back of her head. Dove's eyes are so big and excited. I can't bear the thought of her being disappointed.

Yet, in the wings, I catch sight of Darcy's mom scowling, and my eyes go to Digger's little niece. For the first time, I see her glancing at my daughter and standing a little straighter, lifting her chin a little higher.

Sickness is in the pit of my stomach. The MC takes a glitter-trimmed envelope and steps to the center of the stage smiling.

"And our judges have decided. This year's Princess Peach, who will assume all the duties of Princess Peach and receive a scholarship in the amount of five-thousand dollars is…"

Noel's fingers tighten on my shirt, and my eyes lock on my daughter's.

It feels like time pauses for a breath.

"First runner-up is Dove LaGrange-Rhodes, which means Miss Darcy Hayes is Princess Peach…"

His voice fades out as my gaze tunnels on Dove. She blinks and a true smile splits her cheeks. She's given the first runner-up ribbon and a small tiara, but she also gives Darcy a genuine hug.

Noel is just the opposite beside me. "What?" Her voice goes high. "What a bunch of horse sh—"

"Shh." I put my hand over her mouth and pull her close to my chest. "Hang on a minute. Let's see what Dove has to say."

"She doesn't need a fu-freaking pageant to tell her she's a superstar. That's why I hate these fu… dumb things."

Darcy prances the length of the runway with a crown almost bigger than her head and a bunch of roses bigger than her body. She bows, and her mother stands in the wings preening.

Dove nods a bow and moves to the opposite wing, and we're right there to catch her hands and pull her in for hugs.

"You did so good, baby!" Noel hugs her tight, kissing her cheeks. "I couldn't be prouder of you if you were Princess Peach. I thought you were amazing."

"I know, Mamma." She hugs her mother, but she seems pre-occupied.

"What's on your mind, sweet pea?" I squat beside her, putting my hands on her little waist.

She doesn't answer me right away. She leaves me, and I watch as she goes to where Darcy is entering the backstage area.

"Congratulations, Darcy!" She reaches out and hugs her. "I really liked your song. I thought you were funny to watch doing it. You did a great job."

The woman in the sable lights a cigarette and scowls down at the two girls hugging.

Darcy seems surprised. "Thanks, Dove. I liked what you did with your dog."

"Maybe you can come over and play with me and Boo some-time at the house."

Digger's niece blinks, and her face seems to brighten. "Okay!" She seems really excited, and I'll be damned.

I'm so proud of my baby right now. Dove and Darcy clasp hands and hug each other one more time before my daughter walks back to where Noel and I are standing. I'm sure Noel's face is as surprised as mine must be.

"I'm really tired." Dove catches both our hands, pulling us to the exit. "Let's go home now."

We celebrate Leon's birthday with a brisket Sawyer made, and we all toast Dove as first runner-up Princess Peach. To her credit, she really seems okay with not winning.

She never says it, but I think seeing Darcy's mother in the wings has a lot to do with it. She's curled up on the couch beside Sawyer when we say goodnight before the Peach Ball.

It's been eight years since my last Peach Ball, and not much has changed. The men from the grower's association line the back, nodding and waving to us as we enter.

Noel is more of a celebrity this year because of her successful store opening, and some of her new partners walk over to greet her and set up times to meet and discuss shelf space.

We're out on the floor dancing, and I smile down at her pretty face. I'm in dark jeans, a khaki shirt and blue blazer. Noel is a show-stopper in a short green dress with tiny polka dots all over it. It wraps around her narrow shoulders, and her dark hair sweeps down her back. Her lips are glossy pink, and she is so fucking sexy.

"I won't lie, wife." I lean down to speak right in her ear. "I can't wait to get you out of this dress."

Her brown eyes glow when she looks up at me. "I can't wait for you to take it off me, husband."

Shit. We never stay to the end of these dances. "Let's go." I turn and start to lead her to the door, but she pulls back.

Laughing, she shakes her head. "I need to at least speak to Mrs. Jenny and make an appearance. I'm a business owner now."

"Make it quick."

We actually stay another hour at the ball before I'm able to steal her away. The whole drive back, my hand is between her knees and she leans into my ear, kissing and biting my earlobe, telling me the dirty things she'd like to do to me.

"You're going to make me wreck." It's important for her to know.

I park the Tahoe, and we're out, kissing as we make our way to the door. She laughs when I sweep her off her feet and carry her inside the foreman's cottage. We keep it ready just in case we need it.

We're both sweaty and breathing hard by the time it's over. I've had my face between her thighs, she's ridden me like a pony at the fair, and we lie beside each other satisfied, threading our fingers together and watching the moonlight stream through the windows.

"I was so proud of Dove today." She watches our hands as our fingers cross and turn in the air between us. The light glistens off her moonstone engagement ring and the white-gold band that sits on top of it. "She's getting to be such a young lady."

"She's a good girl." I'm starting to doze, but Noel pulls my hand.

"I've been waiting for a good time to tell you this, but we get so busy…"

My brow furrows, and I shift onto my side. "What's on your mind?"

"Well…" She turns so her cheek is on the pillow and she blinks up at me.

My chest tightens, and I can't help a smile. Everything about her has always been so beautiful to me.

"As you know, we haven't really been paying much attention to birth control…"

The minute the words are out of her mouth, my throat goes dry. "What are you saying?"

"I talked to Dr. Fieldstone last week. It seems we're going to have a new little family member when springtime rolls around."

She lets out a squeal when I flip her onto her back. Whipping the sheet aside, I spread my palm over her flat stomach.

"In here?" I press my lips against her skin, right above her navel.

She laughs and nods her head. "It's too soon to know if it's a girl or a boy…"

Closing my eyes, I lower my forehead to her stomach. She threads her fingers into the sides of my hair.

"Are you happy?" Her voice sounds slightly concerned.

"Noel… I am so happy." My voice breaks, and I hug her closer. "So happy."

She leans back, finding my eyes. "We haven't been married a year. We haven't even had a honeymoon—"

"I'll take you anywhere you want to go, my love." Leaning forward, I capture her lips with mine. "Say the word, and we're there. We've got all the time in the world."

"Oh, Taron." She hugs me, burying her face against my shoulder. "I can't tell you how happy you make me."

Those words are all I ever want to hear. She's given me everything I've ever wanted. She loved me, she waited for me…

Only a few days later, my sweet daughter has a party with her best friend Boo and her new friend Darcy. When Digger drops off his niece, I can't even find it in me to be annoyed by him.

"I guess I have to put up with you." His lip curls as he drops off Darcy.

"I bet you figure it out." Holding out my hand, I'm a little surprised when he shakes it. Then again, I'm used to much bigger assholes than Digger Hayes.

Standing in the kitchen, holding Noel in my arms, my hands are on her stomach as we watch the girls playing.

"You just think your daddy's a prince." Darcy's tone hasn't changed, but my Dove's has.

"My daddy's not a prince," she answers sweetly. "He's a hero. He saved me and Mamma."

My heart rises in my chest, and I slide my palm over Noel's stomach, whispering in her ear, "And you saved me right back."

"I said I'd wait for you."

"Thank God, you did."

Thank you for reading WAIT FOR ME!
I hope you loved Taron and Noel and Dove and all the gang as much as I did.
Stay tuned for the audiobook, coming Jan. 2020.

Sawyer's book is coming Spring 2020!
Be the first to know the title, read the blurb, see the cover, and more...

Sign up for my newsletter (http://smarturl.it/TLMnews) *or get a text alert when it's live by texting TIALOUISE to 64600 now!**
*Text service is U.S. only.

In the meantime...

Read Patton's sexy enemies-to-lovers, workplace romance
BOSS OF ME now!

Keep reading for a short sneak peek... Or get it FREE in Kindle Unlimited Now!
Also available on audiobook.

BOSS
of Me

Patton Fletcher is

✔Demanding,

✔Driven,

✔Sexy AF, and

✔My New Boss.

My sister says don't fall for him. I say don't worry

I'm not about to let some arrogant, young CEO derail my dreams.

Or insult my wardrobe.

I don't care about his deep brown eyes or the way the muscle moves in his square jaw when he's pissed.

I won't fall for his power or how sexy he fills out that suit.

I said I could resist him.

I was wrong…

Raquel Morgan is Trouble.

She's stubborn, independent, and a fighter.

She has long, dark hair, crystal blue eyes, and freckles...

Freckles.

And long, sexy legs.

And a smart mouth.

I've spent seven years building one of the top companies in Nashville, and I'm not about to let some ambitious, cardigan-wearing new kid distract me from my goals.

Raquel Morgan won't tempt me.

I'm The Boss, *and I never lose control...*

(BOSS OF ME is an enemies-to-lovers, military romance with a badass alpha boss and the feisty woman who steals his heart. No cheating. No cliffhangers.)

Prologue

Patton

Seven years ago in a jungle south of the border...

THE CLOCK IS TICKING.

We have to move fast or this will go terribly wrong.

Sweat rolls down my sides, and I exhale slowly, calming my pulse.

The air around us is heavy and close, so thick it's almost visible and so hot it's almost impossible to breathe.

Tropical plants form a dense barrier of wide, shiny leaves around us, and we're hidden in the brush around a small, cinder-block hut.

Our target is a green dot on my screen blinking right in front of us.

He's here.

"Moving in, eleven o'clock." Taron's voice is low in my ear.

"Coming up from the southeast." Sawyer's distinct southern drawl is a quick response.

"No noise. No prisoners." I give the order, firm and clear.

I'm the leader of this three-man rescue mission, and we won't fail.

We surround the unpainted, cinder-block hovel. It's quiet in the shadows. The windows are black holes with no glass, empty squares that could be hiding anything—watchers with guns, lining us up in the crosshairs.

Or he could be alone.

No, it would never be that easy.

He could be dead.

My jaw tightens and I push back on the thought. *What good would he be to them dead?*

Taking a knee, I slowly lift my gun to my eye, setting my sites on the front door. We've been tracking radio signals, emails and IP addresses, until we isolated them here.

Two weeks have passed since Martin was jumped on a routine fuel run. From what we've been able to piece together, they took him down with PAVA spray, a paralyzing nerve gas. Then the videos started.

Two weeks of grainy images of our friend and fellow Marine tied to a chair with a bag over his head. They'd rip it off to reveal black eyes and bloodstained skin. Then the threats started—guns and money. It's what they all want. Until now, the moment of truth in the heart of a South American jungle.

We're tired, thirsty, and focused on retrieving our friend, kidnapped off-duty in a routine stop on our way to a peace-keeping mission in Caracas.

Sawyer checks in from his point, and we watch as Taron creeps across the face of the structure, approaching the weathered wooden door. His gun is at his chest as he carefully reaches out and knocks.

Three sharp raps, and we wait.

Nobody breathes.

No response.

He looks to me, and I give a nod. I'm front and center, ready to cover him.

Nobody gets past me.

Nobody takes my men.

We're brothers—no one forgotten, no one left behind.

My heart beats like a mallet against my ribs. As much as we've trained, this scene is entirely unpredictable. We hope to have the element of surprise. We hope his kidnappers believe we're still in Los Cabos, but they could be smarter than we give them credit for. With low growl, I shake my head. *Not likely.*

These drugged-up gangsters dared to kidnap a Marine. The only thing stopping us from torching this whole place is my belief we can extract him without causing unnecessary casualties.

Taron's jaw is set, the sleeves of his tan shirt showing from beneath the black Kevlar vest are stained with sweat, and his light-brown hair is wet. All our faces are scrubbed with camouflage, making the whites of our eyes seem to glow.

My breath stills. My cheek is pressed to my gun barrel, and the noise of cicadas rises like a chorus around us. It grows louder, a warning.

I shake off the thought. Taron is my focus.

The shadow of Sawyer emerges from the brush at the opposite end of the house. They're acting on my orders, but we're brothers. We've had each other's backs since Day One. This is more than a rescue. Martin is family.

Taron moves away from the concrete wall, and my finger is ready on the trigger. The only thing standing between us and what's about to happen is a wooden door…

He lifts his leg and gives the door a sharp kick, sending it flying against the wall with a blast that rattles the quiet jungle. His back is against the wall again, and he holds, waiting for a barrage of bullets.

None come.

Three heartbeats, three silent breaths—I give him a nod. He

turns quickly, gun at eye level and steps through the space, swinging his weapon side to side. Sawyer is at his side, and I'm out of position moving forward to cover them.

"Marley!" Taron's gun lowers, and he rushes forward. I'm at the door to see him whip the bag off our friend's face, and it hits me like a sucker punch.

His head drops forward, bobbing like a top. I don't understand his mumbles. A thick stream of bloody spit drips from his swollen lips.

Rage mixes with adrenaline. He's been beaten almost to death, and cords of rope cut into his skin. Taron's quickly slicing his restraints as Sawyer and I case the hut. It appears deserted, which puts me on guard for IEDs. The unfurnished room has no interior light, casting long shadows in the corners. With a muted thud, Marley's knees hit the floor.

Taron bends to help lift him, and that's when I see her. Green eyes shining like cat in the darkness.

"No!" I shout as she rushes forward, screaming, just in time for Taron to whip around and see the raised machete in her hand.

Light flashes off the silver blade, the blast of Taron's pistol deafens us in the small space, and she drops like a stone, a bloody splatter like a megaphone fanning out on the floor in front of her small body. Long, caramel hair fans around her head, and she looks seventeen.

"God, no." He lets out a pained groan as the small gun falls to the floor.

For a moment, we're unable to move, unable to look away from the girl lying dead at our feet. My eyes heat, but I squeeze them shut briefly, clenching my teeth against the emotion. Marley mumbles incoherent words. He's barely conscious, beaten almost beyond recognition. I can't even tell if he recognizes us. The machete is at his feet, beside the dead girl.

She would have slashed them both if Taron hadn't done what he did.

Combat leaves no room for second-guessing. Hesitation is how you end up dead, cut in half by a teenager you'd otherwise overlook. A girl who never should have been here. Bastards using children to fight their battles.

"Get him out of here." My voice is a gruff order. When Taron doesn't move, I raise the volume. "I said GO!"

He struggles to lift Marley over his shoulder, and Sawyer steps forward to help him. I'm the last one to leave the hut, giving it a final sweep before I turn, in time to see Taron hit the ground and then cry out in pain.

"Mother—" He rolls to his side, blood soaking his lower back from where he landed on a broken sapling.

"Patton, stop!" Sawyer yells, and I see the trip wire.

How we missed it coming in is anybody's guess. Sawyer hoists Marley onto his shoulders. He's strong as an ox from working on his family's peach farm back home. I throw my rifle over my shoulder and lean down, grabbing Taron's arm.

"Can you walk?"

His face is scrunched in agony, but he manages to nod. "Get us out of here."

My jaw is tight, my brow set, and I force the determination we need to finish this rescue mission. Our ATV is down the hill, hidden in the brush, and we follow Sawyer, Taron leaning heavily on me.

His blood soaks through his clothes onto mine, dripping down to his pants. This injury might send him home, and Marley's worse. We're all worse on the inside. We saved our man, but we're all scarred by what we left behind.

It's too late to change it. We'll deal with the scars later.

When the fighting stops.

CHAPTER

One

Raquel

Present day

A HOT BREEZE WHIPS THROUGH THE STREETS OF DOWNTOWN Nashville, sweeping my light brown hair off my shoulders and throwing my black blazer open. I catch it, holding my bag and clutching my phone to my ear, hanging on my sister Renée's words like the voice of God.

"Make friends with Sandra. She's a good ally." Renée is encouraging, but my stomach is in knots. "Don't ask too many questions. If something doesn't make sense, wait and ask her later."

"I can't ask questions on my first day?" The orange hand appears at the crosswalk, and I take the opportunity to straighten my blouse. "What kind of mind reader do they think I am?"

"Trust me, Patton Fletcher doesn't have time to teach you how to do your job." She sounds like she might be quoting him.

"I've never even met Patton Fletcher."

"Who hired you? Taron? He's the only one who could get away with something like that."

"Ah, yeah." The walk sign appears, and I hustle across the four-lane street. "I interviewed with Taron Rhodes and Jerry Buckingham."

"Hmm..." Her skepticism fans my nerves.

"What?"

"You'll really have to be on your toes, then. If he didn't pick you, he'll be looking to get rid of you."

"Why?" Panic spreads into my chest.

"It's just how he is. He likes to be in control."

"So what do I do? You worked here." I push through the glass doors of Fletcher International, Inc., fresh out of Vanderbilt's Owen Grad School with a shiny new MBA.

Just like my sister, I graduated in the Top Ten in my class, and as such, I landed interviews with the top firms in the city. I wanted to go to Chicago or Dallas, but my advisor said Fletcher was a great starting point, a real feather in my cap if I could get a good recommendation. I assume this Patton Fletcher knows every CEO in the country... or his dad did.

When I searched Fletcher International, I found pages of articles on George Fletcher, not so much on his son.

"Don't let him push you around." Her voice turns thoughtful. "I couldn't tell if he did it on purpose or if it's just his personality..."

"How do I do that? He's the boss."

I wonder if she might tell me what happened to her here. My thoughts flicker back to when Renée started as an accounting intern at FII. She seemed to be doing great, one of *Nashville Magazine's* "Thirty under Thirty" rising stars in local business.

She passed the CPA exam on her first try... Then a year later, she dropped off the grid.

She stopped answering her phone, and when I called the office, a woman said she didn't work here anymore. I had to leave campus in the middle of exams, catch a city bus across town to her low-rent apartment in East Nashville, where it looked like she hadn't left her bed for days.

She wouldn't tell me what happened—she only said she wasn't doing it anymore. "It" meant anything having to do with her accounting degree.

That spring break, I ditched my plans to spend the week in South Walton to help her move back to Savannah, to our parents' tiny home near the watchful eye of Ms. Hazel Wakefield, their old neighbor.

Now she helps run Ms. Hazel's gift shop on Tybee Island and pays for rent by cleaning the old woman's house, running her errands, and cooking their meals. She doesn't have much choice since she walked away from her career with nothing but a crushing load of student loan debt.

"You want my advice on Patton Fletcher?" She huffs a laugh like it will take all day. "Don't mention his dad. It pisses him off."

My brow furrows. "Got it. Anything else?" I'm on the elevator rising too fast. Or she's talking too slowly.

"Never wear all black. He hates that."

"Shit." I glance down at my black slacks and matching black blazer. "I'll have to buy a scarf at lunch."

"Nope, he hates scarves even more."

"What's his problem?" My lips tighten, and my urge to fight starts to rise.

It's how I got my nickname, Rocky. My dad started it because even as a little girl, I never backed down from a bully.

"Remember when we were kids, and you liked to say 'You're not the boss of me'?"

"Yeah?"

"Don't *ever* say that to Patton Fletcher." I'm about to speak, when she adds conspiratorially. "But *never* stop saying it in your head. I think he secretly likes it."

"He sounds evil."

"Well…" Her voice goes higher. "Patton Fletcher is a devil. He's not *the* devil, but he's definitely one of them."

"I'm not afraid of the devil." I have no intention of letting some arrogant young CEO scare me away from my dreams—if that's what he did to Renée.

The elevator stops with a ding, and I wonder if that's the reason I said yes to this particular job offer, to prove the Morgan girls have grit, to prove we're tougher than we look.

"Whatever you do, don't fall for him." Her tone turns serious, and it almost makes me laugh.

"I have no intention of falling for him."

"I checked your star sign this morning. It's a good day for you to start something new."

I'm in the door, and not a moment too soon. When she starts on the holistic remedies and astral predictions, I'm done. "Thanks, sis. Gotta run. Love you!"

"Love you, too. Protect your chin."

"I will." It's our usual sign-off, a boxing reference.

I end the call as a slim young man in a pale blue, button-down and salmon-pink dockers behind the reception desk lowers his phone and gives me a bright smile.

"Welcome to Fletcher International, can I help you?"

"Hi, I'm Rock—ah, Raquel Morgan. I'm supposed to check in with Sandra—"

"Oh! You're the new hire. One moment, please." I wait while he punches a few buttons and speaks quickly into the receiver.

I only have a moment to glance around the immaculate, dark-wood, leather, and glass waiting area before he hops out of his chair, extending an arm toward the door leading to the back offices. "Right this way. Sandra's waiting for you."

"Thank you…"

"Dean." He smiles, turning back to answer the buzzing phone as Sandra appears in the hall.

I can't help noticing her lavender silk blouse and beige pencil skirt. I feel like the grim reaper compared to the two of them…

Which is ridiculous! I look very professional in my suit, and I'm wearing a cream silk blouse… I'll ditch my jacket once I'm in my office. Problem solved.

"Welcome aboard! It's so nice to have another girl at this sausage fest." Her hazel eyes shine behind heavy, tortoise-shell framed glasses, and I like her at once.

"Yeah." I glance down with an embarrassed grin. "I feel over-dressed."

"They say you can never be overdressed, right?"

"I guess…" I'm not sure what to say. I stand out like a sore thumb, and I can't decide if it's a good thing or not.

Sandra leads me down a corridor with offices facing downtown on one side and cubicles in front of computers on the other. "This is your office in the middle."

Does that make me the monkey? I step into a good-sized room with a large window overlooking the river. A dark wood desk holds a newish-looking laptop with a sheet of paper beside it. A banker's box full of files is on the other side and another is on the floor.

I drop my bag in the maroon leather office chair. "This is great."

"Taron is in the corner office to your right." She points across her chest. "And Jerry is just on the other side. I think you met them both already?"

"Yes!" I smile. "They interviewed me."

She gives me a wink. "I think they were both concerned about who would occupy this space. Nobody wants a bad neighbor."

Everything about Sandra puts me at ease and makes me wonder why I was so nervous. I plan to text Renée the second she leaves and thank her for the heads-up when a dark figure glides in behind her.

"Sandra, I need you to open a file on the Madagascar account." A deep, rich voice joins us, and Sandra does a little jump and turns. Dark eyes under a lowered brow land on me.

"Patton Fletcher, meet our new hire, Raquel Morgan. She's taking over the international accounts for Taron."

My heart stutters in my chest, and all I can think is *Wow*.

"For Taron?" The muscle in his square jaw moves, and he looks to the right, toward Taron's office, as if he can see through the wall. For a moment, I wonder if he can... being the devil and all.

"So yes, Raquel Morgan..." Sandra repeats herself, leaving the introduction open as she gestures toward me. "Patton Fletcher."

"Right. Welcome." He seems angry.

I can't seem to find my voice. I've never been in the presence of someone so young yet so formidable in my life.

His dark hair is swept back from his face in glossy waves that just touch the back of his collar, and his shoulders are broad. His biceps strain against the sleeves of the blue blazer he's wearing, and when he extends a perfectly elegant hand to shake mine—long fingers, neat nails—the black tips of a tattoo peek out from beneath his white cuff. *Jesus, take the wheel.*

Our fingers touch, and heat floods my veins. "Thank you." My voice is practiced calm, but I feel weak. *Why didn't anyone tell me how insanely hot this devil is?*

"Then the Madagascar file will go to her." He holds a manila envelope toward Sandra, which she passes to me.

"She's your girl." His eyes narrow, but Sandra continues. "Raquel speaks five languages—"

"Reads," I quickly interrupt. "Sorry... I'm only a fluent speaker in one. Besides English, of course, but I can read the others fluently. For some reason, reading is easier than speaking."

Am I rambling?

Stop speaking, Rocky.

"I hope it's whatever they speak in Madagascar." Patton's tone is dismissive, and he pivots as if to go.

"French." My voice is a bit louder. "They speak French in Madagascar, and you're in luck."

He turns back, and I smile, doing my best to redeem my wobbly first impression. I'm a professional woman, not some swooning school girl.

His dark gaze sweeps up and down my body quickly, and my knees tingle. "Are you going to a funeral?"

The sarcasm in his tone irritates me. I hold my smile steady, and I remember what Renée told me, my mantra. "I'm working at one of the top firms in Nashville. From what I hear, it's a very professional place."

The corner of his mouth twitches, and I'm not sure if he's going to smile or frown. I'm briefly distracted by the fullness of his lips, but I kick that thought out of my brain. Patton Fletcher is testing me, just like my sister said he would. It's a fight or flight situation, and I'm not about to run.

"Try some color next time. We want our clients to feel positive about working with us, not depressed."

Rude! He starts to go, but I can't resist. "I think choosing my wardrobe is a job I can handle." I'm teasing, but only a little bit.

"I guess we'll find out." He glances over his shoulder, and I'm not sure—is he teasing, too?

"I have been dressing myself for a long time." My tone is thoughtful.

I could say as a self-respecting devil, *he* should be the one wearing all black…

But I don't.

"Have you been doing this job longer than me?"

I don't want to answer that.

"Right." He turns to Sandra. "Tell Taron to come to my office as soon as he arrives. We have a video conference with Hastings and Key at ten." I think that's it, and I realize I'm holding my breath. It catches again when he points at me. "Skype meeting with Madagascar tomorrow. Sandra will put everything you need on the G-drive. I expect you to be ready."

"I will be."

He's gone, and I glance at the thin envelope in my hands. *Shit.* What do I need to know by tomorrow?

When I look up again, Sandra is grinning, one eyebrow arched. "Sounds like you'd better get busy. Your passwords and everything you need are on the sheet by your computer. If you need anything else, let me know." She pushes off and leaves me alone in my office, but I hear her last words as she walks away. "This is going to be fun."

Get BOSS OF ME FREE in Kindle Unlimited Now!

Also available on audiobook.

ACKNOWLEDGMENTS

Gratitude. That word stands out in my mind so strongly as I sit here trying to find the words to thank all the incredible people who helped me get this completed novel in your hands.

My family, most of all, I thank you for your patience, for believing in me, for telling me I can do it, and for being the reason I even try.

My readers, who love my books, who tell me they love my books, who leave amazing reviews, send cards, and tell their loved ones to read my stories… I couldn't do this without you!

Huge thanks to **Ilona Townsel** for reading as I wrote and keeping me encouraged… this was a tough one, girl! Thank you for being my rock.

Christine Estevez, who came in like a boss and got my stuff together, organized, and steered the ship while I figured it out. **Dani Sanchez** for the incredible marketing support—also **Kylie McDermott and all the gals at Give Me Books!**

So much LOVE to my incredible beta squad… **Melissa Sagastume, Tina Snider, Renee Mccleary, Jennifer Wolfel**, and **KC Caron**, and to my awesome editor **Kathy Bosman**—you ladies give amazing notes.

To my Mermaid VEEPs, **Ana Perez, Clare Fuentes, Sheryl Parent, Cindy Camp, Carla Van Zandt, Jaime Long, Tammi Hart, Tina Morgan**, and **Jacquie Martin**. You ladies have no idea how much I love you all!

Every author who helped share and promote with me... What would I do without you? **I love you.**

Special thanks to **Lori Jackson** for the masterful cover design, and to **Wander** for the gorgeous, *inspirational* photos. Love you two!

To my **Mermaids** and to my **Starfish**, *Thank You* for giving me a place to relax and be silly, and for showing me all the love...

THANKS to all the **bloggers and bookstagrammers** who have made an art of book loving. Sharing this book with the reading world would be impossible without you. I appreciate your help so much.

To everyone who picks up this book, reads it, loves it, and tells one person about it, you've made my day. I'm so grateful to you all. Without readers, there would be no writers.

So much love,
Stay sexy,
<3 Tia

BOOKS BY TIA LOUISE

BOOKS IN KINDLE UNLIMITED

STAND-ALONE ROMANCES
Wait for Me, 2019
Boss of Me, 2019
Stay, 2019
Make Me Yours, 2019
Make You Mine, 2018
When We Kiss, 2018
Save Me, 2018
The Right Stud, 2018★
When We Touch, 2017
The Last Guy, 2017★
(★co-written with Ilsa Madden-Mills)

THE BRIGHT LIGHTS SERIES
Under the Lights (#1), 2018
Under the Stars (#2), 2018
Hit Girl (#3), 2018

PARANORMAL ROMANCES
One Immortal (Derek & Melissa, vampires)
One Insatiable (Stitch & Mercy, shifters)

eBOOKS ON <u>ALL</u> RETAILERS

THE DIRTY PLAYERS SERIES

The Prince & The Player (#1), 2016
A Player for a Princess (#2), 2016
Dirty Dealers (#3), 2017
Dirty Thief (#4), 2017

THE ONE TO HOLD SERIES

One to Hold (#1 - Derek & Melissa)
One to Keep (#2 - Patrick & Elaine)
One to Protect (#3 - Derek & Melissa)
One to Love (#4 - Kenny & Slayde)
One to Leave (#5 - Stuart & Mariska)
One to Save (#6 - Derek & Melissa)
One to Chase (#7 - Marcus & Amy)
One to Take (#8 - Stuart & Mariska)

Descriptions, teasers, excerpts and more are on my website!

Never miss a new release!

Sign up for my New Release newsletter and get a FREE Tia
Louise Story Bundle!

Sign up now!

ABOUT THE
Author

Tia Louise is the *USA TODAY* bestselling, award-winning author of super hot and sexy romance.

Whether billionaires, Marines, fighters, cowboys, single dads, or CEOs, all her heroes are alphas with hearts of gold, and all her heroines are strong, sassy ladies who love them.

A former teacher, journalist, and book editor, Louise lives in the Midwest USA with her trophy husband and two teenage geniuses.

Signed Copies of all books online at:
http://smarturl.it/SignedPBs

Connect with Tia:

Website: www.authortialouise.com

Pinterest: pinterest.com / AuthorTiaLouise

Instagram (@AuthorTLouise)

Bookbub Author Page: www.bookbub.com / authors / tia-louise

Amazon Author Page: amzn.to / 1jm2F2b

Goodreads: www.goodreads.com / author / show / 7213961.Tia_
Louise

Snapchat: bit.ly / 24kDboV

** On Facebook? **

Be a Mermaid! Join Tia's **Reader Group** at
"Tia's Books, Babes & Mermaids"!
www.facebook.com / groups / TiasBooksandBabes

www.AuthorTiaLouise.com
allnightreads@gmail.com

Made in the USA
Middletown, DE
20 October 2022

13145778R00177